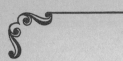

"I have never met a woman who combined modesty and arrogance into such a devilish whole. Is it nature or contrived for your own amusement?"

"Oh, nature, certainly, sir. No woman of breeding would admit to contriving her arrogance."

"The very devil," Lord Cartwright said, smiling down on her.

"I know it is not fashionable to do so, but when have I ever heeded fashion?"

"But this is dreadful, Lady Samantha!" exclaimed Lord Cartwright. "I find myself more and more in agreement with you each passing day!"

"Speaking from vast experience, I should warn you, my lord, that there are dangerous shoals ahead if you pursue such a course."

"I think," Lord Cartwright murmured as he gazed down at Samantha, "that I will enjoy every rock and storm."

Also by Michelle Martin
Published by Fawcett Books:

THE HAMPSHIRE HOYDEN

THE QUEEN
OF HEARTS

Michelle Martin

FAWCETT CREST • NEW YORK

A Fawcett Crest Book
Published by Ballantine Books
Copyright © 1994 by Michelle Martin

Library of Congress Catalog Card Number: 94-94197

ISBN 0-449-22203-9

Manufactured in the United States of America

First Edition: August 1994

10 9 8 7 6 5 4 3 2 1

Chapter One

Lord Simon Cartwright stepped from the badly sprung hack into a large puddle. Muttering imprecations at the puddle, the hack, the weather, and his own continuing bad luck, he paid the driver and wearily made his way to the front door of his London home in Berkeley Square. He had just returned from a grueling five-day trip to Paris to repay the French loans his late father had amassed over a ten-year period. The burden was now removed from Lord Cartwright's ledgers, but not from his mind. He could not forget the disgrace the late baron had brought to his family during his lifetime and at his dishonorable death. Neither could the haut ton. Lord Cartwright entered his house with a bitter sigh. What god had he offended to bring so much misery into his life?

As trouble likes to follow closely on the heels of its brother, it should not have surprised Lord Cartwright, upon entering the warmly lit front parlor that afternoon, to see his sister seated in some consternation at a tea tray near the fire. She rose instantly upon perceiving her brother and, advancing toward him with outstretched hands, cried:

"Oh, Simon, I am so glad you have come! How exhausted you look. You have pushed yourself too hard as I knew you would."

1

"I am fine, Hilary," Lord Cartwright replied, taking his sister's hands in both of his. "Is something wrong?"

"I am not sure," she said. "The most disconcerting thing has happened. I came home from calling on Susan Horton this morning to find someone moving into the Dower House!"

"But ... the Robertses were not expected for another se'ennight," Lord Cartwright said, releasing her hands. "Surely they would not move into the Dower House without first consulting you?"

"I assure you, Simon, that whoever is taking up residence in that house does not bear the Roberts' name," Lady Jillian Roberts replied as she rose gracefully from her chair and moved forward to greet her disheveled fiancé.

"Jillian, I am glad you are here," Lord Cartwright said warmly as he took her hand.

She grimaced slightly at the dirt that covered him. "I came to borrow a key to the Dower House to fix in my mind how I wish to arrange our furniture there," she said. "It seems I am too late."

"But this is absurd!" exclaimed Lord Cartwright. "Hilary, did no one ask permission to gain entrance to the Dower House, offer any explanation?"

"None whatsoever," Hilary replied. "I returned at eleven this morning to find a steady stream of rowdy movers carrying furniture into the Dower House and they have been at it ever since. Simon, do you think it might be ... the Spinster?"

"The Adamson woman? Good God, you don't think—"

A quelling look from Jillian at such language recollected Lord Cartwright to the proprieties.

"I beg your pardon, Jillian. It is just that when I think of the Adamson woman ... It would certainly be like Father to haunt me in this manner. And yet it makes no sense. No woman of good breeding would behave in this brazen fashion and the Adamsons are members of the ton. Well," said

Lord Cartwright grimly, straightening his broad shoulders, "I shall find the matter out directly."

The Dower House, which lay opposite the Cartwright House in Berkeley Square, had been bequeathed by Lord Cartwright's father to Lady Margery Adamson or, if she should predecease him (as she did), to "her spinster daughter, Lady Samantha Adamson, a woman of no character." This legacy had titillated all of London and worried the Cartwrights no end. It particularly worried Simon Cartwright for he had long ago condemned everything his father had delighted in. His father had loved Lady Margery Adamson. Lord Cartwright, therefore, could not tolerate the thought of her ... or her daughter. His fears had been lulled, however, in the last two years, for the Spinster had not stepped forward to claim the property.

But had she done so now?

He stalked from his house, crossed the Square, roughly shouldered his way past the movers on the steps of the Dower House, and entered into Bedlam.

In the pandemonium of jostling workmen, furniture of every description, boxes, parcels, rolled carpets, and lower-class shouts and laughter, Lord Cartwright spied a maid, or perhaps she was a housekeeper. In any event, she possessed an admirable figure which her plain brown dress could not hide. Her mouth was lush; her dark, honey blond hair was caught up and tied precariously at the back of her head.

Images of Raphael's Madonnas came unbidden to Lord Cartwright's weary mind.

Then the woman began to cheerfully shout directions to the movers above her on the stairs in between verses of a rather ribald song concerning the romantic frolics of a young shepherd and shepherdess which she sang lustily and slightly off key.

Lord Cartwright hastily summoned back all thoughts of charm he had nearly bestowed upon the wanton.

Such an atrocious song emanating from a young wom-

3

an's lips—*any* young woman's lips—greatly offended his lordship and this, coupled with the hardships of the last five days, the upset caused to Jillian, and the disruption of any peace he had hoped to enjoy at his homecoming, brought Lord Cartwright to vent all of his pent-up spleen upon this indecorous singer of verse.

"You there, stop that outrageous noise at once!" he demanded as he advanced upon the woman standing at the foot of the grand staircase.

She obediently closed her mouth and turned to regard him with cool, calculating hazel eyes that studied him from head to toe. He was tall, standing well over six feet in height; his figure well muscled; his dun hair disheveled. His eyes were a dark, fulminating brown; his handsome face possessed a long, aristocratic nose tempered by a shockingly sensual mouth now clamped in a grim line. His travel-stained clothes proclaimed Weston's studied elegance. The woman grimaced. She seemed to disapprove of his dirt as much as had Jillian.

Lord Cartwright's blood boiled.

"How dare you sully the gentle propriety of your sex with such a scandalous song?" he seethed.

"It is a simple, amusing ballad, sir, and one that I sing often when I work," the woman calmly retorted. "Who are you, pray, to object to what I sing? An opera critic from Venice?"

Lord Cartwright drew himself with great dignity to his full height, an impressive sight as he well knew.

"*I* am Lord Cartwright, the executor of this property, and I will thank you to keep a civil tongue in your head and remove not only yourself but these men and this furniture from the house immediately!"

The woman carefully placed the writing pad down upon a box, crossed her arms over her chest, and said with great clarity and calm:

"No."

Lord Cartwright's jaw locked. "Where is your master, girl?"

"I am just turned seven-and-twenty, sir, and can hardly be termed 'girl,' though I should thank you for the compliment I suppose, if you had intended it as such. And I have no master."

"Where is your *mistress*, then?"

"I am my own mistress, sir. I am Lady Samantha Adamson, perhaps you know the name? And I will thank *you* to leave *my* home at once!"

Lord Cartwright could only stare at the creature. He felt like a man who, but a moment earlier, had been standing on a strong, tiled floor, but now suddenly found himself mired in quicksand.

"You . . . ?" he managed to gasp.

"I," Samantha affirmed. "It is a terrible blow, I know, my lord, but I am certain you will recover. Good day."

Lord Cartwright became aware of the workmen grinning at him and his fury grew. He had made a fool of himself. . . . No, this woman, this provocateur had made a fool out of him. She *should* have been the housekeeper. No woman of breeding would dress in such a manner or undertake such an unsuitable task. He had been deliberately deceived! All the injustice of his situation came home to him in that moment.

"Leave? Oh no, *my lady*, I have not yet begun! For over two years I have sent repeated notifications of my father's bequest to you and never received a reply. Not even a note of acknowledgment! For two years I have paid your taxes, kept up the house and grounds, and forbore making any use of it myself, although there were many times when I had need of it. Now suddenly, without prior notice, without so much as a *word*, you move in without first informing *me*, my father's executor! How dare you, madam? How *dare* you treat this in such a cavalier fashion?"

5

Arms akimbo, Samantha returned Lord Cartwright's glare.

"You should go on the stage, baron. You've the bombast for it. Your father's will was quite specific. This house is mine and I may do as I like with it. As for your notices of the bequest, they finally reached me in Istanbul two months ago and, as I was even then making plans for my return to England, I thought it best to hold·my reply until my ship docked. I will be only too happy to reimburse you for the expense and trouble of the house these last two years, and I treat this situation cavalierly because I find it wholly ridiculous."

Lord Cartwright gasped. "This is intolerable! Why did you not summon the common civility to call upon me and discuss the bequest?"

"Common civility eluded me, sir. My net was not at hand to catch it."

The workmen laughed; Lord Cartwright counted to five.

"I arrived in London this Monday," Samantha sanguinely continued. "I called at Cartwright House on Tuesday and discovered that you had just gone out of town with no certain date of return. The rest of your family was also absent. I then called upon your solicitor, identified myself to his satisfaction, and obtained the keys to this house. Wednesday I purchased furniture, and today I am moving in. I am sorry if your fine feathers have been ruffled by my refusal to cool my heels in some damp hotel room until your return to town, but I am a woman of action, Lord Cartwright. I needed an establishment, found that I had one eminently suitable to my needs, and took possession of it. Now, have you any further objections to my tenancy?"

Lord Cartwright had several, few of which could be uttered in public.

"I had planned for my fiancée's family to make use of this house for the spring," he replied in clipped accents.

"Their own house is to be redecorated and they are to move in here next week!"

"Well, they will have to change their plans," Samantha said. "I object to sharing my home with strangers, particularly if they are related to *you*."

"But I gave the Robertses my *word*. I have need of this particular house. It is a matter of honor," Lord Cartwright declared. He took a deep breath. "I am a reasonable man, Lady Samantha. I shall find you another residence. There! That is the answer! Sell the house to me, I will give you a fair price, and then you may, with the proceeds, purchase your own home and the Robertses may use this house as we had planned."

"*This* is my home, sir," she retorted. "I have taken a sudden, violent liking to it and I intend to stay! It may surprise you to learn, but the comfort and accommodation of your fiancée's family are the very *least* of my concerns. I would even go so far as to say that my consideration of their well being is nonexistent and is likely to remain so far into the distant future!"

"Why, you poor excuse for a woman!" Lord Cartwright stormed, having passed his boiling point long ago. "Never have I encountered so cold a heart, so unbending a will—"

"For my part," Samantha hotly rejoined, "I have never before met so self-centered and *pigheaded* a man in my life and I hope never to be so unfortunate as to do so again!"

"The will expressly grants me latitude in the disposition of this house!"

"*If* I do not claim it and I have!"

"I say, Sam," came a cry from the first landing, "what's the row about?"

A boy of seventeen and a girl of nineteen—each possessed of black hair and laughing black eyes—ran eagerly down the stairs.

"You can tell us all, Sam," said the girl. "Are we being raided?"

"This uncivil swine," Samantha said, pointing an out-raged finger at Lord Cartwright, "is trying to evict us!"

"I am *not* trying to evict you," he seethed. "I am simply trying to reach an accommodation!"

"No, sir, you are trying to have your own way and are clearly not used to being thwarted," Samantha retorted. "Disappointment and humility are lessons well worth learn-ing, Lord Cartwright."

"Oh, don't get her talking on humility," the girl implored the fulminating Lord Cartwright. "She won't know what she's talking about."

"Remember the time she went on for an *hour* about duty?" the boy said.

"Ye gods, yes," the girl groaned. "Lord, *that* was a croaker!"

"Who *are* these creatures?" Lord Cartwright demanded.

Casting a jaundiced eye at the pair, Samantha moved be-tween them and said:

"The ruddy-faced youth is Peter Danthorpe. His flippant counterpart is his sister, Christina. They are orphans with no appreciation of the higher human virtues which is not surprising for they are also Americans. I am their guardian until their aunt and uncle return to England. Why anyone would *want* to claim the two wretches I have not a clue, but that is the plan at present. The apoplectic gentleman before us, my children, is Lord Cartwright. You may pay homage to him at a later date."

"Lady Samantha," said the apoplectic gentleman, "will you be reasonable and surrender this house to me?"

"My dear sir, I am never reasonable," Samantha replied.

Lord Cartwright glared at her and then, without another word, stormed out of the house, back across the Square, and through the front door of his own home to end where he had begun—the front parlor—once again facing his anx-ious sister and fiancée.

He felt as if he steamed with rage. He wished for an ancient oak that he might uproot it from the ground.

One look at her elder brother's handsome face and Hilary knew the interview had not gone well. Perhaps less observant than she, Jillian inquired:

"And how did you fare, Simon?"

"That . . . that *harridan*," Lord Cartwright seethed as he began to pace the Persian carpet, "is an insult to the name woman! Never have I met a female of such incivility. Her manners are deplorable, her understanding nonexistent. She is ruled by implacable selfishness and a character steeped in the brine of childish stubbornness! A *year* in the pillory could not chasten her!"

Hilary was shocked by this outburst. She had not seen such emotion in her brother these two years.

"Simon," she said carefully, "is it the Spinster?"

"Spinster? Oh yes," Lord Cartwright replied as he stopped at the sideboard and poured himself a healthy glass of brandy, "Father's description was most apt. The woman is all of seven-and-twenty, or so she claims, and it is clear why she remains unwed. There is not a man alive who could be made drunk enough to marry that baggage." This pronouncement issued, Lord Cartwright drained his glass with relish.

"Simon, please," Jillian remonstrated. "It distresses me when you express yourself in such an indecorous manner. Why, you sound exactly like your father!"

Lord Cartwright received a shock at the comparison. Had he really sounded like the late, unlamented baron? Good God, he had! Heaven bless Jillian for her calm in the midst of his storm.

"I apologize, Jillian, for any impropriety of speech or conduct," he replied, carefully setting down his glass. "That woman has shredded my self-control. Never have I encountered so infuriating a creature."

"But what happened, Simon?" demanded Hilary. "What did she say? What did you say?"

"I will neither grieve nor offend you by repeating that abysmal dialogue," Lord Cartwright replied. "Suffice it to say that a wholly objectionable person has taken up residence in the Dower House and refuses to leave."

"She will not honor your prior commitment to my family, then?" Jillian inquired as she calmly reseated herself beside the fire and poured out a fresh cup of tea.

"The woman knows nothing of honor, let alone honesty, civility, or decorum! Why, she was dressed no better than a maid and behaved no better than a swineherd. The difficulty your family is under moves her not at all. She is adamant. She will not go."

"But the house is hers, after all, Simon," Hilary ventured.

"She is forcing me to break my word, Hilary. It is unforgivable."

"I say, Hilary," cried nineteen-year-old Matthew as he ran into the room, coattails flying, "have you seen the to-do at the Dower House? Oh, hello, Simon, welcome back. There is such a ruckus going on over there! Movers all over the place and the most magnificent furniture I've ever seen being carried inside. It's the Adamson woman, I'm sure of it! What a stroke of luck to have her turn up like this! Do you realize what this means, Hilary? We're saved! With the Adamson woman in the house, the Robertses can't move in and hound us day and night. By *God*, what a piece of luck!"

"Matthew . . . ," Lord Cartwright said through clenched teeth, but his brother heard him not at all.

"I can't believe it! Rescued from a daily dose of Jillian's lectures at the eleventh hour. Beats those plot twists of your silly novels all to pieces, Hilary old girl."

"I am sorry that the threat of my presence should fill you with such dread, Matthew," Jillian said in injured tones as she rose from her seat by the fire.

Matthew had the grace to flush.

"You will apologize, Matt," Lord Cartwright intoned.

"Hang it all, Simon, I didn't know she was here!"

"That is the answer I expected you to make," said Jillian to Matthew. "Your head is full of your own pleasures and thinks not at all on the serious business of life, and the decorum with which human interaction should be conducted. If I had been in York just now, I would have hoped you would hold such unkind words firmly on your tongue, directing your thougths not to exultation at my family's plight, but to the injustice suffered by one who is almost a sister and certainly regards you as a brother. It is not of myself that I am thinking, but of your brother who must keenly feel the horror of the path you are following, a path so like that taken by your father that I shudder when I contemplate it. Surely your obligation to your brother alone would curb your wild and heedless nature if you had the heart and mind of a *gentleman*. I begin to despair of your reformation."

"Simon," pleaded Matthew.

Lord Cartwright, though uncomfortable at having his fiancée lecture his brother in such a fashion, held to the proprieties.

"Your apology," he said.

Matthew's color grew. "No! I'll be damned if I'll apologize for speaking the truth!"

He ran from the room, leaving extreme discomfort in his wake.

Lady Samantha Adamson, meanwhile, had been left standing, staring at her front door, which Lord Cartwright had slammed shut.

"Excitable creature, isn't he?" Peter Danthorpe observed as the workmen began once again shifting boxes and furniture.

"Yes, but *very* handsome when aroused," Christina

11

added. "I wonder if he would appear to such advantage in a calmer state?"

"Odious creature," Samantha muttered. "So much ado about nothing."

"But he looked very well while he did it," said Miss Danthorpe.

"Christina, really!" Samantha said in amusement.

"Well, I *like* forceful men."

"You will not think so when you are married and want to have your own way," Samantha replied.

"Now that is a sight I would dearly love to see," Peter declared. "Christina thwarted by her lord and master."

"Don't hold your breath, child," Miss Danthorpe retorted.

"Samantha certainly didn't hold hers!" Peter said with a grin. "Are guardians supposed to let their wards see them in such a temper?"

"I argued the matter calmly and rationally," Samantha retorted.

Her wards hooted with laughter.

"Perhaps I was a little heated," she conceded.

"Heated?" Christina gasped. "I feared that at any moment you would explode!"

"Nonsense. I would, at the most, merely have throttled him. Now, come along, children. We have work to do."

"I don't *want* to unpack any more," Peter complained as Samantha herded her wards back upstairs. "I am tired and hungry and this work will ruin my hands, I swear it!"

This pitiable protest left his guardian unmoved. "What? Threats at this hour of the day? It will not do, my young prodigy, it simply will not do. I shall find you a houseful of servants tomorrow who will coddle you and cosset you, fulfill your every whim, and provide every comfort and pleasure. As for food, *I* shall provide a tea and a supper today unparalleled in the annals of English cookery."

"Hardly a difficult task," Christina observed.

"True," Samantha said with a grin. "Be thankful you have such a considerate guardian, one, in fact, who has gone out of her way to procure her treasured wards a French chef of unmatched skill."

"The only reason you hired Monsieur Girard was to wreak revenge on La Comtesse St. Germaine for hiring away your hairdresser last year," Christina retorted.

"The outraged look on her pink face is one I shall treasure always," Samantha said with a happy sigh. "Monsieur Girard arrives tomorrow, children, and tea will not be until five. So for now, to work!"

Chapter Two

DURING THE SUCCEEDING three days, the Dower House remained a hub of activity as painters and paperers redid every room; draperies were measured, cut, and fitted; servants interviewed and hired; the furniture arranged, rearranged, and rearranged again; and the rest of the moving boxes unpacked. During this period as well, the occupants of the Dower House (saving Samantha) and the occupants of the Cartwright House opposite them (saving Lord Cartwright) made frequent surreptitious sightings of one another.

At breakfast, Matthew Cartwright sliced a second helping of ham and winked at his sister.

"The Adamson woman has hired away Lord Altonberry's butler, Garner, have you heard?"

"Good heavens," said Hilary, "however did she manage that?"

"Doubled his wages and promised there would be no midnight orgies."

"Matthew!" thundered Lord Cartwright as he slammed down his fork. "I will not have you sullying your sister's ears with unsubstantiated gossip about Altonberry."

"Unsubstantiated?" Matthew retorted with a grin. "Doing it too brown, Simon. Everyone knows who provided the funds for the decorations at the last Cyprians' Ball. I've heard, Hilary, that he commissioned painted tapestries depicting the amorous adventures of Zeus . . . and there were lots of 'em."

"No wonder Garner was so eager to enter Lady Samantha's employ," murmured Hilary over her teacup. "She has been charged with many atrocities, but I do not think orgies are among them."

"Adamson, Adamson, Adamson!" fumed Lord Cartwright. "Can you talk of nothing else?"

"I've heard," Matthew said, "that Lady Samantha has the best chef in all of Europe toiling in her remodeled kitchen."

With an oath, Lord Cartwright stormed from the room, leaving Matthew to laugh into his napkin.

"Really, Matt," said Hilary with a severity belied by her smile, "you must not tease Simon so."

"Oh, but Hilary, how can I resist?" said Matthew. "This is the liveliest I've seen Simon since the black day he popped the question to Jillian!"

Within the Dower House later that afternoon, conversation was much less inflammatory.

"It is still snowing," Christina said with a sigh as she turned away from the window overlooking the Square and glanced with little love at the incomplete letter at her side.

"Thank you for that informative announcement," her brother drawled.

"Why is it that every time we come to London it rains or snows?" Christina complained, ignoring Peter entirely.

"It is January, Christina," Samantha replied without looking up from her book. "What do you expect London to do? Have a sandstorm?"

"If I do not see the sun soon I shall wither and die," Christina declared.

"Well, there's hope in that, I suppose," Peter said. "You should never have taken us to Covent Garden last night,

Samantha. She'll be moaning about like an overwrought tragedian for the next se'ennight."

"We must all have our emotional outlets, Peter," Samantha replied, turning a page of her book. "Leave the poor girl alone. Or better yet, play something to cheer her up."

"Well, I *have* been writing this new piece," Peter confided. "I call it 'Dirge for a Dead Love in F Sharp.' "

Samantha looked up from her book, once again grateful she had agreed to chaperone such an entertaining pair. "I was thinking more along the lines of Bach or Handel," she said dryly.

"Oh very well," Peter said and began to play Bach's Concertina in D Minor.

Five minutes later Christina declared that she could not write when Peter insisted upon being so distracting, set her pen down with relief, and turned happily back to the window to watch the comings and goings of the ton in the Square before her.

"Oh, there is Lord Cartwright's sister coming from their house," she exclaimed. "Imagine walking out in weather like this."

"You do not *know* that she is his sister," Peter challenged above Bach.

"Of course I do. They look too much alike to be anything else. Besides, their solicitor said that Lord Cartwright lived with his widowed sister and his younger brother and I have seen her come and go from the house several times."

"Perhaps she is his mistress," Peter suggested.

Christina ignored him. "She is quite pretty—even at this distance one can tell that—and rather young. She can be no older than five- or six-and-twenty. Imagine being widowed so young in life!"

"If she's anything like her brother, she undoubtedly hounded her husband into an early grave," said Samantha.

"Really, Sam," Christina said, chuckling, "you should not be so prejudiced. Good heavens! She is coming here!"

"Who?" Samantha and Peter demanded as one.

"The sister!"

This announcement was confirmed a moment later by the ringing of their front bell. Their venerable (albeit new) butler, Garner, answered the summons and a moment later ushered their guest into the parlor.

"Mrs. Hilary Cartwright Sheverton," he declared in a rather nice baritone.

"Thank you, Garner," Samantha said, rising from her chair. "I think we would all like tea."

With a stately bow, Garner withdrew from the room.

Hilary was left alone to face three of the handsomest people she had ever met. The two youngest—whom Lord Cartwright had termed "rude" and "impertinent"— possessed a dark beauty and a lively curiosity as they returned her survey with the greatest interest.

But it was their guardian—the daughter of the woman Hilary's father had loved until the day he died, the woman who had left Hilary aching with curiosity these last three days—Lady Samantha Adamson who now left her dumbfounded. In his many diatribes against their new neighbor, Lord Cartwright had singularly failed to mention that she was quite possibly the most beautiful woman ever to set foot in London. It was conceivable that in his fury Lady Samantha's beauty had made no impression on him. But studying her now, Hilary did not see how that was possible.

Samantha Adamson was as tall as Hilary, whose height, in her youth, had been termed "lamentable" by more than one patroness at Almack's. Dressed in a simple empire gown of blue and white stripes, she had an air of grace and strength and buoyancy that Hilary found quite alluring.

It was all so very different from what she had expected.

"Mrs. Sheverton," Samantha said warmly as she extended her hand, "how good of you to call on us on such an abysmal day."

"Not at all," Hilary replied with a smile. "I would have done so earlier but I thought it best to wait until the flurry of activity generated by your arrival had calmed somewhat and you had a chance to settle in. I trust you are comfortable?"

"Yes. It is a lovely house."

"It was my grandmother's. She loved it very much. I hope that you will be as happy here. But who is the musician? A spinet, a harpsichord, *and* a pianoforte all in one room? What concerts you must have!"

"They belong to Peter. Come, let me introduce you to my wards, who will be on their very best behavior," Samantha said with a stern look at the Danthorpes that had Hilary close to a giggle.

Introductions and greetings were exchanged.

"But how is it," Hilary inquired as they took their seats, "that a woman of your youth—yes, *youth*, for I have it on the greatest authority that you are not yet thirty and you look no more than three-and-twenty—how is it, then, that you've become guardian of such a charming pair of Americans?"

"Thereby hangs a tale," Peter said, waggling his black eyebrows.

"We were orphans, friendless, destitute," Christina declared with a throb in her voice, "when Samantha rescued us from wretched abandonment."

"What rubbish!" Samantha said. "Mr. and Mrs. Danthorpe died some fifteen months ago and left Christina and Peter to the guardianship of their aunt and uncle who reside in Worcestershire. Christina and Peter, who were in America at the time, obligingly sailed off to meet their aunt and uncle, but their aunt and uncle were not in Worcestershire. Apparently they very seldom are. I was then in Istanbul when I received three letters: a cryptic one from Peter, a far

18

more melodramatic one from Christina, and a third, filled with promises of presents beyond my wildest dreams, from the aforementioned aunt and uncle. They were ensconced in Russia at the time and unable to return to England for at least a twelve-month. I was recruited by one and all to fill the breach and so returned to my natal country, much to the discomfort of some whom we shall leave unmentioned."

Garner placed the tea tray on the table before Samantha and exited.

"That raises a delicate point," Hilary said as she accepted a cup of tea from her hostess. "I must tell you that I was not at all certain of my reception. I came today to not only greet you as a neighbor, but to apologize as a sister. From what I have been able to glean from his vituperative account, my brother used you abominably on Thursday."

"I have encountered ruder and more boorish men," Samantha said. "I am not quite certain where or when, but I must certainly have done so at some point in my life."

"Simon is a dear," Hilary said with a smile, "but he will act without thinking at times. Men are so adept at making complete cakes of themselves, don't you think?"

Samantha laughed at this and knew she had found a kindred spirit. In her experience, men *often* made cakes of themselves.

Two hours later, Hilary returned home to find her irate elder brother and her starving younger brother holding dinner for her.

"Oh, I *am* sorry," Hilary said, kissing each. "I was having such fun at the Dower House that I quite lost track of the time. You may serve now, Clarke," she said to the hovering butler before seating herself at the table.

"The Dower House!" gasped Lord Cartwright. "You cannot mean that you have called on that wretched woman?"

"But that is precisely what I mean, Simon," Hilary said. "I own that I was prepared to dislike her for your sake, but

I find I cannot. Lady Samantha is charming, witty, and attentive, and her wards are a delight. I am certain you would like them, Simon, if you let yourself. My, that soup smells good!"

"Hilary, how could you?" Lord Cartwright sputtered. "How *could* you?"

His sister calmly sampled the soup. "We are her neighbors after all, Simon. She has moved into a house that was once ours. It was but common decency to pay her some sort of call."

"Have you no sense of propriety?" Lord Cartwright demanded. "No sense of loyalty?"

"Loyalty?" said Hilary. "To *your* foolish temper and pride? No, thank God, I do not!"

"You cannot condone her actions," Lord Cartwright said in amazement.

"Of course I can," Hilary replied. "She has acted properly throughout the entire affair. Our solicitor has corroborated her story. And when I recall the foul mood you were in when you went to confront her, I do not doubt that you pushed her into an argument."

"It was *I* who went there the injured party!"

"No, no, no. You only *thought* you were injured," Hilary assured her brother. "But indeed, it is Lady Samantha who has been wronged and I really think you should apologize to her, Simon. You used her abominably, you know."

"I will apologize to no woman who has so little regard for her station in life or the restrictions of her sex that she sets up housekeeping without so much as a chaperone! Why, she strides about London conducting business like a *man*. She is a *profligate*, Hilary. Only look at the ungodly amounts of money she has expended in just three days on furniture, clothing, carriages, *redecorating*!"

"But Simon, Lady Samantha and her wards are to be in town for at least a year. They cannot very well eat, sleep, and sit on boxes. And," Hilary continued over her brother's burgeoning protest, "though you have kept up the maintenance on the house, it has been over two years since it was last occupied. Carpets, draperies, wallpaper, all were in a shocking condition. You must own it, Simon. How could any woman of property and character *not* redecorate?"

Lord Cartwright's napkin was irreparably knotted. "Why do you insist on defending so improper and insulting a creature?"

"Why do you insist on condemning one of the loveliest and most charming women in London?"

Lord Cartwright remained in simmering silence for the rest of the meal.

On Monday morning, Lord Cartwright was astounded when his butler announced that Lady Samantha—whom his lordship had termed a "she-wolf" at breakfast but an hour before—had come to call on him. Grimly he rose and stalked to the morning parlor where she had been installed. He fully intended to have her back on the street inside of two minutes. He flung open the parlor door, stepped in, and stared.

He was, in fact, horrified, for he beheld a gorgeous, golden, hazel-eyed goddess. As he made a curt bow, Lord Cartwright was forced to bitterly concur with public opinion: Lady Samantha Adamson *was* amazingly beautiful and the fact galled him no end. It would be hard to detest a woman who set his heart to pounding, as it was now, at such a furious pace.

Samantha rose gracefully from her chair.

"Good morning, Lord Cartwright. Thank you for seeing me."

"You would not prefer to see my sister?" he grimly inquired.

"Not just now, thank you. My debt is to you, not to Mrs. Sheverton."

"Debt?"

"The taxes and maintenance on the Dower House that you provided over the last two years."

Lord Cartwright impatiently waved away such a purpose. "Our solicitors may handle the matter between them."

"No doubt. But I prefer to view this as a private matter between us and I wish to settle it personally." Samantha drew her purse from her reticule. "I dislike being in any man's debt. What is the sum, please?"

Lord Cartwright almost reeled. "Good God, madam, have you no understanding of propriety?"

Samantha looked up from her purse. Unused to having to look up at a man, she added Lord Cartwright's towering height to the many reasons she disliked him.

"What can be more proper than being beforehand with the world?" she demanded.

"I am not some moneylender for you to come to with your gold."

"Actually, I've brought bank notes. I hope that will be satisfactory? I understand the Bank of England to be fairly solid."

"I should have known *you* would treat a debt of honor so casually."

Samantha's hazel eyes widened. "Casually? My dear sir, I have come to pay the debt. With bank notes. *English* bank notes and a good many of them. There is nothing casual about large sums of money."

For one terrible moment, Lord Cartwright nearly laughed out loud. Fortunately, he recollected his outrage at Lady Samantha's character, activities, and spending habits and instead gave her a fulminating glare.

"That is sheer hypocrisy coming from a woman who has frivolously spent thousands of pounds buying up every stick of furniture, every carpet, and every dress in town! Good God, madam, you've become the sole support of every modiste in London!"

A dangerous flush crept into Samantha's cheeks. "What

I spend and how I spend it is none of your concern, Lord Cartwright!"

"I must and shall condemn the profligacy of anyone so unhappily connected to my family!"

"Condemn?" stormed Samantha. "Oh, the arrogance of the man! You've no more right to condemn me than has a *dog*. There is *no* connection between us, Lord Cartwright, save the distressing proximity of our homes!"

"*Your* home was once mine."

"No, sir, it was your father's. It was his to dispose of as he chose and he chose to leave it to *me*."

"To your *mother*, you mean."

"You will remove the sneer from your voice when you speak of my mother or, by God, I will thrash you!"

Lord Cartwright recollected himself. When had he acquired the habit of insulting women, both living and dead? It was a distressing discovery.

"I apologize, Lady Samantha," he said stiffly. "If you will give me a minute, I will tell you what I have paid on the Dower House in your absence."

He went to his study, collected his ledger, and returned to the morning parlor. He showed Lady Samantha the sum, she counted the bank notes into his hand and, with a curt "Good day," departed.

Lord Cartwright stared after her a moment, then at the bank notes in his hand. With an oath, he flung them across the room.

Lady Jillian Roberts was announced in the next moment.

"Good morning, Simon," she said with a smile as she extended her hand which he dutifully kissed. "Who was that woman I saw leaving just a moment ago?"

"Lady Samantha."

"What? Here? How astounding! I am amazed she had the effrontery to call on you."

"Lady Samantha has an abundance of effrontery."

"Oh, I do sympathize with you, Simon," said Jillian, laying her hand upon his arm. "To have such a woman as a near neighbor must be discomfitting. All of London is talking of her. It seems the ton can talk of nothing else, and little of the Continental reports they spread is reassuring. From what I have gathered, she is an indecorous shrew intent only on her own pleasure. Not only is she an outrageous flirt determined to have every eligible and *ineligible* man dancing attendance on her, she is"—and here Jillian shuddered—"a *matchmaker*."

For the second time that morning, Lord Cartwright nearly laughed aloud.

"No!" he murmured.

"Her matchmaking predilections have even given her the sobriquet 'The Queen of Hearts.' Could anything be more vulgar?"

"I can think of a few others."

Jillian sat in her accustomed place at the fire. "As you said the day she arrived, a wholly objectionable person now resides in the Dower House. I only hope she does not try to force herself onto you to gain entreé into Society."

A wry smile quirked Lord Cartwright's mouth. "Lady Samantha seems disinclined to curry my favor."

"Well, that is a blessing at least. Simon, why is there money strewn about the room?"

"I have become a Shylock."

Jillian regarded her fiancé in some puzzlement. "There are times, Simon, when I do not understand you."

"There are times, Jillian, when I don't understand myself."

Chapter Three

Believing that his family's tolerance of his surly, not to say bearish, behavior in the last fortnight had been above and beyond the call of duty, Lord Cartwright proposed to Matthew and Hilary over breakfast that they should visit the Theatre Royal, Drury Lane, that very night. His proposal was greeted with the greatest enthusiasm. Thus, they descended on Drury Lane that night: Lord Cartwright in white silk stockings, yellow breeches, and blue frock coat, his shirt points nicely pressed but distressingly low, though his cravat was quite presentable; Hilary in a white gown with short puffed sleeves, blue ribbons crossing the bodice and decorating the hem, and blue evening gloves; and Matthew, casting them in the shade with his pale pink silk stockings, gold-and-silver embroidered waistcoat, the hugely padded shoulders of his brown-spotted silk coat and the tightness of his matching breeches, his shirt points rising to his high cheekbones, his neckcloth a very tolerable waterfall, his red locks in fashionable dishabille à la Brutus. Several people turned to regard him as the family made their way into the theater, but Matthew was not certain if they gazed at him in admiration or derision. He wondered if he had the courage to be a dandy.

The theater that night was crowded to overflowing, every

box filled, the pit packed with a boisterous crowd already debating the mixed offerings described by the playbill: a new melodramatic spectacle entitled *Trial by Conscience*, a Grand Asiatic Ballet called *Jasmine and the Vazir*, and a Splendid Harlequinade called *The Elopement*. It promised to be an entertaining evening.

"Look," said Matthew as the Cartwrights nodded and bowed to their acquaintances throughout the theater, "isn't that Lady Samantha?"

Lord Cartwright groaned inwardly. Could he never get away from the wretched woman?

"Where?" Hilary demanded, scanning the other boxes.

"No, no," said Matthew, "not there. In the pit."

"The what?" Lord Cartwright ejaculated.

His brown eyes had but a moment to follow Matthew's direction. He spied a tall blonde with a spray of rubies in her hair to match her evening gown just as the curtain rose on *Trial by Conscience*.

He derived no pleasure from the melodrama for all he did was sit and fume and enrage himself with silent diatribes against a lady of Quality who would demean herself so much as to sit in the pit with a bunch of ruffians. The men of letters, lawyers, students, and artists who were the self-appointed critics of theater fare may well have taken umbrage at being termed ruffians, but Lord Cartwright did not consider this. He was too busy inwardly condemning Lady Samantha.

When the curtain fell on *Trial by Conscience*, Lord Cartwright rose from his chair and grimly informed his brother and sister that he would return.

"Simon," said Hilary nervously, "you do not mean to intervene in Lady Samantha's evening?"

"But I do," said her brother. "The ton knows of our connection. Her actions must rebound upon us and do us harm."

It took several minutes to push his way through the packed theater throng, and when he did so his horror doubled for he discovered that Lady Samantha had actually brought the Danthorpes with her into the pit!

She was flirting cheerfully with a bewhiskered gentleman on her right who might have been her grandfather when Lord Cartwright uttered her name in the most loathsome accents. She stiffened and then turned.

"Lord Cartwright," she said coolly, "what a surprise to see you partaking of frivolity. Are you enjoying yourself?"

"No, madam, I am not!" Lord Cartwright seethed. "How dare you, madam, how *dare* you lower yourself and degrade your wards by sitting in the pit?"

The wards scurried away to seek refreshments and avoid being caught in the crossfire.

"The boxes were all sold out," Samantha replied, her voice calm despite the bright pink spots in her cheeks. "And I had promised the Danthorpes a night at the theater. It would have been craven to disappoint them and insulting to the fine gentlemen I have met here tonight to think I would not be safe in their midst."

"Here, here," said the bewhiskered gentleman.

"I am not thinking of your safety," Lord Cartwright retorted, "but of your reputation!"

"Oh, that was lost long ago," Samantha said breezily.

Lord Cartwright sputtered. "For sheer audacity, you've no equal, my lady."

"Thank you."

"It was not intended as a compliment."

"As condemnation it fell wide of the mark."

"I did not wish to condemn—"

Samantha raised one brow. "No? You would desert your accustomed superiority for some lesser conduct?"

Lord Cartwright stiffened. She might have no understanding of the rules governing Society, but he at least

27

could attend to the proprieties. "I owe you an apology, madam, for my behavior to you on Monday. It is not my habit to insult guests in my own home."

"You amaze me."

Lord Cartwright struggled for a moment with his temper. "I make no excuse for my unconscionable behavior on Monday. I sincerely apologize for any aspersions, intended or otherwise, that I may have cast upon you and Lady Margery Adamson."

Samantha regarded him a moment. "I am indeed fortunate," she said at last, "that I was not raised in London for it appears the rules of the ton wrest apologies from even the most unwilling breast and I can think of many in my acquaintance to whom I would be loathe to apologize. However do you stand it?"

An angry flush crept into Lord Cartwright's cheeks. "Had you any grounding in the most basic rules of civility, you would understand the onus that lies upon me and every other gentleman in the ton to treat a lady with the respect due her station and sex. As you have apparently been raised in a barbarous clime, I must make allowances for your ignorance and seeming inability to conduct yourself properly!"

"How good of you."

A muscle leapt in Lord Cartwright's clenched jaw. "Once again, I apologize for treating you in so base a manner on Monday morning. Now, you will be so obliging as to join my brother and sister and me in our box!"

"I find I take the greatest pleasure in *disobliging* you, Lord Cartwright. I shall remain ensconced here."

"The pit is no place for a woman of your rank!"

"I never let rank stand in my way of a good time."

"Very well!" Lord Cartwright snapped. "I have done what I can. I hope you enjoy the company of your newfound friends. Good evening, Lady Samantha!"

His lordship felt compelled to stride from the theater and

pace the street for several minutes before returning to his box in the middle of the Grand Asiatic Ballet, which he enjoyed not at all.

Chapter Four

LORD CARTWRIGHT WAS walking down the front steps of Brookes the following afternoon when he heard himself hailed and looked up from his gloomy contemplation of the pavement to see Lord Aaron Wyatt smiling at him not two feet away.

"What?" said Lord Wyatt. "Are you just leaving? I was just coming. Be a friend and save me from certain tedium. Shall we promenade arm in arm on this fine February afternoon?"

A smile creased Lord Cartwright's grimly set mouth. Lord Aaron Bartholomew Wyatt was the second son of the Duke of Hensley and determined to distance himself from his dowdy family by cutting a figure in town, as his yellow pantaloons and many-caped greatcoat fashioned by Stultz attested. He was an intelligent, attractive man of thirty years, two years younger than Lord Cartwright whom he had known and loved all his life.

"A delightful scheme," said Lord Cartwright, taking his friend's arm. "A walk will clear the banality from my mind."

Lord Wyatt chuckled. "Brookes and its habitués may be lacking in depth, but it's all such frightfully good ton. Why, only yesterday I heard the most delightful *on dit* there. *Prinny has unloosed his belly.*"

"Good God!"

Lord Wyatt laughed. "Apparently it reaches his knees, but he claims to be happier without his corsets. Come, tell me why you were looking so down in the mouth just now."

Lord Cartwright required no further prompting. He related with some bitterness the trials he had recently endured.

"Between my father's foreign debts," he concluded as they left St. James's Street, "Matthews's losses in some back-alley gaming den, and the damnable presence of the Adamson woman, it has been a hellish fortnight. When I think how closely we are still scrutinized by the ton ..." Lord Cartwright shuddered. "Thank God the banks haven't failed."

Lord Wyatt grinned at his lachrymose friend. "I ran into Tom Wilson the other day," he said. "He's all aquiver over this China venture of yours. Loves the daring, hates the expense was my impression."

"That is my poor banker in a nutshell," Lord Cartwright said with a smile.

"It seems a preposterous scheme on the whole. Can it succeed?"

"It not only can, it *will* succeed."

"You were always such a determined fellow, even as a lad," Lord Wyatt said. "When do you gallop off to China?"

"Not for another year. There are still many matters to resolve."

"I thought things were going well."

"Very well, thank you." Lord Cartwright guided them around a broad woman with a towering hat. "For the first time in two years, I shall breathe the English air as a free man. I should be paying off all my remaining personal loans within the next three months, including your very generous contribution to my salvation."

"It was an investment only and I knew it would pay handsomely. But China?"

"Give over, Aaron," Lord Cartwright said with a grin. "You know you envy me my adventure."

"Not I," Lord Wyatt countered. "I am a simple lover of hearth and home."

"Then when are you going to marry?"

"Now Simon, even you with your nose to the grindstone must have observed that there isn't a woman in England capable of tempting me. When are *you* going to be married?"

"Lord, I wish I knew," Lord Cartwright said with a sigh. "Jillian is in mourning for another five months for her brother and uncle."

"Deuced bad luck their dying just after you had got out of mourning," Lord Wyatt said, nodding sagely, though privately thinking that their demise could not have been more opportune.

"Bad luck hounds me, Aaron, you know that. My betrothal to Jillian must be the longest on the books: two and a half years and no altar in sight. The odds at White's of our ever marrying have become most distressing."

"Ah," said Lord Wyatt, "but the devotion you two have exhibited through the years is touching to behold and a valuable example to us all."

"Reprobate! Jillian is a marvelous woman and you know it. I doubt if there is another who would have stood by me these last few years."

"Lady Jillian has grit, we have all remarked it."

Lord Cartwright stared at his friend. "Jillian? *Grit?*"

The two gentlemen howled with laughter.

"Jillian is an amazing young woman, truly," Lord Wyatt averred, despite his chuckles. "How many other ladies of the ton would tolerate spending their honeymoon in China?"

"You have a vile sense of humor," Lord Cartwright said. "You know damned well, Aaron, that I have not mentioned a word of China to Jillian."

"And you know damned well, Simon, what her response will be when you *do* tell her. You may be deserted before you are wed. By all accounts, Lady Jillian Roberts abhors travel, particularly to foreign climes."

"She will come around," Lord Cartwright proclaimed, not at all convincingly.

"No, she will have *you* come around and pontificating in Parliament before the wedding bells have stopped pealing."

"That she will not. I dislike politics as you well know."

"Yes, but does Jillian know? And would she care if she did?"

Lord Cartwright stiffened. "You will kindly forbear casting aspersions on the woman I am to marry."

Lord Wyatt shrugged. "Pity her tastes do not incline toward those of Lady Samantha Adamson. I understand her to have a passion for travel . . . as well as contretemps with irate gentleman callers."

"You have been talking to Hilary again," Lord Cartwright muttered.

"She likes Lady Samantha very much, you know."

"It has been brought to my attention."

Lord Wyatt lifted his gold quizzing glass to survey a passing curricle. "Hilary's judgment has always been excellent. If she likes the woman, I daresay you could, too."

"Thank you, no."

"Oh come, Simon. A great beauty, a wit, a world traveler—what is there not to like?"

"Everything," declared Lord Cartwright. "She besmirches her sex with every action, every word. She sits in the Dower House and laughs at every rule that guides our society."

"I can't fault her for that. Some of our rules are pretty laughable."

Lord Cartwright stared at his friend. "Aaron, when you deride the precepts of our world, you pull down the very structure of our lives!"

"But what if the structure doesn't suit you and needs to come tumbling down?"

"We were discussing the Adamson woman's affront to society, *not* anarchy, and I tell you straight, Aaron, I cannot abide the woman. *She does not suit me.*"

"Very well, I'll cease nagging you," Lord Wyatt said. "But it would be devilishly amusing if it turned out you were wrong."

He suddenly jerked his friend to a stop, his expression rapt, his gaze fixed on some startling object across the street.

"Aaron, what on earth—" Lord Cartwright began.

"La Belle Flamme," Lord Wyatt breathed in reverential tones.

Startled, Lord Cartwright followed his gaze and beheld a titian-haired beauty arrayed in a pale blue walking dress partially revealed by a pink pelisse, a norwich silk shawl draped over the whole, a stunning face framed by a large poke bonnet.

"And who is the golden beauty with her?" Lord Wyatt said. "Another welcome emigrée?"

It was, of course, Samantha Adamson. When Lord Cartwright informed Lord Wyatt of her identity, his friend stared up at him in amazement.

"And *she* doesn't suit you?" he gasped.

"How could any woman parading on the arm of Europe's most notable courtesan suit me?" Lord Cartwright demanded with some heat.

Lord Wyatt stared at him a moment. "You have lost your mind."

"*I* am not the one intent on destroying whatever character I have left in the ton by openly flaunting my friendship with a notorious member of the demimonde! Has the woman no sense? Come along, Aaron," Lord Cartwright said, beginning to pull his friend across the street, "we must rescue Lady Samantha from her own folly."

"Simon, I don't think it's our place to—"

"I will detach Lady Samantha from La Belle Flamme if you will be so good as to escort the courtesan wherever she wishes to go."

"Simon," said Lord Wyatt with deep emotion, "you are too good to me. Truly you are."

Lord Cartwright had but a moment to cast an amused glance at his friend before they had stepped in front of the feminine duo, bringing them to a stop. Each woman carried four or five books in her arms and looked up at them in some surprise.

"What of him?" demanded La Belle Flamme in pleasingly accented English.

"*No*, Celeste," Samantha said firmly. "He won't suit you at all."

"*Hélas!*"

"Good afternoon, Lady Samantha," said Lord Cartwright.

"How do you do, Lord Cartwright?" Samantha replied with an equal lack of enthusiasm. "May I present my friend, Madame Celeste Vandaun? She, too, has recently arrived in London."

Lord Cartwright gave Madame the curtest of bows.

"My friend, Lord Wyatt," he said.

Lord Wyatt swept both women an elegant and heartfelt bow.

"I am enchanted, ladies," he said. "To be in the presence of the two most beautiful women in Europe has quite overset my reason."

Madame Vandaun beamed at this flattery, but Samantha, made wary by the look in Lord Cartwright's brown eyes, could find no answering smile.

"You are very kind, Lord Wyatt," she said. "Celeste and I have just met again, in the booksellers of all places, after a three year separation, and were on our way—"

"Lady Samantha," interjected Lord Cartwright, "I must beg the favor of a private tête-à-tête. Perhaps Lord Wyatt could escort Madame Vandaun to her destination?"

La Belle Flamme beamed at this for the cut and style of Lord Wyatt's clothes proclaimed him an Exquisite ... a *wealthy* Exquisite. Thunderclouds, however, settled upon Samantha's brow.

"Surely whatever you have to tell me can wait until—" she began.

"No, it can't," Lord Cartwright said bluntly. "I must speak with you on a matter of the greatest importance."

"Samantha, *chère amie*," said Madame Vandaun, her gray eyes twinkling, "I am happy to exchange escorts. You will talk to me only of Molière and Monsieur Coleridge, while I feel convinced that Lord Wyatt will converse on the lofty plane of beauty and charm, a much more delightful engagement, you must agree."

"Very well," Samantha said glacially. "You will still come to lunch tomorrow?"

"Mais certainment!" Madame replied, kissing her friend on both cheeks.

Samantha returned the salute and, after a brief struggle in which Lord Cartwright gained possession of her books, she turned and walked down the street with this far less agreeable companion.

"How could you?" she burst out. "How could you insult one of my oldest friends by publicly informing her she is not fit to walk at my side?"

"She is *not* fit to walk on the same street with you!" Lord Cartwright replied with a like fury. "How could even *you* openly court the reprobation of the Polite World by parading yourself on the arm of a notorious *whore*?"

Had they not been on a public street, Samantha would have slapped his lordship with all the strength at her command.

"Celeste Vandaun is the respected and admired friend of every notable family in Europe!"

"Indeed?" Lord Cartwright sneered. "Tell me, is *Madame* an honorary or descriptive title?"

Samantha did slap him then and with such force that the imprint of her hand remained on his cheek.

For one breathless moment it seemed as if he would return the blow. Only his remarkable self-control prevented his lordship from shaking her silly.

"Don't do that again," he said in clipped accents.

"Don't provoke me again!" Samantha retorted. "Celeste Vandaun was married at sixteen to a man she had not met prior to the wedding. Her husband proceeded to run through her fortune and his and then died in a drunken brawl in a far from savory house of pleasure. Her intelligence, warmth, and beauty were all Celeste could rely on to save herself from the streets. What woman of courage would not accept carte blanche from a respectable gentleman of means? How, then, is she any different from Mrs. Jordan, or the Prince Regent's morganatic wife, Mrs. Fitzherbert, or any of his *chère amies* like Lady Jersey?"

Lord Cartwright's face was darkly flushed as he jerked Samantha across the street.

"They were not the paid concubines of any man rich enough to keep them!" he snapped.

"Weren't they? Weren't they paid off with jewels and clothes, carriages, horses, *houses*, and pin money?"

That she had him dead to rights only fanned the flames of Lord Cartwright's outrage.

"Can you not understand, you caper-witted *fool*, that to be seen arm in arm with La Belle Flamme reduces you in the minds of all observers to one of her profession?"

Samantha stopped dead. "You're mad."

"I am the sanest person on this street," Lord Cartwright informed her as he pulled her along. "If you do not want every man you meet to offer you carte blanche, then I suggest you give up your afternoon promenades with Madame Vandaun!"

They had reached Berkeley Square by this time, but Samantha was too enraged by Lord Cartwright's interference and this reference to the mendacity of the ton to pay any heed to her surroundings.

"I shall go wherever I want with whomsoever I want and you've no right to stop me!" she cried.

"If you persist in flaunting your dubious associations in this manner I *will* have the right to bar you from ever entering my house again!"

Samantha gasped. "Your sister will have something to say to that, I think!"

"I am the head of my family and Hilary will do as she's told!"

"Make me your enemy, Cartwright," Samantha said, dragging her books from his arms, "and you'll have to watch your back for the rest of your life!"

"Ruin yourself in the ton, madam, and you will find yourself denied every acquaintance and privilege of your class!" Lord Cartwright retorted.

They turned from each other with equal fury and marched into their respective homes, slamming their front doors with equal force.

The following afternoon, Lord Cartwright stalked from his dining room, brushing past his sister without a word.

"Not *another* row?" said Hilary as she advanced into the room.

"I am sorry, Hilary," said Samantha from her place before the remains of their considerable luncheon. "I don't know what is wrong with me lately. He came looking for you and . . ."

"What was it about this time?" Hilary said, taking the chair beside her new friend.

"Oh, the usual: my character, my lack of a suitable duenna, and my residence at the Dower House. He does not seem to enjoy our close proximity."

"Yes, well, your appearance was rather inopportune," said Hilary with a wry smile. "Jillian has been nagging at

38

him this last fortnight. How shocking of you, Samantha, to move into your own house!"

"Oh, I don't mean to argue with your brother. But why must he always be so grim?"

Hilary began to pleat the tablecloth. "The last two years have been . . . hard on him."

"I do not understand. Did something happen?"

"What did *not* happen?" Hilary said with a little shudder of memory. "Having been out of the country, you may not be au courant with town gossip. You know that Father killed himself?"

Samantha paled. "No, in truth, I did not."

"He placed . . . a gun . . . to his head. Simon found him."

"Good God!" Samantha grasped Hilary's hand and received a sad smile in return.

"Horrible to lose a father like that," Hilary said softly. "Horrible to learn of his legacy. You see, although we had been worried beforehand, it was only upon Father's death that we discovered in what a frightening condition he had left our finances. He made us virtually paupers. I know, you look around at our present comfort and wonder how that could be. It is all Simon's doing. He has devoted himself every moment of these last two years to saving us from destitution. He swallowed his pride and borrowed money from his friends. He sold nearly all of our estates at an outrageous loss. He had no time for gaiety and pleasure, only worry and humiliation. The ton treated him abominably, the spiteful cats! Now, even though he has rescued us and himself far better than anyone could have foreseen, the rigors of the last two years remain. His soul is . . . scarred. I doubt if he even knows what pleasure is any longer. Samantha, he is so wretchedly different!"

"In what way?"

Hilary looked, not at her friend, but beyond to a tender memory. "He once had a passion for riding and boxing and fencing. I have not seen him with a foil in his hand since Father died. He used to adore dancing. He has not stood up once at Almack's or in our own ballroom in over two years. He used to be the greatest scamp, Samantha, *much* more scandal prone than Matthew. Why, he once cajoled his innocent sixteen-year-old sister into attending the Cyprians' Ball."

"You didn't!" Samantha gasped.

"I most certainly did," Hilary retorted. "I even received five proposals of a most dubious nature, I am happy to say."

Samantha gazed at her with open delight. "An adventuress. You used to be an adventuress!"

"In my day I enjoyed a bit of renown."

"Well, I am fairly flummoxed. Do you not miss such adventures?"

Hilary hesitated slightly. "No. No, of course not. I am not a silly schoolgirl any longer. I am a widow. I have responsibilities. Matthew gets into enough scrapes for the both of us."

An hour later, Samantha returned home thinking of all she had just learned of the Cartwrights.

A gun to his head.

She shuddered. How had Simon Cartwright survived such an horrific discovery? And then to shoulder the monstrous burden of his father's debts: the humiliation of borrowing from friends, the pain of selling off one family estate after another. It was no wonder her glib prosperity outraged him.

She cringed as she recalled lecturing him at their first meeting on humility and disappointment. He had suffered more from each than any man of pride could tolerate.

She was the greatest harridan to have used him so abominably in this last fortnight. How could she have abandoned herself to such ill temper? Whither had her remarkable self-control fled?

Well, she would reclaim it now and hold firmly to it, whatever the provocation. Knowing now some of his history, she would strive to be ever civil with Lord Cartwright, forbearing to add her anger to the burden wearing away at his broad shoulders.

Recalling Lord Cartwright's intolerance and inflexibility, Samantha believed she had set herself a monumental task.

Recalling the abuse *he* had heaped upon *her*, she began to reconsider any claims he might have to her civility.

Still mentally debating the matter, she entered her bedroom and was removing her yellow pelisse when Christina entered after a quick knock on the door and threw herself onto the bed with a huge sigh.

"What is troubling you, my child?" Samantha intoned.

"A terminal case of ennui," Christina replied, propping up her head on her hands. "I am sick to death of this dull existence. It was bad enough in Worcestershire rambling around that rackety huge house and knowing no one in the neighborhood, but now at last I reside in the greatest metropolis on earth and who is my only companion? *Peter!*"

This last was said with a wealth of disgust. Her guardian could not but smile.

"Samantha, I am nineteen and unmarried," Christina complained bitterly. "Why, I am nearly on the shelf! Help me to meet at last a man of sensibility and beauty, a man who can stir the most violent of palpitations within my breast, a world-weary man needing the soothing balm of my gentility and love. Oh, Samantha! I long to unburden my heart to a kindred spirit, to meld my soul with his, to rejoice in a union of sympathetic feelings!"

Samantha regarded her ward with growing horror. "Good God, Chris, have you been reading *novels*?"

"Oh, honestly, Sam, have you no sensibility at all?"

"None, thank the gods. I warn you, Christina, if you succumb to just one fit of the vapors, if you should—God forbid—dare to faint upon a sofa or, even worse, the floor, I shall send you packing posthaste back to Worcestershire

41

where you may wither in your rackety solitude until Armageddon!"

Christina could not repress a smile as she sat up. "I shall abandon all pretensions to vapors, I promise, Sam. But in recompense—for I really should like to know what it feels like to faint just once—you must do me a good turn. I long to enter into Society, but we have no friends save Mrs. Sheverton, no connections, no entrée into the ton, and I cannot bear it! How am I to find a husband when I am forever trapped in this house? Can you not *do* something, Samantha? Can you not pull a few strings? Bribe somebody? Blackmail *someone* to make something, anything, happen?"

Samantha was suddenly arrested just before stepping out of her gown, and turned to stare at her ward.

It had occurred to her in a flash of remarkable brilliance that she was suddenly in a position to help two women of whom she was inordinately fond: Christina ... and Hilary Cartwright Sheverton. That Hilary was in dire need of assistance Samantha had not a doubt. Once a gay, intrepid adventurer, the pain of her husband's death four years earlier had pulled Hilary back from life to such a degree that she was stagnating in her sheltered pool of widowhood and did not even know it. But Samantha did. She could not yet see her way clear with the brother, but as for the sister ...

Samantha beamed at her ward and won a crushing embrace in return.

She was accosted in her well-stocked library twenty minutes later by Peter Danthorpe.

"Hullo, Sam," he said as he threw himself into a chair, draped his legs over the far arm, picked up a magazine, and idly began to flip through the pages.

"Hullo yourself," Samantha said with a smile as she looked up from the pages of *The Way of the World*. "Practice much this morning?"

"Five hours," Peter replied, his dark head hidden by *La Belle Assemblée*.

42

Samantha set down her book. "You must be joking."

"There isn't much of anything else to do, now is there?"

"I have heard this refrain before."

"Christina got to you first, did she?" Peter said with a grin as he threw down the magazine. "She always was a headstrong wench."

"The affection you two feel for each other moves me deeply."

"I suppose you found something for the baggage to do?"

"I believe so."

"Any glimmerings for me?" Peter asked hopefully.

Samantha studied the boy for a moment, her hazel eyes suddenly narrowing. "I think that I do," she said slowly.

"Oh no," Peter groaned as he slumped further into his chair. "I fear that look. That look had me taking swimming lessons in Bluefish Lake in midwinter for three weeks. Oh, why did I even come in here?"

"It showed a remarkable lack of good sense, I must say."

"Well, I've made my own bed, I might as well lie in it," Peter said with a sigh. "What are you planning for me?"

"A return to the ample bosom of Education."

"Alack, cut down in me prime!" the poor boy groaned. "Is there no justice in life?"

"None that I have observed."

"You're a hard woman, Sam Adamson."

"I'll find you a tutor this week."

With a groan, Peter made his way to the kitchen for a restorative scone, leaving his guardian in a pool of growing melancholy.

It was all very well to arrange Hilary, Christina, and Peter's lives to some purpose, but what, Samantha wondered, was she to do with herself? As this question had plagued her more and more in the last few years without any satisfactory reply, she returned to her book but not, alas, with the pleasure Mr. Congreve's work deserved.

Chapter Five

"YOU HAVE FOUND a place to live, then, while your house is being redecorated?" Hilary inquired.

"Yes, we have rented the Dillywyr house in Brook Street for the winter and spring," replied Jillian, gracefully accepting a cup of tea from her hostess's hands. "It really is too large for us—there are only the four of us after all—the Dower House would have suited us perfectly. But as that situation is no longer possible ..." She let the sentence hang.

Hilary secretly wished that Jillian would go hang herself.

They sat in the yellow saloon, half a dozen portraits of long-dead relatives staring down at them from the walls, the fire near Jillian burning vigorously.

Lord Cartwright crossed one long leg over the other. "The Dillywyr house, though large, will suit you, I think. You are only in lavender gloves for another four months and then will wish to begin entertaining on a larger scale."

"Larger, certainly," Lady Jillian replied, "but *not* lavishly."

And what, Hilary wondered, could one say to that? Her brother seemed to be wondering the same, for silence descended upon the room once again. Jillian thereupon began an interminable discourse on her recent dinner at Carlton

House which was only interrupted when Clarke entered to announce that Lady Samantha had come to call.

"Show her in, Clarke, show her in!" cried Hilary, grateful for this reprieve and uncaring that her brother and Jillian might view the matter in any other light.

The three of them rose as Samantha entered the room, her blond locks swathed in an ermine turban, her dark brown gown dotted with white ribbons.

"Samantha, I am so glad you called!" Hilary cried, advancing on her guest. "Come, you must meet Lady Jillian Roberts."

"Must I?" Samantha murmured.

"Yes!"

"Good afternoon, Lady Samantha," said Lord Cartwright, stepping forward and making a negligible bow.

"Good afternoon," Samantha replied with determined brightness. "I've just returned from a barbarous clime and thought I'd drop in. The onus lies heavily upon you still?"

"It does," Lord Cartwright replied with a suspicious quirk of his sensual mouth. "Permit me to present you to my fiancée, Lady Jillian Roberts."

Samantha carefully scrutinized the cool beauty before her. Jillian was a tall young woman in her early twenties possessed of thick, light brown hair that glowed in the room's light. It was skillfully arranged to emphasize the regal beauty of her face and particularly her startling dark green eyes. She held herself with a maturity and confidence far beyond her years.

"I am glad to meet you at last, Lady Samantha," said Jillian with cool civility. "Hilary has told me much good of you."

"And your fiancé much ill," Samantha said with a smile.

"No, no," murmured Lord Cartwright, studying the portrait of a grimly bewigged relative. "The truth, only the truth."

Samantha flashed him a startled grin.

"It is my belief," said Jillian dampingly, "that a correct opinion can be formed only from a comparison and appraisal of diverse reports. Then, of course, one must make one's own observations before reaching an appropriate conclusion."

"You would make an excellent scientist, Lady Jillian," Samantha replied, her amusement growing.

"If I were a man. But if that were the case, I would enter the political world, not the scientific. I find the awesome power within the political arena to be quite intoxicating."

"But since you *are* a woman, you will marry Lord Cartwright, a man who is neither a scientist nor a politician," Samantha observed.

"Lord Cartwright has been too involved in his family's difficulties to attend to national and international concerns. The time will come, however, when he will take his rightful place among his peers."

Lord Cartwright regarded his fiancée with dismay and sought sanctuary in a cake at the tea table.

A small silence fell on the room.

"The winter is unusually mild this year, is it not?" Jillian said at last, for silence of any duration in a conversation was anathema to her.

"I would not know," Samantha replied. "It is many years since I was last in London."

"Ah yes, you *travel*," Jillian said.

"On occasion."

"For my part, I do not understand this mad passion to roam about the world that moves so many young women nowadays," Jillian stated. "England provides our every need: comfort, culture, art, music, similar society, language, and experience. It is my belief that if one cannot be satisfied in England, one cannot be satisfied anywhere."

"Very commendable."

"One thinks of that awful Lady Hester Stanhope woman

cavorting about on Mouth Lebanon with horror and disgust."

"I don't think of her at all, actually."

"You have never married?"

"Not that I can remember," Samantha replied.

Lord Cartwright, hand trembling slightly, poured himself another cup of tea.

"I daresay you met no one suitable in your foreign travels," said Jillian.

"On the contrary, I have met many suitable men. *I* am simply not suited to marriage."

"Not suited . . . ?" Jillian stared at Samantha as she would a freak at Bartholomew's Fair. "You are absurd, Lady Samantha. You are a woman. The church, society, and our very nature teach us that Woman was created solely *for* marriage."

"Ah, but I am more ambitious."

Jillian regarded her with growing hostility and would have replied save for the clock on the mantel beginning to chime three o'clock.

"Oh dear," she said, "I must leave. I promised to call on Princess Esterhazy before four o'clock. Had you another call to make, Lady Samantha? May I drop you somewhere?"

"Thank you, no," Samantha replied, her hazel eyes twinkling merrily. "I shall be ensconced here a while yet."

"I'll come with you to the door," said Lord Cartwright.

"I am glad to have met you at last, Lady Samantha," said Jillian coolly as she extended her hand.

"And I you."

They shook hands and Jillian sailed from the room, Lord Cartwright in tow.

"Well," said Jillian, drawing on her fur-lined cloak at the front door, "she is all that I had heard and more. How can she have the impudence to call upon you in such a brazen manner?"

"I suspect it was Hilary she came to see. They have become fast friends."

"Really, Simon, as head of this family, I think you would extend yourself to protect your sister from such a creature."

"Hilary is old enough and wise enough to choose her own friends," Lord Cartwright replied mildly.

"Indeed?" said Jillian. "Then she should know that Lady Samantha Adamson is an unregenerate *philistine* who poisons all about her. I dislike leaving you with that woman in the house."

Lord Cartwright smiled down at her. "I think I will be safe."

"It was her place to leave first."

"But, Jillian, she has just arrived."

"I wish you will not willfully misunderstand me, Simon. You know I have always deplored your levity. It appears at the most inappropriate times."

"I'm sorry, Jillian."

She accepted the apology, presented her cheek, which Lord Cartwright duly kissed, and then sailed out the door.

Lord Cartwright stood in the entry hall lost in uncomfortable thought. Jillian's ill-treatment of a guest in his house roused him to reconsider his own treatment of that selfsame guest. He had, as Hilary had said more than once, treated Lady Samantha abominably. And, while she had most certainly responded in kind, he should at least summon common civility when in the wretched woman's presence.

He was a gentleman. He would act like one.

"I daresay London must seem rather dull to the Danthorpes after all their adventures," Hilary was saying as Lord Cartwright drew near the saloon.

"As it happens," Samantha said slowly, "they have both come to me seeking greater activity in their days. Peter's lethargy is easily resolved; I intend to find him a tutor."

"Poor boy," Hilary clucked sympathetically.

"Poor *me*. I have no idea where I am to find such a creature."

"If you had need of a governess, I might be able to help you, but tutors, I fear, are beyond my province."

"Do not even *mention* the word 'governess.' Christina is just turned nineteen and cannot tolerate the sight of them. She locked her last governess in a trunk over a year ago and . . . er . . . lost the key."

Lord Cartwright firmly repressed a chuckle and strolled into the room.

"I could not help but overhear, Lady Samantha," he said as he took his place beside his sister on the gold brocade sofa, "that you are in need of a tutor for your ward. Perhaps I might be of some assistance?" He was rewarded by a momentary look of shock on his opponent's face. He hid a smile and continued. "My brother, Matthew, has quit the schoolroom comparatively recently and I still have access to the addresses of several reputable men who would, I believe, serve your ward quite well."

Samantha, it must be confessed, was momentarily nonplussed by such graciousness.

"You are very . . . kind. I gladly accept your offer."

"Excellent," Lord Cartwright said with the first smile he had ever given her. "I shall prepare a list of possible tutors and have it delivered to you before the day is out."

He rose from the sofa, made his farewells, and strolled from the room.

Samantha blinked and tried to recall herself to a sense of her surroundings. Lord Cartwright had the most charming smile!

"My word," she murmured.

Hilary smiled. "Come, we were discussing the lethargy of your wards. Peter's ennui has been resolved for the present. What of Christina?"

"Ah yes," Samantha said, shifting in her chair. "Well, that involves my asking you for a very great favor."

"Really? What is it?"

"I must tell you that you are entirely to blame for my request."

"I?"

"You. If you had not spent every visit with us recounting the many supposed pleasures in London, Christina would not now be hounding me into an early grave. It is time to make restitution, Hilary."

"Shall I describe, instead, the squalor and poverty all about us?"

"No, no, I depend upon you to take more direct action. Christina is nineteen and of a gregarious nature. She longs to enter into Society. Actually, what she really wants is a husband, which means she must enter Society. As an inveterate matchmaker I must not only applaud such a decision, but support it. She, of course, has set her heart on a ramshackle hero, but I am determined to find her a steady fellow who will be utterly devoted to her. My question to you is: how is this to be accomplished? Christina is an American raised abroad, and I am an Englishwoman raised abroad. *I* have never even had a formal debut. Consequently, I know none of the patronesses at Almack's, none of the dragons of the ton who could give Christina carte blanche. I know no reputable matrons who could invite her to a party and introduce her to the people who seem to matter . . . save you."

"Would you like me to give her a party?" Hilary inquired. "It is the simplest thing in the world!"

"No, no, no," Samantha calmly broke in. "I do not want you to merely give her a party. I want you to sponsor Christina's debut."

Hilary gaped at her friend.

"You have had a shock," Samantha said. "Shall I ring for the smelling salts?"

"What an absolutely marvelous idea!"

"I beg your pardon?"

50

"I have always longed to sponsor a debut and, as I will have no daughter of my own, this is the perfect opportunity to do so. I *adore* parties and balls and Christina will be such a sensation!" Hilary rhapsodized. "I trust she has money?"

"Oh, she's full of juice," Samantha drawled.

"An heiress! Even better. She will reduce to ashes that dreadful Letty Maxwell—thirty thousand pounds a year and determined to queen it over the lot of us. But we must start at once! The Season doesn't get fully under way until spring, but the town is very far from being thin. We can launch Christina now and have her ruling the roost by April. Oh, what fun I shall have!"

Looking at her friend glowing from head to toe, Samantha doubted that Hilary realized the revolutionary change that would soon transform her life. She was about to reenter the world of the living with a vengeance and Samantha could not have been more pleased. She felt that she was terribly clever and was sufficiently proud of herself for being so.

Hilary broke in on these happy ruminations.

"And I shall find a worthy husband for you as well, Samantha. See if I don't."

"Thank you, no!" said Samantha in some alarm. "I want no suitors, no courtship, and *no* husband. I will go to my grave a spinster and glad of it."

"But you have said that you are a matchmaker!"

"And a very good one."

"But why make matches for your friends and not yourself?"

"Because I have more sense than any of my friends," Samantha retorted. "I am too independent and too intelligent to tolerate a master's hand guiding me through my days. Marriage places a woman's life, livelihood, and happiness directly in the hands of her husband. Such a loss of control over my own destiny terrifies me!"

51

She held up one hand. "You will urge me to marry for love—I see the words hovering on your lips—and I tell you straight, Hilary, you would wish misery upon me. I have seen in what a vulnerable position marital love places women. My own mother was such a one. She adored my father to the exclusion of anything else, including her own needs and well-being. I have a horror of such an unhealthy dependence on another human being and that is what a marriage of love creates."

Hilary clasped her friend's hand. "You are wrong, Samantha. Such dependence is but a part of character. You are very different from your mother. You would not succumb to such slavish devotion."

Samantha carefully removed her hand. "I find it infinitely safer not to make the experiment."

She would discuss the matter no further, and instead turned the conversation back to Christina and her forthcoming debut. Hilary allowed herself to be distracted and they spent a happy hour planning Christina's life before Samantha bid her adieu and returned to the Dower House.

Garner opened the door to her and intoned after she had taken but two steps into the house: "The Duke de Peralta has called, my lady. I have installed him in the Blue Drawing Room."

"What? Phillip? Here? Oh, how marvelous!" Samantha cried. "Whatever is he doing in England?"

"The duke made some mention of . . . ahem . . . wife-hunting, my lady."

"Oh lord, is he out of pocket again? Isn't that just like him? Well, it looks like I'm going to be busy, Garner. Better batten down the hatches."

Aware that there could be no suitable reply to such a statement, Garner said nothing as Samantha ran up to the first landing, gaily shouting at the top of her lungs:

"Phillip! Phillip, you old dog, where are you?"

"Mi flor inglés!" reverberated all the way down the stairs.

Samantha threw open the door to the Blue Drawing Room and then threw herself into the arms of Phillip, Duke de Peralta, who hugged her as if he would crush every rib in her body.

The duke was of but medium height, barrel chested and stocky. But his beautiful black eyes, lit now with the greatest happiness, and his full mouth which promised the sweetest smiles and the most passionate kisses, gave him an appearance of beauty which his wardrobe and the dramatic sweep of his black hair did everything to augment. The duke was forty-eight years old, his dark face unlined, his dark hair untinged with gray. In short, he made an impressive figure.

"Dearest, darling Phillip, it's been an age!" Samantha said breathlessly when the duke at last released her.

"Three years, five months, sixteen days," said the duke. "Ah, I have missed you, my lovely Samantha. What a surprise I received when I learned you were in London. How many times have you sworn never to step foot in this city of pomposity?"

"Innumerable times, no doubt, and they've all come back to haunt me. *Cómo está usted?* What brings you from the warmth of the Mediterranean to our endless fogs and cloudy skies?"

"Ah, Samantha," the duke said woefully, "the gods have not smiled upon me. You know that I loved Sophia dearly . . ."

"You were utterly devoted to her, I know, Phillip," Samantha said, guiding him to a blue satin couch and sitting beside him. "I was so sorry to learn of her death."

"Your letter was most kind and most welcome. It came just after I received the shattering news that I was to receive a mere competence from her estate."

"But Phillip, how is this possible?" Samantha demanded

with great surprise. "You always carefully investigate your future wives' financial background before going down on your knee."

"The fortune is there, *mi amiga*, but in the coffers of Sophia's cousin, Piero. It is a tangle of Italian documents I still cannot understand," the duke said with a grimace, "but the result is all too clear. A competency, a mere competency, Samantha!"

"You poor dear," Samantha said, sympathetically patting his hand. "You've run through it, of course."

"Who would not?" the duke demanded. "I am amazed that I contrived to make it last so long. Three wives, Samantha. Three! And I am as much without funds as the day I was born."

"You have been sadly misled in matrimony, Phillip," Samantha said, looping her arm through his. "For Evangelina to lure you into marriage before you had even become of age and not leave you a peso at her death was bad. For Angelique's family to provide you with property and francs that did not last the length of the marriage was worse. But for Sophia to leave you a mere competency . . . ! I wonder you have not turned to drink."

The duke's black eyes twinkled at her. "You are a rogue, Samantha. I have often said it. A rogue. Very well, I come to you in the state I was born. A magnificent title and nothing behind it but centuries of impoverishment. Spain, France, and Italy have all failed me. Can you contrive a rich marriage in England for such a man?"

Samantha considered the matter. "I believe England has a goodly number of rich widows. I'll see what I can do."

"*Diosa!*" said the duke, pressing her hand to his lips. "You would not consider offering yourself up as my bride?"

"Phillip, you know that I love you dearly, but I am determined never to marry."

54

The duke sadly shook his head. "A waste. A terrible waste. *Qué lástima!*"

Samantha held back a chuckle. "Where are you staying?"

"The Clarenden," the duke said with a shrug. "It is tolerable."

"It is expensive," Samantha retorted. "Can you pay your shot?"

"In a word, no."

"Well, since you have engaged my matchmaking services, the least I can do is provide you with the necessary Clarenden funds. And you certainly may dine here as often as you choose. Every day if you wish."

The duke beamed at her and kissed her hand again. "*Muchas gracias.* You are the soul of generosity."

"But I will pay no tailor."

"Samantha!" cried the poor duke.

"No, Phillip."

"But I must make myself presentable if I am to woo and win a wealthy English lady."

Samantha's gaze took in the duke's gleaming Hessians, biscuit-colored pantaloons, cream waistcoat, and coat of forest green superfine. "You look more than presentable right now. How many trunks did you bring with you?"

"Five. Only five."

"I daresay five Spanish trunks must hold a surfeit of clothing," Samantha said. "No tailors, Phillip."

"Very well," said the duke with a sigh.

"As for gaming—"

The duke brightened. "I have been remarkably fortunate thus far."

"Excellent. Retain your winnings and promise me no more wagers of any kind until you are riveted to a suitable female."

"Not to gamble?" said the duke with the utmost horror. "Samantha, of what can you be thinking?"

"Debts of honor which I refuse to pay for you."

"But Samantha—"

"*No*, Phillip."

The Duke de Peralta moved a few inches away on the couch, his expression petulant, his manner cold. "You are hard, very hard. I find I don't wish to marry you after all."

"Oh very well," she relented, "I grant you whist. But no debts over a thousand pounds."

"Samantha!" the duke cried, returning to her side and fervently pressing his lips to her hand. "You are munificence itself."

"Samantha!" called Christina from the stairs. "Samantha, are you there? Oh, there you are!" she cried bursting into the room and stopping dead when she saw her guardian and an older and clearly experienced gentleman holding her hand on the sofa. "Oh, I beg your pardon. I didn't know you had company."

"*Hola!* Who is this ravishing child?" exclaimed the duke as he rose.

Samantha performed the introductions, suppressing a smile as the duke executed one of his most romantic bows and kissed Christina's hand with a warmth tempered by reverence.

"I am enchanted to make the acquaintance of so deliriously beautiful a young woman," he declared.

"She's wealthy, too," Samantha commented.

"Her perfections are clear to the meanest intelligence," the duke informed her, kissing Christina's hand once again.

"To think that I should meet the Duke de Peralta at last!" Christina exclaimed. "Samantha has told me so much about you."

"*Mil rayos,*" said the duke.

"*No importa*, Phillip," Samantha said with a fond smile. "You couldn't have her anyway. While you certainly meet Christina's criteria of a romantic suitor, she has enough sense to marry someone a trifle closer to her own age."

"But your love, Christina, would be my fountain of

youth," the duke proclaimed, pressing Christina's hand to his heart. "I could be a mere stripling in your arms!"

"Samantha, he's *wonderful!*" Christina exclaimed as she gazed up at the duke.

"I could say he's had years of practice," Samantha said with a grin, "but the truth of the matter is that Phillip was born wonderful."

"Mujer angélica."

"You know, your arrival is most opportune, Phillip," Samantha said. "You can help give Christina some town polish."

This stopped the duke for a moment. "Polish?"

"Samantha, what are you going on about?" Christina demanded.

"Why, your debut, of course. It's all arranged."

"Samantha!" Christina screeched as she hurtled herself into her guardian's arms. "You dear, sweet, wonderful woman!"

"Homage is always welcome, Chris, but you are strangling me."

Christina freed her guardian and began to dance in ecstasies around the room.

"You have your hands full, I see," commented the duke.

"I always like to keep busy," Samantha said.

"You do not do yourself justice, *amiga*. For you, to be busy is an obsession."

Chapter Six

Mrs. Hilary Cartwright Sheverton determined that, prior to the debut of Miss Danthorpe, a testing of the social waters was required. Thus, she resolved to hold a dinner party for her protégée in which some of the haut ton (and others not of their league but far more entertaining) were invited. Invitations were sent out for Friday evening and responded to in a most satisfactory fashion.

On Friday, a stunned silence greeted the Danthorpes and Samantha as they entered the Cartwright drawing room. Unintentional though it was, they could not have shown themselves off to better advantage. Samantha's golden fairness placed between the handsome darkness of the Danthorpes created a marvelous contrast. The room erupted into hysterical conversation.

Lord Cartwright—dressed in simple black evening dress that did everything to flatter his tall, muscular frame—made the trio his bow.

"You will be the talk of the town tomorrow," he said.

"My dear sir," said Samantha, "I am always the talk of the town!"

"No retort, if you please, Simon," Hilary intoned.

"But you ordered me to enjoy myself tonight!" Lord Cartwright expostulated.

"*Not* at Samantha's expense," his sister retorted.

"It's quite all right, Hilary," Samantha said with a grin, "I can take it."

"Of course you can," Hilary replied. "I only wish you would not tempt it. Go away, Simon, and play the polite host."

Lord Cartwright was not so easily shifted. "It would, perhaps, be impolite of me to observe that Lady Samantha and the Danthorpes should have been the first to arrive, rather than some of the last."

"Yes, it would," said Samantha with a grin. "But I try to encourage rudeness in the upper classes whenever possible. Also, I wanted to make an impression on your guests, my lord, for Christina's sake. I trust we succeeded?"

Lord Cartwright surveyed her low-cut evening gown of green netting over white satin in such a way that Samantha unaccountably blushed.

"That is an understatement," said he. "Unlike you, madam, I value my reputation in the ton. I implore you to employ a modicum of propriety while in my house tonight."

"You are in luck, sir. I've just a modicum left."

Lord Cartwright sighed heavily and withdrew to the more decorous company of Lady Jillian Roberts.

Hilary ordered Peter and Matthew to enjoy themselves without destroying the house or scandalizing her guests, and then took Christina and Samantha on a tour of the ton.

She led them first to Lady Susan and Lord Cyril Horton. His lordship was a genial, sociable, but rather obtuse viscount. His wife, a matron of four-and-thirty years and the mother of three children, was a growing force amongst those women aspiring to dragonhood. Introductions were made. Lady Horton beamed at Samantha and Christina as if they were long lost relations happily reclaimed.

"Lady Samantha," she said fondly, taking Samantha's hand, "this is a *very* great pleasure. We have a mutual

59

friend, you know. Besides Hilary, of course. Count Rintoul. Do you remember him?"

"Deep bass voice? An overfondness for diamonds?" Samantha asked.

"*That's* the fellow!" Lady Horton exclaimed. "Oh, the stories he told of you! I do hope they were true."

"I daresay they were."

Hilary led Samantha and Christina around the rest of the room, introducing them to damsels and dandies; the lesser dragons of the ton; and to Princess Esterhazy and Lady Jersey, two of the formidable patronesses of Almack's.

"Your taste was always excellent, Mrs. Sheverton," said Princess Esterhazy to Hilary as she scanned Christina standing demurely before her. "She will change the fashion from blondes to brunettes within a se'ennight. I commend you." The Princess had always been proud of her own, carefully maintained, black locks.

"Rather a shabby trick to play on your own sister-in-law, though," Lady Jersey opined. "How can you sponsor so formidable a rival to Miss Ellen Sheverton?"

"Because nothing worth having, including an excellent husband, should come too easily," Hilary serenely replied.

"Bosh!" declared a musical voice.

They turned to behold a vision in diaphanous white, her blond hair a mass of curls upon her head, her heart-shaped face smiling upon them, her blue eyes twinkling with laughter.

"Everyone knows," continued the vision, "that you and my brother fell in love at first sight and were married within three months. Where was the hardship in that?"

"Completing all of the wedding plans in time," Hilary retorted with a smile. "Lady Samantha, Miss Danthorpe, I present my sister-in-law, Miss Ellen Sheverton. Take everything she tells you with a large lump of salt."

Miss Sheverton wrinkled her nose prettily at her sister-in-law and then extended her hand to Christina. "Oh, I am so glad to meet you! Shall we confound the masses and become the best of friends?"

"Yes, lets," Christina said dimpling as she took the outstretched hand. "I think we will show each other off to great advantage."

"My thoughts precisely!"

"You are fortunate, Mrs. Sheverton," said Lady Jersey with an amused smile at these new bosom-bows, "in having so understanding a relation."

"Now Lady Jersey, you know what a minx Ellen is," Hilary replied with a fond smile at her sister-in-law. "She is a trial to us all. You have often remarked it."

"Yes," said Lady Jersey. "But a charming trial for all that. Your parents are in negotiation with Lord Farago, are they not, Miss Sheverton?"

"The lawyers are battling it out even as we speak," Ellen gravely replied.

"You are to be congratulated," said Princess Esterhazy. "The Farago fortune and lands are extensive."

Ellen merely bowed as the two dragons made their way toward new victims.

"They are rather awesome, aren't they?" Christina commented, gazing after them.

"Yes," Ellen agreed, "and no matter what anyone tells you, their bark *is* as bad as their bite."

The two girls erupted into laughter and, arm in arm, moved off to enjoy a private chat.

"I like her, Hilary," Samantha announced. "You have excellent taste in sisters-in-law."

"You are too kind. Ah, here he is at last!" Hilary suddenly exclaimed, deserting Samantha to hurry across the room to greet Lord Aaron Wyatt who was, as usual, looking quite splendid in black evening dress, cream-colored ribbons at his knees. She caught his hand in hers, laughed at something he said, and then dragged him back across the room, introducing him to Samantha as her oldest and dearest friend. "My two best friends must be best friends as well. I insist upon it."

"Anything to oblige you, Hilary," said Lord Wyatt with a warm smile that interested Samantha no end. "But we must disappoint you in our introduction. Lady Samantha and I have already met. How are you, Lady Samantha?"

"Very well, thank you," Samantha said with an amused smile. "And you?"

"Enthralled with your friends who know how to flatter in all seeming innocence. I have been looking forward to meeting you again, Lady Samantha," Lord Wyatt said as he took her hand. "Hilary has told me so much about you."

"That is what everyone has been saying," Samantha said with a groan. "I had not realized Hilary has such an active tongue in her head."

"She uses it sparingly, save on those of whom she is fond," Lord Wyatt replied. "Hilary is . . . a remarkable woman."

Something about Lord Wyatt's tone of voice, rather than his words, made Samantha regard Hilary and him with a more scrupulous attention.

"I think you and I," she said, "will not fail Hilary. We shall become friends. I suspect we have much in common."

With the arrival of the last of Hilary's guests, dinner was announced and all adjourned to the larger of the two Cartwright dining rooms. Samantha was sufficiently distant from Jillian Roberts to retain her wry amusement at so perfect a young gentlewoman, and close enough to Lord Wyatt to follow his every word and movement. This consisted chiefly in his blue eyes straying continually toward Hilary during the course of the meal. That he was hopelessly in love with his hostess was all too clear to a woman of Samantha's experience and she found herself, upon reflection, well pleased with such an interesting development. Perhaps Christina would not be the only one to pull Hilary from her safe and secluded widowhood.

At the conclusion of dinner, the gentlemen withdrew into masculine solitude to enjoy their cigars and port, while the ladies returned to the drawing room where they had all first gathered. There they broke up into small groups enjoying tea or wine or coffee and a myriad of conversations. Hilary, having spoken first with Princess Esterhazy and then with Lady Jersey, hurried up to Samantha, gripped her arm with great strength, and pulled her into a corner.

"She is a success!" she cried.

"Who?" Samantha inquired, taking a sip of wine.

"Throw off the pose and pay attention. Christina has triumphed! Both Princess Esterhazy and Lady Jersey have commanded me to bring her to Almack's on Wednesday. They will both send her vouchers. Her success is assured!"

Samantha's brow was creased in puzzlement. "With Christina's beauty and vast fortune, how could she not be a success?"

"And is this the thanks I get for all my efforts on your behalf?"

"Ignoring for the moment that you have enjoyed and thrived on every single one of your efforts, I do thank you, Hilary, for making Chris so happy. I certainly could not have contrived such a debut. I wish you joy of your sojourn at Almack's Wednesday."

"But you must come as well!"

"Good God why?" said Samantha aghast.

"Because you are her guardian. You must be seen with her at every major function at first, to give your countenance to her debut, and to reassure the ton that she is properly supervised and connected."

Samantha regarded Hilary with open horror. "If I had known the baggage would be leading me into the insipid social whirl of this grimy town, I would have removed us all to Moscow weeks ago."

Hilary clucked with mock sympathy.

"Oh, I know your sentiments very well," Samantha said.

"You love attending every dreary rout, dinner, ball, and assembly the town can offer, while I"—she stopped and considered—"might be able to put them to some use after all."

"Samantha," said Hilary in some alarm, "what are you thinking?"

"Merely that Celeste Vandaun has asked me to find her a suitable protector. Where better to look than in the drawing rooms of the haut ton?"

Hilary stared at her in stupefaction. "You can't! You mustn't!"

Samantha smiled imperturbably. "But I will."

Filled with foreboding, Hilary went off to see to the rest of her guests. Samantha was soon captured by Lady Susan Horton who fondly looped her arm through hers.

"I am so glad you have landed in London, my dear," said Lady Horton. "You've given us all so much to talk about! How glad I am to discover that there is more to you than a pretty face."

"Others do not share your generous opinion," said Samantha, rousing herself from the deep depression into which Hilary had dropped her. How was she to survive a London Season? "Lord Cartwright has frequently conveyed his disapproval of my character to me in a manner which left little doubt that he would prefer me decorous and accommodating."

"For an intelligent woman you are amazingly stupid," Lady Horton declared. "Simon Cartwright adores strong, opinionated women; comes from having Emma Cartwright for a mother. Why do you think he shackled himself to Jillian Roberts? Because Jillian, for all her stuffiness, has a good head on her shoulders and a strong will. Cartwright could never tolerate a woman who quietly bowed to his every decree, and Jillian has certainly never done that!"

"No, I don't imagine she would," Samantha said with an

amused smile. "If she unbent even a little, the crack of ice around her would deafen the nation."

Lady Horton gurgled with laughter as the gentlemen entered the saloon.

Lord Cartwright had but a moment to wonder how Lady Samantha could contrive to look so ravishing and so mischievous at the same time before his attention was claimed by Lady Jersey and all such wayward thoughts were put aside.

Some time later, he observed his fiancée conversing with Peter Danthorpe. Seeing the color slowly rise in young Mr. Danthorpe's face, Lord Cartwright drew near.

"You must remember," Jillian was saying, "the duty you owe your guardian and to Society when you appear in company and not put yourself forward or demonstrate the backward social graces of our former colony. Hilary tells me that you play the pianoforte."

"A little," was Peter's sullen reply.

"You must remember to practice every day if you wish to become proficient. I, myself, am a notable harpist and insist upon practicing one hour each and every morning, saving Sunday of course, to maintain and improve my skill. Do you play Haydn?"

"A little," Peter grimly replied.

"Handel?"

"A little."

"Oh nonsense, Peter," Hilary protested, for she had been shamelessly eavesdropping on this conversation as well. "Samantha tells me that you play a great deal of Handel and that you play him superbly, as you do everything else. Peter," she informed Jillian, "is considered something of a prodigy."

"Indeed?" Jillian replied. "It is a pity he has nothing prepared. I should have enjoyed listening to him play this evening."

"My dear ma'am," Peter gravely said, "a prodigy is always prepared. It would be my very great pleasure to perform before so august a company . . . if I would not be putting myself forward."

"No, no," Hilary said with a grin, "not at all."

Peter solemnly advanced to the harpsichord, sat down, and indicated to Hilary that she could now introduce him. This done, he plunged into Handel's Air and Variations in E Major from Suite Number Five.

The twenty people in the drawing room were stunned into silence.

Lord Cartwright stared at Peter in shock. The boy's long fingers moved with great power and speed over the keys, his face a study of intense concentration as the complexity and rapidity of the piece grew. The boy was magnificent!

The tension that Handel and Peter's skill created built into an unbearable knot within his listeners until the final crashing notes released them from his spell. The audience burst into wild applause and vociferous pleas for him to continue. But Peter merely bowed, shook his head with a smile, and returned to Lord Cartwright, Jillian, Hilary, and Samantha, who had joined them during the performance.

"That was very well done," Jillian said. "The first ten measures were perhaps too strident, too erratic, but on the whole you performed very well indeed. I commend you."

Lord Cartwright stared at her.

But Peter suddenly smiled. "Your ladyship is too kind," he said. "Such praise from so accomplished a musician as yourself is most gratifying."

With a grin at Samantha, he then strolled off to receive accolades from the rest of the Cartwright guests. Jillian was called away by Lady Jersey, and Hilary went to attend Lord Wyatt.

Lord Cartwright, recollecting his vow to practice civility whenever in her presence, remained with Samantha.

"Jillian was . . . too severe. Your ward is a remarkable musician," he said.

"I quite agree," she replied.

There was an awkward pause.

"I have not yet had the opportunity, my lord, to thank you properly for recommending Mr. Victor Speer to me," Samantha said with great determination. "He is an excellent tutor. Peter and he will deal extremely well together."

"You have already engaged him?" Lord Cartwright said with surprise.

"Certainly. You cannot think I would let such a find get away! Once a scheme is hatched I cannot sit idly by. I told you once, I believe that I am a woman of action. Peter's lessons begin on the morrow."

Lord Cartwright preferred not to recall their first meeting. "Rumor has it that you have also engaged Madame LeCarron to instruct Mr. Danthorpe on the pianoforte."

"Blast Hilary! That was meant to be a secret until I unleash her on Peter tomorrow."

"My lips are sealed, I assure you," Lord Cartwright vowed. "It is true, then?"

"From the outrageous fee I have paid her, it is *very* true."

"Genius does not come cheap."

"And Frenchwomen even less so."

"I shall ignore the double entendre," Lord Cartwright intoned.

"Drat," Samantha said with a grin. "You will not even chastise me for the impropriety?"

Lord Cartwright smiled down at her. "I will allow your conscience to apply the burning balm."

"I lost my conscience in a game of vingt-et-un several years ago and haven't missed it since."

Lord Cartwright's brown eyes were lit with laughter. "That I can easily believe. Shall I lend you some of mine?"

"Thank you, no. I've a dislike of stiff necks."

Lord Cartwright sighed heavily. "I might have known you could not get through one night without insulting your host."

"I never knew a man to have such thin skin," Samantha said impatiently. "You take in bad part every word that leaves my lips."

"Perhaps the fault lies in your conversation and not my thin skin. I advise you to guard your tongue whilst in London. Your cavalier conversation will soon do you harm if you do not reform it."

"I will speak as I like when I like and no starched-up *slowtop* shall make me do otherwise!"

"Then you will reap the consequences of your own imprudence," Lord Cartwright stated and strode off for a badly needed glass of wine.

Lord Wyatt quickly took his place but Samantha, staring mutinously at her host's broad back, did not see him.

"*How* can I be civil with such an odious man?" she muttered.

"I have offended you already," Lord Wyatt moaned.

Samantha stared at him in some surprise. "Not you; Cartwright!"

"You have had a row. I see it by the fire in your beautiful eyes. Was this quarrel over indecorous songs as well?"

"You have heard that tale, have you?" Samantha said, smiling at the memory of her first (and victorious) meeting with Lord Cartwright.

"With Hilary, Simon, *and* Matthew as my informants, how could I not hear of your every action and word? You are a tonic, Lady Samantha. A kick in the pants is just what Simon needs and so I have said for over a year now. . . . Why do you stare at me so?"

"Are you quite certain you are Lord Cartwright's *friend?*" Samantha queried and Lord Wyatt chuckled. "You are not at all what I expected. In fact, you are remarkably charming."

Lord Wyatt bowed. "It is no difficult task to be charming in such charming company."

"Lady Jillian Roberts would not agree with your assessment of my company, I think."

"Ah yes, but Jillian holds herself to a higher standard."

Samantha regarded Lord Wyatt. "You do not like the lady?"

"Not much, no," he calmly replied. "She promotes all of the worst aspects of Simon's beliefs and behavior and thereby increases the unhappiness of his family and friends."

"An odd pair," Samantha murmured, studying the affianced couple as they stood conversing at the opposite end of the room.

"A disastrous pair," Lord Wyatt amended. "They are so completely unsuitable for each other that it is frightening to contemplate their future together. Yet each is caught within the rules of the ton, and neither seems aware that one has only to shuffle the deck to start a new game."

"An interesting theory and applicable to more than one in my acquaintance. Hilary informs me that you and she have known each other from the cradle. . . ."

Matchmaking always put Samantha in good humor. Thus, she was able, some hours later, to take her leave of Lord Cartwright with perfect cordiality, which he met with the stiffest propriety.

Chapter Seven

Within half an hour after her arrival at Almack's on Wednesday night, Christina was surrounded by a bevy of gentlemen all eager to gain her attention and she was just as eager to grant their wish. Christina liked these men. She liked them all, even the dull and the plain and the arrogant. They entertained her, flattered her, intrigued her. They represented her future in all of its glory and folly.

But would she ever look upon a man she could love? Hear his voice? Utter his name? She had been infatuated several times in the past, but her heart had never been truly touched. Where was the hero of *her* romance?

Lord Michael Palmerston stepped through the crowd (with some difficulty) and up to Christina to remind her that she had promised him this quadrille. She smiled engagingly up at his square face and allowed him to lead her onto the floor.

"I begin to feel that I play the part of some intrepid adventurer," Lord Palmerston said with a smile as they made each other their bows. "Forcing my way through your jungle of admirers, pressing my claim forward, carrying you off. It seems like some huge game and I the champion, for a brief time at least, as I claim the grand prize: your delightful company, Miss Danthorpe."

Christina liked this little speech very much indeed, let her partner know it, and continued to converse with him on this lofty (and thoroughly enjoyable) plane for the rest of the dance.

Samantha was far less pleased as she stood, weary with boredom, in the decorous hall of Almack's Assembly. The dancing was decorous, the conversation was decorous, the refreshments were decorous to the point that she actually found herself drinking watered lemonade. Christina's triumphant success this evening did nothing to alleviate the throbbing headache that tedium had created. Silently cursing Hilary for trapping her into entering this bastion of propriety, Samantha looked around desperately for some means of entertainment.

She spied Lord Cartwright, who had not partaken of a single dance all night, in conversation with Lord Wyatt.

No, she would not be tempted.

Yes, she would.

She adopted one of her brilliant smiles and descended upon the gentlemen.

"How do you do, Lord Cartwright? You are in your element at last, I see. And Lord Wyatt, you are just the man who is needed on an errand of mercy."

"I am always eager to oblige you, ma'am," Lord Wyatt said.

"You see that attractive woman over there?"

Lord Wyatt dutifully looked in the direction she had nodded and saw Mrs. Plonkett strapped into a gown of red-and-silver stripes. By no stretch of the imagination could she be considered attractive.

"No, no, the one in yellow," Samantha said, pointing with her fan to the far corner of the room where two women were joined in a private tête-a-tête.

"What? You mean Hilary?" Lord Wyatt gasped.

"The very one," Samantha replied with a beam. "As you can see, she is trapped in the dregs of conversation with the

71

Countess Iseley, a woman of mean intellect, no humor, and all the charm of a gnat. I speak from experience for I spent an interminable minute at her side earlier in the evening. Be a gentleman, rescue Hilary from her unhappy fate, and lead her out into the dance."

"But—but do you think I should interrupt? The countess is an extremely important—" Lord Wyatt stammered, a flush creeping into his cheeks.

"Do not dillydally, Wyatt," Samantha commanded. "Hilary's eyes are beginning to glaze over. Would you have her think you a knight-errant or a mouse?"

"The former is certainly preferable," Lord Cartwright murmured.

Lord Wyatt's flush deepened. "Hilary has always enjoyed the cotillion," he remarked as he started across the room.

Affection welled in Samantha's bosom for the gentleman.

"You appear to be overfond of ordering people about," Lord Cartwright observed.

"I issued no order," Samantha retorted as they watched Lord Wyatt disengage Hilary from the company of the Countess of Iseley and lead her out onto the dance floor. "I merely made a request. Lord Wyatt is well past his majority. He acts as he chooses."

"And in the process does your ward a disservice."

Samantha regarded Lord Cartwright with frank curiosity.

"The countess," he said, "is one of the most important dragons of the ton. Her favor can raise any girl to the greatest heights of Society. Her disapprobation can ruin any girl's chances of success."

"No one person should have so much power," Samantha declared, "particularly a person who has so little to recommend her."

"I pray you, Lady Samantha, take heed what you say in such a public place. Whether you approve or not, the countess possesses great power and will not hesitate to use it against you or Miss Danthorpe."

Samantha bridled. "What an arrogant, mean-spirited harridan she must be to terrorize the already terrified debutantes embarked upon your wearisome Season."

"Of whom can you speak with such disapprobation?" a stern feminine voice demanded.

Samantha and Lord Cartwright turned to observe the imposing presence of Lady Jersey at their side.

"The Countess of Iseley," Samantha promptly replied, observing Lord Cartwright cringe from the corner of her eye. "Her lack of outer beauty extends inward with a fierce determination. I wonder London can tolerate her."

Lady Jersey's aspect was glacial. "The Countess of Iseley," she intoned, "is a universally admired wife, mother, and patroness of Almack's. His Royal Highness, the Prince Regent, has been conspicuous in his marks of favor toward her. Yet you stand there, a stranger to this town, and dare to condemn one of the most highly regarded women of the ton? I am appalled, Lady Samantha. Yes, appalled. I had heard you described as a hurly-burly female and I find, to my everlasting regret, that reports of you were more than correct."

Lord Cartwright turned to an approaching waiter, liberated a cup of lemonade from his tray, and was thus able to whisper in Samantha's ear, "I did warn you."

"I shall see to it," Lady Jersey continued, "that you are not received by the haut ton. Miss Danthorpe, of course, is a delight and I shall insure that she is not harmed by your distasteful conduct or the censure you so rightly deserve."

Lord Cartwright, noting Samantha's stunned look being overtaken by a mounting anger, hurriedly stepped into the breach.

"You are too severe, my dear Lady Jersey," he said soothingly. "Lady Samantha, it is true, speaks with a greater freedom than we are used to, but she was raised in a barbarous clime and must be forgiven her unintended errors in conversation and action. Surely you, an acknowledged leader in the haut ton, should not condemn such an innocent, but instead instruct and mold her to be a fit member of the class into which she was born."

Samantha, who had not been called an innocent since the age of thirteen, stared at Lord Cartwright and wondered if he had gone quite mad.

"A barbarous clime, eh?" Lady Jersey said, her mouth grimly set despite a growing twinkle in her eyes.

"She has freely admitted to me the shocking lack of care taken in her upbringing," Lord Cartwright continued, warming to his subject, "her consequent ignorance of even the most basic tenets of civilized behavior, and her eagerness to learn how to repair the lamentable reputation she has unknowingly acquired through the years."

Samantha thought Lord Cartwright had gone well past the bounds of civilized behavior and opened her mouth to denounce such fustian, but his heel grinding into her foot effectively aborted the speech hovering on her lips.

Lady Jersey unfurled her fan and waved it studiously near her ear. "You are quite right, of course, Simon," she said complacently. "I spoke too rashly. It seems I am prone to the same errors which threaten to sink Lady Samantha beyond redemption. As I am therefore tainted, I shall make you my deputy. I depend upon you to instruct Lady Samantha in the ways of the ton. Any errors she makes will be on your head. Good evening, Simon. Lady Samantha."

Lady Jersey swept away in a rustle of silk as Lord Cartwright and Samantha stared after her. Then Samantha began to chuckle.

"So, you are to be my keeper, are you?"

"It will be a cold day in—" Lord Cartwright forcibly held himself back. "I will no more tutor you in the ways of the ton than I would a . . . a *mule*, for neither of you have any desire to learn."

"Too true," Samantha said with a grin. "But will you disobey a direct order from on high?"

"Lady Jersey may rule Almack's. She does not rule me."

"Manfully said. You've only yourself to blame for this hobble, you know. If you had not spoken without thinking, you would not now be reaping the consequences of your own imprudence."

A muscle twitched in Lord Cartwright's cheek. *"Touché."*

Samantha laughed. "Why on earth did you rescue me from my own folly?"

"I had a sudden fit of light-headedness. I pray it does not happen again."

"Now, now. You acted the knight-errant very well," Samantha assured him. "I was most impressed. I certainly have learned my lesson, I assure you, Lord Cartwright. You need not fear me putting you to the blush again . . . at least in Almack's."

"I am grateful for any crumb," Lord Cartwright said feelingly.

"Come," Samantha said with a smile, "let us abandon me as a topic of conversation; it will undoubtedly make you bilious. Who is the stout gentleman dancing with Miss Ellen Sheverton?"

Lord Cartwright gazed into the cotillion and perceived his sister-in-law on the arm of a gentleman nearly fifty years of age. Stout was an apt description. Florid was another as he energetically partnered the lovely Miss Sheverton. Lord Cartwright's mouth returned to its grim setting.

"That is Lord Barnaby Farago, Miss Sheverton's future husband."

"What!" exclaimed Samantha, staring at the pair aghast. "You cannot mean it."

"Unfortunately, I do."

"But he is old enough to be her grandfather!"

"His age is tempered by a respectable title and a vast fortune. Miss Sheverton is considered quite fortunate in attaching him."

"Fortunate!" Samantha exploded. "Oh, how can you say so? It's monstrous to chain that lovely girl to a fossilized Midas who hasn't civility enough to stop leering at his prize."

Lord Cartwright gazed down at her in some amusement. "I thought you had learned your lesson and meant to repair your conversation while in Almack's."

"Oh, but 'tis unjust, sir! Unjust!"

Lord Cartwright paused. "Nevertheless," he said, "we must not quibble when the Shevertons have given the match their full approbation. Nor has Miss Sheverton been browbeaten into an engagement. She enters it willingly, with her eyes open. She knows both the disadvantages and the advantages of such a marriage and is, I believe, content."

Samantha studied him a moment. "You abominate the match as much as I, don't you?"

"I . . . could wish her a different husband," Lord Cartwright said carefully. "But the Shevertons are not rich and there are younger daughters to provide for. Such a union will benefit many."

"Yes," Samantha drawled, "that is the usual excuse for any marriage alliance contracted for fortune, politics, or family aggrandizement. How much simpler the whole thing would be, and how much happier Miss Sheverton would be than she appears now, if she simply married for love."

Lord Cartwright was startled from his noted composure. "What? Is the determined spinster a romantic?"

"No, no," Samantha said hastily, "I am a very practical sort. I believe marriage to be what is claimed in the church service: a union of heart, mind, body, and soul. I cannot recall fortune or policy or family being mentioned in the vows."

"Amazingly, Lady Samantha, I find myself in agreement with you for the first time in our acquaintance."

It took a moment to recover from such a declaration.

"Well, I have never been one to let opportunity pass me by," Samantha replied. "Since we agree on this, perhaps we will agree on horseflesh, which I sadly lack. I have already sent the order for our carriages to Tattersall's, but have not the horses to pull them. Nor do I have suitable mounts for my wards or myself. The situation is quite intolerable. Can you tell me what a fair price is for a good horse at Tattersall's?"

A disapproving frown had settled upon Lord Cartwright. "Tattersall's is hardly a suitable place for any gentlewoman, however well traveled. You would look very foolish if you were to visit there and only embarrass yourself. If you will, tell me what sort of horses you desire and I shall purchase them for you."

"Lord Cartwright," Samantha said frostily, "I have purchased horses in America, the Caribbean, Arabia, Turkey, Italy, and France and have been well satisfied with each of my selections. I shall do very well at Tattersall's, I assure you. I require only your hint as to a fair price—"

"Lady Samantha," Lord Cartwright replied, "I have said that Tattersall's is not a suitable place for a woman, *any* woman. Society would condemn you for so unfeminine an undertaking."

"I do not give a *snap* for your society's condemnation of my actions!" Samantha hotly retorted. "I have made what I consider a simple request. You may comply or refuse it as you will. *However*, our brief acquaintance does not give you the right to condemn my intentions, let alone my abilities of which you know nothing."

"You are, by your own account, in a foreign country and therefore unaware of the customs that guide our behavior," Lord Cartwright calmly stated. "If you will not think of your own reputation—which has a high value in our society—then I must, as a gentleman, do so for you. The rules of the ton are just. You must not kick at them so vehemently."

"That is quite enough. I need no lecture from *you*!"

"You once accused me of wanting to have my own way in a matter of some importance. Cannot the same be said of you now?"

Samantha stopped, glared at him, and snapped, "Yes!"

She then stalked off, Lord Cartwright watching her departure with both amusement and satisfaction. Curiosity supplanted both as he observed her stop halfway down the hall and stare at the gentleman who had just entered. She was not alone in this, for several people of the highest rank turned to regard the newest entrant into the staid frolics at Almack's.

He was a very handsome man dressed in impeccable evening clothes, his golden locks beautifully curled, his Hessians blinding. He raised a golden quizzing glass to one blue eye and surveyed the room with an aspect of ennui . . . until he spied Samantha.

She blinked at the blond god. "Derek? Good God, it *is* you!"

There was an audible gasp in the room, which she heard not at all, as she threw herself into the god's arms, kissing both his cheeks. He, in turn, kissed both her hands and stared at her with rapt adoration.

"The last I heard, you were in Italy," he said.

"The last word I heard of you," Samantha happily retorted, "you were in Austria wooing a very young, very beautiful, and very *wealthy* princess."

"Henrietta? She meant nothing to me, my Queen of Hearts. You shall always take precedence."

"Dear Derek," Samantha said fondly, "you haven't changed a bit."

"But you grow more lovely with each new year," Derek said with a rapturous sigh, "and your manners more lamentable. Throwing yourself into my arms in a public forum. For shame, Samantha! What will people think?"

"Everything lowering, I assure you. Oh, it is so good to see you again, Derek! But what are you doing in London? You told me once you could not bear consorting with your

78

backward countrymen, yet here you are: dashing as ever and looking quite at home."

"I have come back to reclaim my heritage, O Queen of Hearts. Political dominion."

"The world is doomed."

The beautiful gentleman snapped open a gold snuff box and took a pinch of snuff. "I will have you know, wench, that I shall make a superb prime minister."

"Prime minister?" Samantha wrinkled her nose in concentration and then nodded. "Yes, you would attain the greatest heights in any career you undertook."

"Angelic creature. You know me so well."

"But when do you start?"

"Start? I have already begun. I have wined and dined and flattered boring government officials and boorish M.P.s the whole of this last se'ennight. I dined with the Prince Regent this evening."

"And will form a new government by morning," Samantha murmured.

The orchestra began to play again.

"A waltz!" Samantha gasped. "Oh, do be generous and dance with me, Derek. I have not waltzed all evening."

"Have you received permission to waltz from the patronesses of Almack's?"

"What?"

"No woman may waltz at Almack's until she has been given permission."

"Of all the absurd ...! I have been waltzing since the Germans invented the dance, Derek."

"Nevertheless, I will not put up the backs of the powerful women who have organized this establishment by flouting the rules they have created.

"Oh very well, very well!" Samantha muttered. She grasped the blond god's hand and towed him behind her to Lady Jersey and Princess Esterhazy who were locked together in an earnest debate over when these two would post the banns. "Your Highness, Lady Jersey," Samantha said with a deep curtsy. "I have come to throw myself at your feet. You alone have the power to grant me the greatest happiness of my life. This is Lord Derek Barnett—"

"We have met," said the Princess. "I am so glad you could come tonight, Lord Barnett."

"I treasure the very kind note you sent with my voucher, Your Highness," Lord Barnett said with a graceful bow.

"Ah, if you know Lord Barnett," said Samantha, "then you can understand how deeply I yearn to partake of the waltz with him. He is a demigod when executing the most fashionable dance on the continent. But, alas, he will not waltz with me. No, he will not! He values your regard too highly to flout it by dancing with a mere social solecism. You see," she said humbly, golden head bowed, "I have not yet received your permission to waltz."

Lady Jersey was hard put not to laugh out loud at this performance. "That is quite enough, Lady Samantha," she said with great severity. "Clearly Lord Cartwright has instructed you well. As it is Lord Barnett who will partner you, you have our permission to waltz."

"Oh, thank you, my lady!" Samantha cried with a brilliant smile. She curtsied once again, Lord Barnett bowed, and they swept onto the dance floor.

The sight of these two blond Incomparables locked in each other's arms as they swirled around the room left many gaping in open admiration.

Except for Lord Cartwright. He disliked the way Lady Samantha smiled so radiantly up at her partner. He particularly disliked the way the beauteous Lord Barnett beamed at her with such open devotion.

Chapter Eight

RAIN STREAMED DOWN the trees and houses in the Square. Looking out her sitting room window at the gray, wintry scene, Samantha held back her sigh. Such a scene inspired introspection. Her introspection inspired sighs.

Ever honest, she took stock of her life: twenty-seven and useless. Yes, that summed it up nicely.

Shopping, paying calls, annoying the London nobs. What a purposeless existence she led! Travel and even match-making no longer satisfied the yearning that gnawed at her vitals. She needed happiness in an increasingly unhappy life and had thought Christina and Peter would provide it. But, though she loved them dearly, they were not the solution she had sought. What was?

Samantha's sigh escaped at last. She needed challenge in her days and contentment in her soul. Both eluded her.

"What an awful mess," she muttered to herself.

"Mrs. Harriet Hunt?" Christina inquired.

"Oh heavens!" said Ellen Sheverton with a pretty shudder.

"She would not know pâté de foie gras from chopped ham if you labeled both and held them directly under her nose. Ignore her," Hilary commanded.

Christina, Hilary, and Ellen sat together before a crackling fire in Samantha's private sitting room. A fortnight had passed since Hilary's dinner party and, as she had promised, Christina had been buried by a mountain of invitations over which they now bent, black head and fair brown locked together in earnest conversation. Balls, routs, assemblies, driving in Hyde Park (and riding when weather permitted), her presentation at Court, appearing at Almack's Assembly rooms—every minute of Christina's days was now filled to the brim and she was quite simply ecstatic.

"Oh look!" Ellen cried, handing an invitation to Christina.

"Lady Helen Chitwood?" said Christina.

"Heavens, yes; grab her, girl!" Hilary said. "She always has the best food, the gayest music, and the most charming young men at her parties."

"Then by all means let us go," Christina said with a smile. "Do you think Lord Palmerston will be there?"

"Oh, he's divine, isn't he?" said Ellen with a rapturous sigh.

"*So* handsome," Christina agreed, "and so romantic! He quoted Shakespeare to me at dinner last night. *Romeo and Juliet*."

"*Lovely,*" said Ellen.

Peter burst into the room just then, his unbuttoned coat heavy with snow, his cheeks flushed with exercise and excitement, his black eyes sparkling.

"I've just had the most smashing time!" he declared to the three women as he advanced into the room, lifted the last of their cakes from its lonely vigil on the serving tray, and began to munch happily upon it. "Matt's been showing me around town and introducing me to all his friends. I've never met such jolly fellows! They laugh all the time. We've all agreed to go to the theater next week. We're going to discuss everything tomorrow. Matt's a capital fellow, bang up to the mark. Well, I'm off to practice," Peter declared after popping the last of the cake into his mouth, "after I raid the kitchen, of course."

With that he trooped happily out of the room, banging the door shut behind him.

"That child is so easily amused," Christina sniffed.

"Well I, for one, am glad that Peter has made such a good friend," Samantha retorted. "Matthew is introducing him to boys his own age which is precisely what Peter needs and has longed for."

"I would not be too eager to embrace Matthew's aid, Samantha," Hilary said uneasily. "Some of his friends are too unthinking, too uncautious, too wild. Matthew is constantly falling into one scrape after another."

"But that is what boys *do* at this age," Samantha replied with a smile.

"Nevertheless," Hilary persisted, "Matthew has done several things that have left Simon and me quite perturbed."

"Hilary, I do see and understand your concern and I thank you for it," Samantha said. "But Peter is a sensible and honorable young man. He will do nothing against his conscience and I trust his conscience completely. He is perfectly capable of taking care of himself."

Hilary was silent.

"Mrs. Follingale?" Christina inquired as she studied an invitation.

"Yes, she's quite suitable," Hilary replied, forcing away her concern.

"Oh, this one is for you, Sam," Christina said, handing her guardian an official-looking envelope.

"This doesn't look like an invitation," Samantha said. "It looks like a summons to court. Heavens, what have I done now?"

"If you'd like me to enumerate—" Hilary began.

"Thank you, no," Samantha retorted, her ward bowing her head to hide her smile as Samantha opened the envelope. She read the letter quickly, the color springing to her cheeks, her mouth becoming decidedly pinched.

Christina was grateful that the next moment brought a summons to a fitting for a new ball gown and she quickly escaped, Ellen in tow. She had no wish to be anywhere near Samantha when she exploded.

"Great galloping goats!" Samantha thundered, shocking Hilary no end.

"My word, what has happened?" she gasped.

"This," Samantha said, shaking the letter in front of her, "*this* is a communiqué from the Adamson family banker informing me in the most superior tone that I may not draw more than two thousand pounds from my account in a month. I cannot draw out my own money! I will horsewhip him through the streets! I'll gouge his eyes out! I'll—"

"Find another bank?" Hilary suggested mildly.

Samantha stopped and stared at her friend. A smile peeped onto her mouth. "Yes, that would be nice. Withdrawing an account worth tens of thousands of pounds and placing it in another bank would be the perfect form of revenge on a supercilious, pompous, narrow-minded, dimwitted banker, wouldn't it?"

Hilary laughed. "You are never shy in expressing your opinions, are you?"

"Never. But which new bank shall I choose?"

"Why not ask Simon for advice?" Hilary said. "He's awfully clever about finance and banking and the Exchange."

"Oh, I couldn't!" Samantha cried.

"Whyever not?"

Samantha considered the matter. Her smile bloomed. "It might be quite an enjoyable romp at that. He's such fun to torment."

"That was not precisely what I had in mind," Hilary said dryly.

"He has never apologized for his abominable behavior at our first meeting, let alone our last," Samantha said righteously. "Prosing to me about propriety ... such arrogance! He needs to be taken down a peg."

"He needs to be happy again," Hilary riposted.

"Why can I not achieve both?" Samantha demanded. "He's stuck in such a rut of propriety that my larks are bound to be good for him. You should have heard him rattling on to Lady Jersey. She nearly split her seams to keep from laughing and if he can make her titter there's hope for the old boy yet."

"He's neither old nor a boy and you'd best watch where you tread," Hilary advised. "You may get yourself into a fix not even you can escape."

"I can only assume it is our brief acquaintance that makes you so fallible a judge of my abilities," Samantha retorted. "There isn't a scrape I can't get myself out of—if I choose to get out of it. Some scrapes are quite entertaining, you know."

"I begin to fear for my poor brother."

"Yes," Samantha said with a saucy smile, "you should."

Lord Cartwright sat in his large, leather chair in his study. He had removed his coat upon entering the room and sat now in shirt sleeves, his feet propped up on his desk as he contemplated the ceiling.

He thought not of the excellent Jacobean woodwork above him, but of his own life.

This is why he frowned.

At twenty-one he had had a clear understanding of who he was and what his life would be. At thirty-two he now wondered how reality could be so different from that youthful vision. At twenty-one he had anticipated love and romance and adventure. Yet here he was, battle-scarred from the last two years, not from an adventure of his own choosing, but from the hell his father had bequeathed him. He had once believed that he would marry for love, yet he had repudiated romance and become engaged to a woman his

85

father would never have chosen, which was certainly a mark in Jillian's favor. Lord Cartwright admired her for her strength, her intelligence, her beauty. But he did not love her, nor did she love him. That had been clear from the beginning.

And now he had begun to wonder, could he live within the narrow worldview that guided Jillian and that she meant to guide him?

And why was he wondering about all this now?

"Lady Samantha Adamson wishes a word with you, my lord," intoned Clarke from the doorway.

"What?" gasped Lord Cartwright, removing his feet from the desk and sitting upright in his chair.

Clarke apparently took this ejaculation as consent for he withdrew from the room and Samantha Adamson soon took his place.

She was dressed in a gown of green silk that did remarkable things to her eyes ... and figure. Her thick, honey blond hair glowed in its soft sweep to her shoulders. And she was smiling at him.

Samantha Adamson was the last person he had expected to see standing (and smiling) before him now. He started to rise but she quickly stepped forward and urged him back into his chair.

"There needs be no formality between such old friends as we," she assured him.

"You will forgive me, madam, but I do not recall the friendship," Lord Cartwright retorted.

To his surprise, her smile only grew.

"Perhaps the friendship does not exist, but then neither does the formality," said Samantha. "We abuse each other cheerfully and with great abandon and that alone should keep you in your chair. I daresay you are wondering why I have called."

"The thought *had* crossed my mind."

"That is precisely what I like about you," Samantha declared. "Your mind does not muck about with idle ruminations, but cuts straight to the heart of the matter. An admirable quality."

She jauntily perched herself on Lord Cartwright's desk and beamed down upon him.

"Would you not prefer . . . a chair?" he suggested.

"Oh no, I am perfectly comfortable," Samantha assured him. "Now then, I have called because I have need of some of your invaluable advice on a financial matter. I wish to change banks—"

Lord Cartwright held up one large hand. "You will forgive me, Lady Samantha, but why come to me? Surely there are others you can turn to who are more knowledgeable than I?"

"Nonsense," Samantha said briskly. "I know you to be an intelligent, honorable (albeit pigheaded) man and I would trust and follow your advice completely (as long as I agreed with it). I see no need for our quarrel—well, it is a feud actually, isn't it, since we quarrel over everything—I see no need for our feud, then, to interfere with my financial needs. Besides, everyone raves about your business acumen and I know so few people in London just at present with that skill, so you're elected."

"Could you not use your family's bank?" Lord Cartwright inquired faintly.

"But that is just the point! I *am*! And I am miserable. My banker is even more backward in his view of the appropriate feminine sphere than are *you*. He took a *month* getting approval from my brother to deal directly with me and to allow me to draw on my own account!"

"Your brother? Good God, do you mean there are *more* of you?"

"Two," Samantha said with a grin. "A brother and a sister. But rest assured, Lord Cartwright, they are not at all like me."

"I own I *am* relieved. I do not believe that I have ever heard you mention these siblings of yours."

"I do so as little as possible. We do not get along."

"Why does that not surprise me?"

"Odious creature," Samantha said, wrinkling her nose at him in a perfectly charming manner. "My brother, Reginald, is eight-and-thirty, and my sister, Lydia, is *six*-and-thirty, and I shall roast in the fires of eternal damnation for revealing that dark secret. Their greatest joy in life comes from thwarting and maligning me at the least provocation. *I* am the baby of the family."

"Of what can your parents have been thinking?"

"Procreation."

"But they already had an heir. If they had just practiced a little temperance in their relations—"

"I do see your point," Samantha said, her hazel eyes lit with amusement, "but I fear they were very intemperate in their love for each other, even after all those years of matrimony, and I am the result, and you are forced to suffer the consequences."

"I am indeed," Lord Cartwright said with a smile that belied the charge. "But I remain curious. Why haven't you mentioned your brother and sister before this?"

"Their memory is too painful for me to bear."

"Oh, I am sorry," Lord Cartwright said, flushing in confusion. "I did not mean to—"

"Reginald," Samantha said with great disgust, "is a pompous ass with a bubbleheaded wife and *five* hideous children. They reside on the Adamson family estate in the black depths of Yorkshire and have never evinced the slightest interest to leave that hellhole."

"And your sister?" Lord Cartwright inquired with a grin.

"Lydia married a Shropshire knight who made his fortune in long-tailed sheep. *She* has three of the most obnoxious children ever to decimate a nursery. I could forgive her the husband, the children, even the sheep. But I could never forgive her Shropshire."

Lord Cartwright burst into laughter. "Lord, if I don't pity you," he said in something akin to amazement.

"Well, I do think you ought to," Samantha said, "and I thank you very much, but we are straying from the point. You have given me excellent advice in the past where Peter was concerned and I do not see why you should not do the same for me. You were, if you recall, rather churlish about the horses and I was forced to venture to Tattersall's by myself."

"So I heard."

Samantha grimaced. "Apparently the whole of the town has heard and can think of nothing else to feed their scandal-broth. But that is neither here nor there. My stables are now full and I am content. Lord Wyatt has been particularly vocal in his praise of my purchases. Which reminds me," said Samantha brightly, "would you object to having Lord Wyatt as a brother-in-law?"

It took a moment for Lord Cartwright to realize that his mouth had fallen open. He quickly closed it and fortified himself with a deep breath.

"Not . . . in theory," he managed.

"Excellent! If you would do me the very great favor of occasionally reminding Hilary of his many superb qualifications as a husband to her, I would be most grateful."

"Why?" demanded Lord Cartwright.

"Because I am fostering a match between the two of them."

"Why?"

"Because they will make each other happy, of course."

Lord Cartwright's expression was daunting. "You are matchmaking."

"How very observant of you."

"The terrible rumors from the Continent are true, then?"

"Enough not to dither about. Indeed, in casting my mind

89

over the dozens of couples I have helped to the altar, I cannot call one unhappy union to mind. Hilary and Lord Wyatt will only add to such a satisfactory record."

Lord Cartwright privately agreed. He shuddered. "I begin to lose my grip on sanity. We have, it seems, strayed once again from the purpose of your call. You wished advice."

"Yes. I wish to change my bank. My trouble lies in that I know nothing of the other financial institutions in London. That last time I was in town I was only twelve and not yet in the habit of dealing with bankers."

"You amaze me," said Lord Cartwright and won a smile in turn. "As it happens, I had occasion to change banks and advisors a few years ago and am more than satisfied with the exchange. My present bank is comparatively young but quite solid and forward looking."

"They sound exactly the sort I want. Will you give me their address?"

"You are determined to deal with them directly, I take it?"

"But of course," Samantha said smoothly. "How could you doubt it?"

"I did not," Lord Cartwright replied with the barest trace of a smile before he dipped his pen in the inkwell behind and to the left of his desk-sitting guest. He wrote the bank's direction on a piece of paper and handed the sheet to her. "I would appreciate your not mentioning China in any of your conversations with Tom Wilson. He's rather touchy on the subject of late. I would also recommend writing to the gentlemen I have listed. To ease the shock."

"How very considerate you are, to be sure," said Samantha, tucking the paper into her reticule. "Now that we have solved my difficulty, I require your help with Peter. He still has some few unfilled minutes in his days which I intend to stuff with physical activity. Unfortunately, I have no knowledge of the male sporting institutions in London, one of the many glaring gaps in my education. I was wondering if you might know of some suitable activity for a lad of seventeen?"

"I know of one or two," Lord Cartwright gravely admitted. "I would be quite willing to sponsor him at Jackson's Boxing Saloon. There are other means of exercise at Jackson's besides boxing that will not imperil your ward's hands. I'll walk out with young Mr. Danthorpe to Jackson's tomorrow morning if that scheme is agreeable to you."

"Very agreeable," Samantha said, not entirely hiding her shock. "You are generous in your aid, sir."

Lord Cartwright leaned back in his chair. "It is, surprisingly, my pleasure, Lady Samantha."

"I really am going to have to pay you back some time for your many kindnesses to me and mine."

"If you would but marry and retire into domesticity—perhaps in Cumberland—that would repay me nicely."

"Thank you, no," Samantha said with a startled grin, "for if I followed your example, I should have to marry someone the opposite of my temperament, views, and needs, and I should soon learn to hate the poor fellow, which would not at all be a pleasant way to spend the rest of my life, particularly in Cumberland. Good day, Lord Cartwright!"

Samantha jumped off his desk and strode from the room as Lord Cartwright goggled after her.

Jillian was not . . . No, of course she wasn't! And he didn't! And . . . oh, blast that wretched woman!

Chapter Nine

FRIENDLY TIES ACROSS Berkeley Square that had been introduced by Hilary, embraced by Samantha, advanced by Christina, and furthered by Matthew and Peter, were now strengthened by Peter and Lord Cartwright. For Peter to enter the rarefied atmosphere of Jackson's and see his sponsor sparring with the champion himself was more happiness than he could assimilate. For his part, Lord Cartwright was grateful to Peter for such avid enjoyment of these sporting sojourns, and of his youthful worship of his prowess with a pair of fives. Because of the boy's enthusiasm, Lord Cartwright was returning to the sporting world he had once loved.

As he began to exercise muscles long unused, to reaffirm an agility and strength he had nearly forgotten, a peace Lord Cartwright had not known in years settled upon him and seeped into his soul.

Less than a fortnight after he had returned to Jackson's, Lord Cartwright sat easily astride his new black Arabian as the gelding moved at a majestic canter through Hyde Park. A crisp snow crunched beneath the beast's hooves. A breeze played with Lord Cartwright's dun hair and stung his cheeks.

Oh, this was glorious! The sun shone brightly overhead,

he had a good steed beneath him, and all was right with the world.

Slowly he drew the Arabian down to a walk, letting the reins go slack. The gelding snorted and tossed his dark head and Lord Cartwright laughed, patting the strong black neck affectionately. It had been a long time since he had owned such an animal. He had forgotten what joy it could give. With a contented sigh he gathered his reins and walked out of the park and into the Promenade thick with the elegant bustle of the ton. He presently found himself hailed and, scanning the crowd before him, spied Jillian Roberts calling him from her barouche.

He moved his horse easily between carriages and horses and pulled to a stop beside her.

"Good afternoon, Jillian," he said with a fond smile. "You have finally consented to rejoin the Promenade, I see."

"When one is in lavender gloves, one may indulge in some of the milder frivolities of the town. Is that a new horse?" Jillian inquired. "He is very handsome."

"He is magnificent, isn't he? I concluded the bill of sale last week."

"How glad I am that you have a proper mount once again. I was quite heartbroken when you were forced to sell Solarious. I doubt if there was a more perfect horse in all of England."

"He was a grand animal," Lord Cartwright said with a wistful sigh.

"You had trained him yourself, had you not?"

"Bred, raised, trained, groomed, and rode him. Mother once told me that she would not have been surprised if I had insisted on bringing Solarious into the house to take family tea."

"Dear Lady Emma," said Jillian with an indulgent smile. "Oh dear, the bells are tolling five o'clock. I must fly, Simon," Jillian said. "Give my love to Hilary and Matthew.

Lady Emma and Timothy returned to town shortly, do they not?"

"In a fortnight."

"What a comfort that will be for you. Come to tea tomorrow?"

"I look forward to it," Lord Cartwright said with a bow.

"Dear Simon," Jillian said with a smile and then bid her coachman to drive on.

Lord Cartwright's answering smile died as quickly as Jillian's team of matched bays pulled her barouche away. He remained where she had left him, thinking of Solarious and the black week when he had been forced to sell that beloved animal along with the largest of his mother's dower estates and the Cartwright emeralds. All of them were grievous injustices, but together they were a terrible blow. Personal and family treasures sold, because of his father.

The late baron's heedless disregard of anyone and anything save his own pleasure had brought them untold misery. Had he been a gentleman who honored his responsibilities, his family would not have suffered.

Had he been a gentleman . . .

The most damning phrase of all, and the most true.

Libertine, profligate, adulterer, suicide . . . traitor. His father had been all of those and more. But he had never been a gentleman. The rules of Society had not been for him. Why should he think of others when it was so much more pleasant thinking of himself? Why be considerate of his wife's feelings when it was so delightful to be madly in love with Margery Adamson? Why be polite to guests when he wanted to be off at one of his clubs anyway? Why protect his fortune when it was his to spend as he chose?

Lord Cartwright recalled the horror he had known when he had attained his majority and entered upon the pleasures of the town only to acquire a full knowledge of his father's character instead. With the horror had grown an equal determination to counteract his father's misdeeds with his

94

own irreproachable conduct. And still the ton had turned on him.

Suddenly hearing himself hailed, Lord Cartwright looked up to find Samantha Adamson, in a severely cut dark blue riding habit, trotting toward him on a large dapple gray mare.

"Good afternoon," she said cheerfully. "Was that Lady Jillian who just drove off? 'Twas a very stylish coach. I am impressed more and more with the excellence of her taste, though I cannot admire her slavish devotion to propriety."

Lord Cartwright glanced at her sharply.

"Is this not a magnificent day?" Samantha continued. "I quite long for miles and miles of open country over which to gallop. London seems so very confining at times, don't you think?"

"Indeed," Lord Cartwright replied. "Are you with a party?"

"Not at present. I am to meet Lady Susan Horton in half an hour or so."

"Then where is your groom?"

"Samantha Adamson trailed by a groom? Never!" Samantha declared. An impish grin peeped out. "It would shatter my scandalous reputation in the ton. Besides, with so many red-blooded Englishmen out and about, I do not lack for any number of knight-errants, should the need arise."

"Very sound thinking," Lord Cartwright agreed.

"And that is a very sound animal beneath you," Samantha said admiringly. "There is a great deal of strength in those haunches and chest, and a good deal of speed in those legs if I am not mistaken. The color, the breeding, the style . . . I grow quite envious!"

Lord Cartwright could summon none of his earlier joy. "He is an excellent mount, of course. But he is nothing to Solarious."

"Solarious?"

"A horse I once owned. He could run forever. He was magnificent." Lord Cartwright was silent a moment, bleak and lost in thought. "What kind of man would deny his own son those things a son holds most dear?" He flushed when he realized he had spoken aloud.

"A very foolish man, or a very cruel one, perhaps," Samantha replied. "What sort of man cannot say good-bye to the dead?"

"A very foolish man, a very loving man, or," Lord Cartwright said slowly, "a very bitter one."

Samantha spoke with a casualness that was almost, but not quite, convincing. "We seem to have suffered a similar plague. My father was the most selfish man I ever met. He wanted to travel and so we traveled, though Mother was never very strong. But father didn't think of that. He must needs see Greece, Egypt, the Americas, and off we went. When my mother developed consumption, she asked to return to England but Father was certain that a sojourn on the Black Sea would put her to rights. As she grew weaker, she asked again to return to England that she might die in her own country, but Father would not hear of her dying. He loved her. She could not and would not die and that was that. He thought India was the place for her to recoup, and then it was Venice, and then it was the Holy Lands ... and then she died. He abandoned himself to a frenzy of grief. All he could think of was what he had lost, not what he had. Such rodomontade! How could any father abandon all claims to happiness when he had a daughter like me?"

Lord Cartwright was startled into a laugh.

"There, that is much better," Samantha said approvingly. "You make a very handsome satyr, of course, but Pan suits you better. Come, we've two strong mounts and a glorious day, all we need is a wager to make the day perfect. A guinea says I beat you to that old beech tree some two hundred yards off."

Lord Cartwright sighed in exasperation. "Lady Samantha, members of the ton do not race each other in Hyde Park."

"Whyever not?"

"It is just not done."

"But the field is perfection. We would have a superb race."

"We would be sniggered at and dropped from every guest list of every important hostess."

"That's not much of a loss."

"It is to me, my family, and my fiancée."

"Oh, bother!" Samantha said in exasperation. "I am sick to death of your pigheaded refusal to enjoy life simply because propriety forbids it! You may have your tenets of civilized society, for all the good they'll do you. I am going to have a race . . . with Lord Barnett," she said, pointing her riding crop at the gentleman who was trotting toward them on a huge white gelding, "and that *will* do me a world of good!"

With a sharp snap of her crop, she set her mare to a thundering gallop that quickly brought her to Lord Barnett's side. Lord Cartwright's fury grew as he saw that paragon raise Samantha's hand to his lips, pulling her closer to share some secret.

"He's welcome to her!" fumed his lordship as he spun his Arabian around and set him off at an indecorous gallop away from the infuriating duo.

Chapter Ten

SAMANTHA STOOD IN Peter's schoolroom, arms folded across her chest, foot tapping incessantly, a forbidding frown marring her lovely face. She glanced at the clock on the fireplace mantel. Three-fifteen.

With a muttered imprecation, she began to pace the room. She stopped to spin the globe standing near a large window. She stopped it suddenly. She glanced down. China. This made her think of Lord Cartwright, which only added to her spleen.

She paced again, picked up a Latin text, thumbed through it, put it back down, glanced with no love whatsoever at a book of mathematics, and then stopped before the clock on the mantel.

Three-nineteen.

The door crashed open and Peter lunged into the room, half out of his greatcoat.

"I'm sorry, Mr. Speer. I—Sam!" the boy gasped, flushing to the roots of his hair.

"Ah, you are not suffering from amnesia, then," said his guardian.

"Amnesia?"

"You remember me, this house, this room. Do you remember what you are to be doing in this room?"

"Sam, I'm so sorry. I—"

"Mr. Speer was here for your afternoon lessons promptly at one-thirty. He waited and he waited and he waited. Finally growing concerned, he informed me of your absence. As I had no knowledge of where you had gone when you should have been eating your lunch—and even less knowledge of when you might return—I sent Mr. Speer home to his wife and many children who, I am convinced, will treat his company with the happiness and respect he deserves."

"I'm so sorry, Sam."

"Are you?" Samantha said witheringly. "You said you were sorry last Friday *and* this Tuesday. Am I to believe you are sorry a third time in one week?"

"I'm not a child in knee pants!" Peter said, flaring up. "You needn't treat me like one."

"And Mr. Speer is not your servant to come and go at your whim. He is a highly educated and well-paid tutor. Have I ever mentioned to you, Peter, how much I abhor wasting my money?"

"It won't happen again, Sam, on my oath."

Samantha sighed. "Very well. I shall cease playing the ogre. What was it this time?"

"Matthew heard there was to be a championship cockfight and—"

"Cockfight? You abandoned Homer and mathematics to watch two birds rip each other to shreds?!"

"Females," said Peter with the greatest superiority, "have no understanding or appreciation of masculine pursuits."

"No, we bloody well don't! Cockfights," Samantha said with a shiver of disgust. "You will immerse yourself in Homer and Plato until dinner, Peter. There must be something that can elevate your mind."

Peter, thinking it wisest not to mention a forthcoming jaunt to watch a champion bullterrier demolish over a hundred rats in less than ten minutes—an expedition he was looking forward to with the keenest excitement—merely uttered a dutiful "Yes, Sam," sat down, picked up his Homer, and pretended to read.

Samantha regarded this performance with a jaundiced eye and left the room without a word. She had just started down the stairs when Christina dashed past her.

" 'Bye, Sam!" she called.

"Where are you off to now?"

"The Wildings' rout, of course!"

"Oh yes, of course," Samantha muttered as Garner held the door open for her ward.

Christina was gone in a rush. The front door closed. Silence remained.

It struck Samantha with unpleasant force that she had arranged her wards' lives very well, but had done nothing for herself. In short, she was threatened with boredom.

This was intolerable.

She could not call on Hilary for Hilary was escorting Christina to the Wildings' rout. She could not call on Phillip for the duke habitually played whist at White's in the afternoon. She could not call on Derek for even she understood the impropriety of a woman visiting a gentleman's lodgings. Celeste always took an afternoon nap to gird herself for the evening's revels, or what passed for revels in the ton. Heloise Zanuch, Bavaria's most immoral export and one of Samantha's most entertaining Continental friends, was in the midst of one of her grand passions and was undoubtedly still in bed.

Samantha stood halfway down the stairs. The lack of direction in her life and the silence of the house combined to oppress her. It was not the first time.

"I shall go for a drive," she decided, even though it was not the fashionable hour to drive on the Promenade. Escape was far more important than fashion.

She called to Garner to order her phaeton and turned back to her room to change.

Twenty minutes later, her team of chestnuts trotting in all

their glory, Samantha drove into the Promenade and looked for some means of entertainment.

She spied it at last in Lord Wyatt who was standing beside an ancient coach and patiently conversing with its occupant: old Mrs. Foxthwaite, a bombastic female of at least seventy years who had an opinion, always negative, on every subject. She expounded each opinion with such volubility that half of London knew what she was saying at any given point in time. A warm glow settled in Samantha's heart. Despite their brief acquaintance, she liked Lord Wyatt. He was honest, intelligent, and hopelessly in love with her best friend. It was time she acted.

She hailed him in a voice that would have done Mrs. Foxthwaite proud, reminded him of their fictitious appointment, and soon had him installed at her side in the phaeton.

"You're a godsend, Lady Samantha," said Lord Wyatt as she expertly flicked her whip and moved them into the flow of traffic.

"Very true," Samantha said complacently, "and far more than you can guess. I have an ulterior motive."

"You terrify me!"

Samantha cast an amused glance at his lordship. "I have been observing you these last few weeks, Wyatt, and I must make plain to you that I find your method of courting Hilary Sheverton quite horrendous."

"I should be prostrate, I suppose, by such condemnation; but as it happens, I am *not* courting Hilary," Lord Wyatt mildly corrected.

"You are in love with her; it is the same thing."

"But the lady does not return my regard."

"Oh, the blindness of men," Samantha said with a weary sigh as she jockeyed between a mail coach and a smartly turned-out curricle. "Whenever she speaks of you, which is often, she speaks of you as her best friend. She praises you constantly and openly admires your many worthy qualities. These things do *not* bespeak indifference, my lord."

"No," Lord Wyatt agreed, "they bespeak, at most, a kindness and sisterly affection. We have been friends all our lives. That is how she has always regarded me and I must be content."

"Your thinking is all muddled. Look here, Wyatt, pay close heed and I shall instruct you in the intricacies of human nature. Have I your attention?"

"I sit worshipfully at your feet, Mistress."

"Excellent. Now then, even you, in your provincial ramblings, must have observed that one's actions are predicated upon the treatment one receives at the hands of others. A valet, abused by his master, will give his employer's boots an indifferent shine. A shepherd, whispering sweet nothings into the ear of a shepherdess, will receive a like reply. A gentleman dealing with a lady in strict, friendly propriety will receive like treatment at her fair hands. Treat her as a lover, however . . ."

"And she will regard and treat him as a lover in return," Lord Wyatt concluded.

"Your understanding is excellent. That is my point precisely," Samantha said with great condescension.

Ten minutes later she drew her team to a stop. "Good afternoon, Lord Cartwright," she said frostily.

Dazedly, Lord Wyatt looked down to see that they had stopped before the Marble Arch and his friend who was standing, somewhat grimly, on the pavement.

Lord Cartwright bowed. "How do you do, Lady Samantha?"

"You may get down now, Wyatt," Samantha informed her passenger.

Lord Wyatt blinked and then hurriedly jumped from the phaeton. Samantha drove off in the next moment, the two men staring after her.

"Do not stand there with your mouth hanging open, Aaron," Lord Cartwright advised his friend. "It is most unseemly."

"Simon," Lord Wyatt said, turning upon him with wide, glowing eyes. "I have just been helped to the most momentous decision of my life. I am going to court and win a lady!"

"Finally going to woo Hilary, are you? I must say, it is about time."

Lord Wyatt stared at Lord Cartwright. "You knew?" he gasped.

"For years," Lord Cartwright blithely stated. "It is not difficult to unearth so deep and dark a secret when I love the principals involved. I wish you luck with your wooing, Aaron. You may certainly count on me for any assistance you require."

"You mean you . . . I . . . I have your blessing?"

Lord Cartwright roared with laughter. "Oh, I shall hold this over your head for *years*!"

"Dash it all, Simon, you know what I mean," Lord Wyatt said with some heat.

"Yes, of course I do, you nit. As for blessings, it is I who am blessed. I could not wish for any greater happiness than to have my best friend as my brother-in-law."

"Thank you, Simon," Lord Wyatt said quietly. "That means a great deal to me."

"Tell me, what finally made you decide to storm the ramparts of my fair sister's heart?"

"Lady Samantha Adamson," Lord Wyatt reverently proclaimed.

"She begins to matchmake in earnest, then," Lord Cartwright said with a sigh. "Heaven help us all. Must she meddle in everyone's affairs?"

"I think not," Lord Wyatt replied soberly. "She meddles only in those affairs she cares about. I know not how, but I seem to have earned the lady's regard and, being no fool, I have no intention of losing it."

"You *are* keen on the creature," Lord Cartwright marveled.

"And you are too harsh," Lord Wyatt riposted. "You should soften in your stance to Lady Samantha . . . and to the rest of the world while you are at it. Do you even *like* the man you've become these last two years?"

"Aaron—"

"You chose this grim role. You can choose another, you know."

Lord Cartwright's brows rose. "This seems to be a day for advice."

"At least I have the good sense to heed it."

"Touché," Lord Cartwright murmured.

Lord Wyatt strolled off to contemplate the unexpected broadening of his horizons.

Lord Cartwright stood gazing after his happy friend for several minutes. Then, slowly, thoughtfully, he continued on his way to St. James's Street.

He walked through the door of White's and was instantly hailed by half a dozen friends who all wanted him to have a drink and confirm the latest rumors about Lady Samantha Adamson. Despite all of his protests to the contrary, it was a universal belief amongst the male members of the ton that his enforced association with the lady made him a treasure trove of information about her past and present. In vain did he deny such knowledge.

He joined his friends, drank a glass of port, and listened to incessant discussion of the newest rumors about Samantha Adamson. With one breath his friends chortled over her reputed adventures on the Continent and with the next breath condemned all of her scandalous friends who she insisted on inviting to every rout, ball, and assembly she gave.

"Wouldn't be surprised if she invited those two highwaymen of hers to tea," harrumphed old Admiral Blair as he drained a large glass of whiskey.

"What highwaymen?" Lord Cartwright could not help but ask.

Eagerly, six gentlemen took up the tale. His lordship had to piece together the half dozen contradictory reports and at the end declared that they were all drunk and didn't know what they were talking about.

"God's truth," Lord Cyril Horton pronounced. "Have it on the best of authority."

"Yes, but have you confirmed it with Lady Samantha?" Lord Cartwright demanded.

"Hell's bells, Simon, can't go askin' a woman about *that*," said Lord Horton.

Lord Cartwright was struck by a sudden fit of whimsy. He set down his glass of port.

"I shall ask her about it directly," he announced and was not displeased to see his friends gape at him.

"Now, Simon," began Lord Horton.

"Don't you want to know what really happened?"

"Well, yes, but—"

"Who better to ask than the principal concerned?"

"Well, of course, but—"

"Shall we meet back here at nine o'clock?"

The others rather uncomfortably agreed, and Lord Cartwright strolled off to beard the lioness in her den. It required far more effort than even he had imagined.

Garner was all cordiality when he opened the Dower House door to his lordship, but became more and more evasive with each passing minute.

"I should like to see Lady Samantha," Lord Cartwright announced.

"Ah," said Garner. "I am afraid, my lord, that that is a little difficult just at present."

"Is she not at home?"

"Well, she is and she isn't."

"Come, come, Garner. Lady Samantha is either on the premises or she is not."

"On the premises is a very good way of putting it, my lord. But her ladyship's . . . occupied."

"She has guests?"

"No, sir."

"She is indisposed?"

"No, sir."

"Garner, I like a riddle as much as the next man, but the time has come to reveal the mystery. What is Lady Samantha doing?"

"She is cooking, sir."

"Cooking?" said Lord Cartwright faintly.

"Yes, sir. Monsieur Girard has quit ... again. He is French and you know what the French are—temperamental. He quits at least twice a month. He always comes back, of course, usually in time to prepare the next meal. Not today, however."

"His feelings were particularly lacerated today?" Lord Cartwright inquired.

"Yes, my lord. He took umbrage at her ladyship hiring caterers to assist him for tomorrow night's ball. He spent ten minutes yelling in French and stormed out of the house in high dudgeon vowing never to return. He will be back by breakfast, but there is still dinner to be got through."

"Hence Lady Samantha's presence in the kitchen?"

"Yes, sir. Marvelously handy in a kitchen is Lady Samantha."

"This I must see," Lord Cartwright declared. "Take me to the kitchen, Garner."

"But, my lord—"

"I won't be denied. I shall be the envy of White's. To the kitchen, Garner."

"Yes, my lord," said the butler with heavy resignation as he led his lordship downstairs.

Lord Cartwright was soon standing in the kitchen doorway staring in amazement at the scene before him. As a scullion rigorously scrubbed out a huge copper pot, Lady Samantha Adamson was expertly chopping up a variety of vegetables with a large kitchen knife which she wielded as one born to the culinary arts. She was swathed in a huge white apron, strands of blond hair brushing against her flour-smudged face.

"I wouldn't have believed it if I hadn't seen it with my own eyes," Lord Cartwright declared.

Samantha looked up, her knife not missing a beat.

"One cutting remark about my cooking and I'll carve you up and serve you for dinner," she said.

"I'm too tough. I'd ruin your marvelous collations," Lord Cartwright said as he strolled to the stove and lifted the lids from each of the pots simmering there. "This *does* smell marvelous!"

"Of course it smells marvelous. I cooked it!"

Lord Cartwright turned and grinned at the impromptu chef. "You can't abide false modesty, can you?"

Samantha sighed. "What do you want, Cartwright?"

"Where on earth did you learn to cook?"

"Mrs. Danthorpe, Christina and Peter's mother, taught me when I was fifteen. It was either that or learn to scrub floors. I chose cooking. It's easier on the knees. Now be a good boy, Cartwright, and tell me why you have invaded my kitchen."

"I've come to grill you on your scandalous past . . . no pun intended."

"And the moon's made of green cheese. Here," said Samantha, tossing him an apron, "put that on."

"Whatever for?"

"If you want to stay in my kitchen, you have to work."

"But I can't cook!"

"You'll never know until you try."

Lord Cartwright hesitated and then met the sardonic gleam in Samantha's eyes. Deciding it might be wisest to leave this part out of the tale he recounted tonight at White's, Lord Simon Cartwright removed his immaculate, tight-fitting coat by Weston, and replaced it with the apron.

"And now?" he inquired.

"You whip these egg whites to froth," Samantha said, handing him a bowl and a whisk. "I am making a meringue."

Lord Cartwright eyed the bowl and the whisk with the greatest suspicion. "You cannot make a meringue out of this glop."

"I have no intention of doing it. *You're* going to do it."

"Oh yes, of course. How silly of me."

Lord Cartwright tentatively placed the whisk in the bowl and began to whip the egg whites.

Samantha, meanwhile, had removed a towel from another bowl. Glancing across at her, Lord Cartwright was knowledgeable enough to recognize the tan ball as bread dough.

"Very well," Samantha said, punching down the dough and turning it out onto a floured bread board, "what do you want to ask me? Keep whipping."

Lord Cartwright moved the whisk with greater vigor. "My mind is confounded by a story to which I, knowing something of your audacity, must give full credence. Did you really capture single-handedly two French highwaymen on the road to Paris?"

"Not at all," Samantha said, mangling the dough.

"You disappoint me."

"They were *German* highwaymen."

"German?" said Lord Cartwright, his mouth quirking.

"They mistook the road to Cologne."

"*How* could they have mistaken the road to Cologne?"

"Well, all of the signposts had been destroyed during the war, and the poor dears could not speak a word of French, only German; and the French, you know, refuse to acknowledge any language save their own."

"*How* could you have captured two German highwaymen on the French road to Cologne?" Lord Cartwright demanded.

"Oh, it was simplicity itself, I assure you," Samantha replied, shaping the dough and plopping it into a greased bread pan. "They did not expect a woman to do anything to thwart their robbery. That is one of the few advantages of being female: men never think we will do anything unexpected. Once I had shot Herman in the shoulder, Erick very quickly surrendered himself and we all had a jolly ride to the nearest local magistrate. They were very entertaining fellows in their way."

"You shot a German highwayman in the shoulder?" Lord Cartwright said faintly.

"It seemed the appropriate thing to do at the time," Samantha said with a shrug.

Lord Cartwright, to Samantha's surprise (and pleasure), suddenly burst into laughter.

"I must know," he said, still chuckling, "where on earth you found a gun. Did you wrestle it from their criminal hands?"

"There was no need for I always carry one of Harding's pocket pistols on my person," Samantha replied. "One never knows what dangers one may encounter on the road or in a London kitchen, after all."

"Come now," said Lord Cartwright, "you do not mean to tell me that you have a gun on your person at this very moment?"

"But I do," Samantha replied and, seeing that Lord Cartwright doubted this pronouncement, she wiped her hands on her apron, leaned down, raised the hem of her gown, and removed a small pistol from the holster strapped to her calf. She held the gun for him to see and was more than a little pleased when he gaped at her in silent awe. She then returned the gun to its holster.

A light warmed Lord Cartwright's brown eyes. "By God, if I do not begin to like you."

"I am honored, sir," said Samantha, placing the bread pan in the oven. "But do you think you should go so far?"

"Never fear, my lady, I shall undoubtedly think better of it on the morrow."

"Undoubtedly. Well, I am never one to be behindhand in

taking advantage of momentary lunacy. You have a broad acquaintance in the ton, do you not, Lord Cartwright?"

"I do," he replied with the greatest suspicion.

"Excellent! Then you can, perhaps, advise me. I am searching for a protector for Celeste Vandaun."

Lord Cartwright coughed. "The ladies of the ton will tremble at the news."

"I had not meant to publish my intentions," Samantha said dryly as she inspected the growing froth in his bowl, "and I don't want a married man for Celeste. I think single would be best for her at this point in her career. He must be rich, of course, very rich. Celeste must save for her old age, after all. And I think he must be young. Past his majority, certainly, but still years away from thinking of marriage. A young, rich man who will appreciate the bounty he has in Celeste and treasure her for several years to come. Do you know such a man?"

It struck Lord Cartwright with the greatest absurdity that he *did* know such a man. "The Marquis of Lockwood," he pronounced before he knew what he was about.

"But he is one of my guests tomorrow!" Samantha exclaimed. "I don't know him, of course. I've only seen him here and there. Passably attractive and a bit shy was my impression. Tell me about him."

His amusement growing at his own collusion in such a mad scheme, Lord Cartwright obliged her. "His father has told the world that should the marquis marry before he is thirty, he will be disinherited. The duke had the misfortune to marry in the throes of calf love and has regretted it these twenty-five years since. The Marquis is now but four-and-twenty. Will he do?"

"He is perfection!" Samantha cried. "You've hidden talents, Lord Cartwright."

His lordship bowed. "Nevertheless," he said, "I shall leave the matchmaking to you, my lady."

Samantha smiled up at him with great warmth. "I shall

interview the young marquis tomorrow and, if he meets my requirements, lead him to his future happiness tomorrow night."

She set happily to work on a large ham, Lord Cartwright watching her, an amused smile playing about his lips.

At least La Belle Flamme would be removed from circulation. A good many ladybirds, wives, paphians, and hopeful debutantes would rest easier tonight. Perhaps he *did* have hidden talents.

Finally gaining release from his kitchen apprenticeship, Lord Cartwright removed his apron, put on his coat, suggested that his efforts had produced the lightest meringue ever seen in London, won a scoff for his pains, and returned abovestairs.

He entered the front hall. Garner opened the door, Lord Cartwright stepped out, stopped, and retraced his steps.

"There is one thing, Garner."

"Sir?" said the impassive butler.

"Those painted tapestries of Altonberry's. Were they . . . faithful to the Olympian frolics?"

"Grievously so, sir."

"Did he keep any after the Cyprians' Ball?"

"Several. There is one of Leda and the swan that I recall with particular horror."

"I really must call on Altonberry some time," Lord Cartwright murmured as he once again made his exit.

He returned home to change for his evening storytelling at White's and walked into pandemonium. Trunks, valises, and bandboxes littered the front hall. Excited voices and laughter poured from the drawing room. Hurrying upstairs, he burst into the drawing room, crying, "You were not expected until next week!"

"Simon!" cried his mother as she enveloped him in a long and loving maternal hug.

The dowager was a woman of fifty graceful years. Her once brown locks had turned to a salt-and-pepper gray, but she had maintained her trim figure, her lively brown eyes giving the lie to her age.

"We have only this minute arrived. Oh, look at you! Dear Simon," Lady Cartwright said as she took his hands in hers and gazed lovingly into his brown eyes. "You look well."

"I am, Mama."

"No, no, you look far better than I have seen you in ages. You seem rested, peaceful, even . . . happy?"

"On occasion, Mama," Lord Cartwright said with a fond smile, "especially when I may look upon you and hold you close."

"My dear," said the dowager, hugging him and giving him another kiss.

"My, it is good to be back in this house," Lady Emma Cartwright exclaimed as she released her son and surveyed the room. "How I have missed you all! Matthew, my darling, my youngest, my baby, how you have grown!" she cried, her hands resting upon the younger Mr. Cartwright's shoulders. "You will outstrip Simon, I am convinced of it."

"Looking forward to it, I assure you, Mama," Matthew said with a grin.

"Hilary, dearest!" Lady Cartwright said, catching both of her daughter's hands in hers. "You are simply blooming! Just look at you. Never have I seen you in greater beauty. Are you in love?"

"*No*, Mama," Hilary said, laughing.

"Well, I cannot remember when I last saw you looking so well. You quite take my breath away. Why *aren't* you in love?"

"I am too busy," Hilary replied with a smile.

"Ah yes, the Season," the dowager said with a sigh. "I would much rather you were in love than busy, Hilary."

"Yes, Mama."

"Simon, have you no friends who can steal your sister's heart?" the dowager demanded as she turned to her firstborn.

"I believe there's a local matchmaker working on the

problem," Lord Cartwright replied, "but if you're eager to kick the chick out of the family nest, I'll be happy to ask around at White's."

"It would probably be best to trust to providence," said his mother. "Well, you all look splendid. It is clear you have no need—"

"Well, I like that!" said Timothy. He was a gentleman of eight-and-twenty years. His hair was dark brown and simply cut, his eyes blue, his body straight and lean, the bones of his angular face sharply defined. One empty coat sleeve was pinned to a riding coat. "You greet these three with armloads of compliments but do you spare one small accolade for your second and most worthy child? No!"

"Nincompoop," Lady Cartwright said with a loving smile.

"What a tongue he has with his own family," Lord Cartwright marveled. "Pity he cannot find it when in company."

"I have too poor an opinion of myself to venture forth conversation in company with those who are more intelligent and adept at speaking than myself," Timothy gravely replied.

"I think we've just been given a set down," said Lord Cartwright.

"*I* think he has been mucking about with the sheep too long," Hilary opined, which set everyone to laughing.

Slowly the family separated into smaller groups; Timothy and Lord Cartwright drawing together as their mother bantered with her two youngest children.

"Well, brother," Lord Cartwright said, "*have* you been mucking about with the sheep too long?"

"I begin to think so," Timothy replied with a rueful smile. "I have been experiencing lately an unaccountable desire to come to town and . . . socialize."

"At last. This damned shyness of yours has kept you on the outskirts of the Marriage Mart for too long. It is time we got you riveted to some good female with a fondness for sheep."

"Please, Simon, I beg you, *don't* help me!"

Feigning injury, Lord Cartwright turned to his mother for succor and found her deep in conversation with Hilary.

"But how fun!" Lady Cartwright exclaimed. "I haven't been to a masquerade ball since I was a girl. I shall go incognita and find the truth out for myself about Lady Samantha Adamson."

"What about Lady Samantha, Mama?" Lord Cartwright inquired.

"I was telling Mama," Hilary said, "that she and Timothy will meet Samantha and the Danthorpes tomorrow night at the Adamson Masquerade Ball."

"The letters I have received in the last month," said their mother, "describing the many entertainments Lady Samantha has provided the ton, both formal and otherwise, have filled me with the greatest desire to meet such a fashionable scapegrace."

"You *want* to meet her, Mama?" Lord Cartwright said in some surprise.

"Yes, of course. Who would not?"

"I had thought you ... would derive no pleasure from associating with the daughter of the woman who caused you so much misery."

"Simon, what on earth are you talking about?" the dowager demanded.

"Lady Margery Adamson, of course," her eldest replied in some confusion.

"Margery? Cause me misery? Simon, I begin to think you harbor an excess of sensibility in that otherwise impressive brain of yours. Margery and I were bosom friends practically from birth. She never caused me a moment's pain."

"But ... but," Matthew sputtered, "Father loved her instead of you ... didn't he?"

"To the point of idiocy, yes," Lady Cartwright said with a fond smile. "But then, so did half the male population of England." A sudden thought occurred to the dowager and she stared at her four children with growing wonder. "Have you all been thinking . . . ! No, you couldn't! Oh, it is too ridiculous! You haven't been imagining me suffering from a broken heart because the baron loved Margery, have you?"

"Well," Hilary said, blushing profusely, "it would only be reasonable that you would be . . . er . . . wounded by Father's preference for another woman the whole of your marriage."

"Oh what folderol," Lady Cartwright gasped. "You silly children. Margery and your father and I were lifelong friends. I knew the baron always adored Margery and, as I was not in the least in love with him, I couldn't have cared less. Certainly I was sad to see him so pained when she fell in love with Lord Adamson at first sight, but it had no other effect upon me. The Cartwrights and my family arranged *our* marriage two years later. I not only want to meet Samantha Adamson, I am eager to see how she compares to her mother and if she had inherited the friendship her mother had for me."

"But the Dower House!" Lord Cartwright expostulated. "Good God, Father left us in penury and that woman an unencumbered home within a stone's throw of our own!"

"Yes, at my suggestion."

"What?" cried the four younger Cartwrights.

"We wanted Margery to have an excuse to return to England," their mother explained, "and thought the Dower House the perfect means to an end. In some ways it has served its purpose. It couldn't bring the mother back, but it has returned the daughter and in the nick of time from all that I've heard. Lady Jersey wrote that Samantha Adamson needs a bit of civilizing."

"She needs to be bound and gagged and sent post to China!" Lord Cartwright cheerfully declared.

"Why how shocking! I await our meeting with bated breath."

"That's right, Mama," Lord Cartwright said, "enter the fray with a suitable amount of terror and you may survive."

Chapter Eleven

On THE FOLLOWING evening was fixed the Adamson Masquerade Ball. Samantha's character, conversation, and activities provided the greatest part of London's *on dits*. But she was rich, which excused most of her faults, and she was titled, which excused the rest of her faults. She was, therefore, as great a hit as Christina Danthorpe, a greater hit in some circles. Dragons who thought nothing of terrorizing an obtuse countess who had the misfortune to not understand one of Lady Jersey's witticisms embraced Samantha like a lost child and happily pulled her into the fold.

She found it all very disconcerting. She was quite used to having every man who could breathe admire and dance attendance on her, but this . . .

Her ballroom hosted a string quartet, the oak floor gleamed from the feverish polishing the three parlor maids had given it that morning. A large chandelier cast the room in a brilliant golden glow that brought out the frothy artistry of the wall and ceiling paintings of gods, goddesses, and cherubs frolicking about in half-naked abandon. The supper room was packed with a dozen tables of food of every description. The largest drawing room had been converted to the enjoyment of those who preferred cards to dancing or food.

Christina, of course, had chosen Juliet for her costume, Peter was dressed as a jester, while Samantha was dressed in a white Greek gown that swept to her ankles, her feet clad simply in sandals, a quiver of arrows at her back.

"Cupid?" inquired Christina with an arch grin.

"Artemis, you abominable child," Samantha retorted. "I thought that a staunch spinster should dress as the Greek's most determined virgin."

The front bell sounded in the next moment.

It was the Cartwrights. Hilary entered first, dressed, at Samantha's urging, as Titania, a crown of flowers gracing her head. Unbeknownst to her, Samantha had cajoled Lord Wyatt to come as Oberon. She kissed Hilary on both cheeks, praised her costume, turned to Lord Cartwright, and burst out laughing.

He wore a huge, floppy Italian hat, an old jerkin, a pair of old breeches thrice turned, a pair of boots that had been candle cases (judging by the multicolored dabs of candle wax all over them), one boot buckled, the other laced, and an old rusty sword with a broken hilt.

"Heaven preserve us!" she gasped. " 'Tis Petruchio come to be wed!"

Lord Cartwright executed an extravagant bow. "On the contrary," he replied, "I have come to enjoy myself at your scandalous soirée."

"You anticipate no pleasure, then, in the wedded state?" Samantha inquired.

"Viper!" Lord Cartwright said good-humoredly. "Who would have thought of such a tongue in Cupid?"

"Artemis."

Christina, meanwhile, had hurried past them to the dowager, taking her hand in both her own as she smiled eagerly into the dowager's brown eyes.

"Ah, *you* are Lady Emma Cartwright," she said. "I have so looked forward to this meeting!"

Lady Cartwright, dressed as Mrs. Malaprop, was charmed and greeted Christina with equal warmth.

"Hilary has excellent taste," she declared. "My dear, you are breathtaking. You deserve, at the very least, an earl for your husband . . . or one of my younger sons. Simon, I fear, is spoken for."

"I am devastated," Christina said. "I shall retire to a nunnery."

The dowager smiled. "Oh Hilary, how clever of you to sponsor such a charming debutante. My dear," she said, squeezing Christina's hand, "I like you enormously."

She then turned to Samantha and saw high-spirited good humor in those rich hazel eyes.

"And you are Lady Samantha Adamson," she said. "How I have longed to meet you. You are quite like your mother, you know, only much more ravishing. And my dear, the things I have heard of you have left me quite agog!"

"Odious, *odious* reputation to proceed me wherever I go," Samantha said. "Pay it no heed, ma'am, I implore you. I am not at all the scandalous harridan you may have heard me to be. Hilary," she said, "why did you not set your mother aright before she came?"

"But I did!" Hilary replied. "I am the one who reported you as a scandalous harridan."

"This is your doing, my lord," Samantha accused Lord Cartwright.

"Not I," he protested. "I think you merely a scandalous meddler."

"First," Samantha retorted, "I am not scandalous. I am, at most, determined. And second, I do not meddle. I merely organize people's lives for them when they have not the sense to do so for themselves."

"An apt description of a meddler."

"How you harp upon that single chord! I urge you, Lord

118

Cartwright, to expand your repertoire before I am put to the yawn."

"Ah yes," Lady Cartwright murmured with a smile, fascinated by this exchange, "I had heard something about a feud between you two. It would appear, Lady Samantha," said the dowager, "that you enjoy harassing and tormenting my eldest son."

"You grossly understate the matter, Mama," said Lord Cartwright.

As he and Samantha continued to banter with Lady Cartwright, Christina continued to act the hostess and greeted Matthew, who essayed the role of Pan, pipes and all. She then turned and stared at the last Cartwright to enter her home.

It was Harlequin, a black mask over his face, his blue eyes luminous, an empty sleeve pinned to his costume.

Her heart suffered a sudden spasm that she was at a loss to explain.

"You are Mr. . . . Timothy Cartwright?" she murmured, her face suffused in a blush.

Mr. Cartwright's cardiovascular system stopped all together. His face felt hot, his toes numb. Somehow he pulled himself together under the full force of Christina's radiance to make his bow.

"Miss Danthorpe," he murmured, he knew not how, "it is a *very* great pleasure to make your acquaintance."

"The . . . the *pleasure* is all mine, sir," Christina murmured in an equally dazed fashion.

Samantha stared at the riveted pair for a moment, ruefully shook her head, and then returned her attention to the rest of the Cartwrights.

"Hilary!" she exclaimed. "I am more and more impressed by your gown. You should wear green more often. I heard Lord Wyatt mention only the other day that green is his favorite color. He was commending a morning gown Miss Letty Maxwell was wearing. Have you seen it?"

Lord Cartwright suffered a sudden coughing fit which his mother was at a loss to understand.

"Miss Maxwell and I are not intimate," Hilary retorted with a certain grimness.

"No?" said Samantha. "But I thought any friend of Lord Wyatt's must be a friend of yours. Ah well, you may further the acquaintance tonight. She assured me only yesterday that she would come as Helen of Troy. A hostess cannot have too many pretty heiresses at her ball."

Hilary's reply was—perhaps fortunately—unintelligible.

It required almost an hour for the sixty guests—invited to partake of dinner before the ball—to arrive. Among them were Celeste Vandaun dressed as Aphrodite and the Marquis of Lockwood who essayed Prometheus. Samantha, who had spoken to both earlier that day, introduced them and let nature take its course.

She devoted herself instead to a close surveillance of Timothy Cartwright. He had propped himself up in a far corner of the main drawing room, his blue eyes never leaving Christina as she greeted the rest of her guests in a rather distracted fashion for she was continually glancing toward *Timothy* during that intense span of time, blushing furiously and looking away whenever their eyes met.

"You seem quite interested in my brother," Lord Cartwright commented as he came up to Samantha.

"Oh, I am," she replied, her hazel eyes intently studying the flushed Mr. Cartwright.

"Planning on setting your cap for him?"

"What? And find myself trampled beneath the feet of a more determined pursuit? Thank you no, sir. I shall keep my cap where it is."

"What can you mean?"

Samantha, in response, glanced briefly toward Christina who was gaily laughing (she was, in fact, quite giddy) at something Lady Susan Horton had said.

"Miss Danthorpe?" gasped Lord Cartwright. "You cannot be serious. They only just met!"

"Mm," Samantha said. "And never before have I seen the look of incredulity that graced Christina's face when they were introduced."

"Yes, but . . . Oh, this is pure fantasy!"

"Perhaps," Samantha conceded in some amusement.

"You intend to muck about with this affair as well, I suppose," Lord Cartwright said with a sigh.

"But of course! In fact, with what I consider a masterstroke of unconscious genius, I have made your brother and Christina dinner partners tonight."

Lord Cartwright stared at his hostess. "No one in London is safe from your powers."

"I know," Samantha said, dimpling. "Isn't it delicious?"

"Is . . . is not the . . . um . . . soup . . . delicious?" Christina stammered some twenty minutes later at the crowded dining table.

"Superb," Mr. Timothy Cartwright said with a rapturous sigh.

Both, from shyness, were at a loss for anything further to say. The soup was removed and salmon offered in its place. Desperately Christina racked her addled brain for something, *anything*, to say.

"You . . . do not come to London often, Mr. Cartwright?" Christina tried again.

"No. I spend most of the year in Gloucestershire managing our estates there."

"It seems you have shouldered a great deal of responsibility."

"Yes, but I like the work," Timothy said with a shy smile. "It is good to feel useful."

"Yes," Christina replied softly. "One does not get the opportunity for being of much use in London."

Silence fell once again between them. Both searched

their brains for even a snippet, however dull, of conversation to hold the other's attention. Finally, Timothy happily hit upon the innocuous question of whether Miss Danthorpe had ever been to Gloucestershire.

"No," she conceded, "but I understand it to be quite beautiful."

"Oh, it is!" Timothy said warmly and continued by enumerating the county's many charms, for on the topic of his home country, Mr. Cartwright could wax poetic. "Grenwick, my estate, used to serve as little more than a hunting lodge in my grandfather's time," he continued, "but I have managed to turn it into a profitable working farm. It finally began to pay for itself for the first time last year. The neighborhood was in an uproar."

"I can imagine," Christina said, chuckling. "I congratulate you on accomplishing what few men would even dare attempt. I admire you enormously for such an ... heroic reformation."

"Miss Danthorpe," Timothy breathed, wholly out of his mind with joy, "I realize that I am only the second son of a baron, a mere country farmer and a complete stumblekins, and I know it is wholly improper for you to even consider such a thing at your own ball, but would you grant me the very great honor, the infinite joy, of bestowing on me your hand for the first dance of the evening?"

"Mr. Cartwright," Christina said fervently, "you have spoken the greatest wish of my heart."

The two grinned at each other in complete and utter ecstasy and remained oblivious to everyone else in the room for the rest of the meal.

Samantha, meanwhile, though not as ecstatic, was well pleased with her dinner companions. She had claimed the Duke de Peralta and Lady Emma Cartwright for her partners.

The duke, dressed appropriately as Vincentio, Shakespeare's Duke of Vienna masquerading as a friar, had arrived shortly after the Cartwrights and had made an immediate hit with them. He had discussed the Peninsular campaign with Timothy, detailed the newest Continental fashions to Matthew, assured Hilary that Miss Maxwell's costume in no way compared to *hers*, and, upon Samantha's introducing them, poured the lion's share of his charm upon Lady Cartwright.

"If you are matchmaking for my mother," Lord Cartwright had commented to his hostess as he removed an infinitesimal speck of lint from his coat sleeve, "I will strangle you."

Samantha grinned at him. "How can I matchmake for her when I have just met her?"

"A paltry handicap to a woman of your skills, ma'am. Who is the fellow?"

"But I told you: the Duke de Peralta."

"Don't play the innocent with me, Lady Samantha, for you are as transparent as glass."

Samantha's smile produced a dimple. "Very well, Phillip's lack of funds is in direct proportion to his abundance of charm."

"Somehow I am not surprised."

"Now don't jump to conclusions. Phillip was born impoverished. The Peraltas ran through their fortune two centuries ago. He acquired the title and nothing else. His intelligence and good nature have brought him every success."

"And what success would that be?" Lord Cartwright inquired with the lift of one brow.

"Three excellent wives who adored him and whom he treated like goddesses."

"Three? How charming. A bigamist."

Samantha choked. "Lout! He has been widowed three times and don't start about how he drove his wives to their graves for it was in his best interest to keep them alive: they controlled the purse strings."

Lord Cartwright smiled down at her. "The people you know, Lády Samantha, are an education. My horizons broaden with each soirée you give. A future prime minister one night, an Italian roué the next, the illegitimate and lascivious heiress to a Bavarian brewer another night, and now a bluebeard. You lead a full life."

"You are laughing at me, I know, but I shan't rise to the bait for you are a guest in my home and there are rules that bind all hostesses to civil treatment of their guests."

"Rules?" said Lord Cartwright vaguely. "Rules, did you say? Whatever can you mean?"

"I mean," Samantha said grimly, "that I shall save the boxing of your ears for a more appropriate occasion."

"Yes," said Lord Cartwright with a smile, "I thought that was what you meant."

"Ah Samantha," the Duke de Peralta cried as he turned to his hostess, Lady Cartwright's hand clasped in his own, "you have made for me this night a Pantheon of all the feminine graces for they dwell within this delightful creature who smiles so engagingly and blushes with such charm."

"You are too effusive, your Grace," said the dowager.

"*Qué disparate!* How can the truth be effusive?" the duke demanded.

"She is all that you say, Phillip, of course," Samantha said, her eyes twinkling. "But she is not rich. I warn you from the start, she is not rich."

"But Samantha, are you so corrupted by the practicalities of the world that you cannot see that Lady Cartwright's beauty and charm are wealth enough for five lifetimes? Ten!"

"Indeed, Lady Samantha," said Lord Cartwright, "how could you voice such a common protest? My mother is the embodiment of the feminine ideal. No man of character would even consider looking at her purse."

124

"Ah," said the duke with great satisfaction, "you, sir, are a *man*."

"He is drunk," Lady Cartwright retorted with some asperity.

"No, no, *querida*," the duke said, raising her hand to his lips, "he spoke the truth. What man would think of money when he can gaze into your velvet brown eyes?"

He and the dowager had continued their flirtation with the greatest happiness throughout dinner, ignoring their hostess completely.

"To Cupid," she said to herself, raising her wineglass to her lips, "wherever he flits."

Recollecting other duties, she handed a previously written note to an attending footman and bade him deliver it to Lord Wyatt. She watched as he read the brief missive. A flush stole into his cheeks. She could not suppress her smile. Clearly this was a night when matchmaking would reign supreme.

The rest of Samantha's guests streamed into the Dower House and, when not remarking Miss Danthorpe's distracted demeanor, the proprietary way the Marquis of Lockwood attended La Belle Flamme, Enrico Sabatini's stunning entrance as Sir Galahad, the Duke de Peralta's attentions to Lady Cartwright, and Mrs. Hilary Sheverton's chilly acknowledgment of Miss Maxwell, debated between themselves if Lord Barnett would attend that night, if he and Lady Samantha really were on the point of announcing their engagement, and what Lady Caroline Evers would say to that, for all of London knew that she was passionately in love with Lord Barnett and had taken to sitting on his doorstep at night. When Garner advanced into the ballroom and uttered in clear tones Lord Barnett's name, there was an instant hush and all eyes turned eagerly to the door. Garner stepped aside and there stood Derek Barnett in all his glory.

He had come dressed as Henry the Fifth and bitterly did many a maiden wish she had thought to come as Princess

Katharine. With admirable calm (and a hint of superiority) he surveyed his audience ... and was not unpleased.

Samantha moved quickly across the room to greet her friend, adding to the gossip already running riot in the room.

"Derek, you conceited exhibitionist," Samantha said in a low voice, chuckling as she permitted Lord Barnett to carry her hand to his lips. "That was magnificently done. You have awed them to their toes."

"Thank you, my dear Cupid," Lord Barnett drawled.

"Artemis."

"Whatever. The issue, of course, was never in doubt. I perceive several political figures here this evening. I am grateful. And several beauteous maidens as well! Samantha, you are too good to me."

Forbearing to point out to him that the ball was not being held in his honor, Samantha led him slowly around the room, allowing him but a word or two with each guest before leading him to the next introduction.

Lady Jillian Roberts, who had come as Portia, felt her heart erupt into a series of often violent palpitations as she observed Lord Barnett advance through the room for she at last beheld her secret ideal. She had, of course, glimpsed Lord Barnett at other functions, but now, for the first time, saw him where he belonged: at center stage. Her green eyes followed his every move; they would not leave his tall, handsome figure.

It was only Jillian's remarkable self-control and pride that allowed her to keep her countenance as Lord Barnett advanced toward her at last. His blue eyes widened as his gaze met hers. He bowed over her hand, murmured that he had been longing for an introduction, and could not describe the pleasure he felt at knowing her name at last. His lips seemed to caress her fingertips for the briefest moment and in that instant Jillian knew, as she had never in the past known, what it was to be vulnerable.

She was oblivious to everyone around her, to everyone in the room, in fact, and so missed the startled glance Lord Cartwright gave them both, his brown eyes narrowing speculatively. He was then distracted by observing Lord Barnett loop Samantha's arm through his as she led him away, laughing at something he had said.

"I've invited Lady Caroline Evers tonight," Samantha said to Lord Barnett.

"Damn!"

Samantha grinned at him. "I only give balls to amuse myself . . . and Lady Caroline is frightfully amusing. Look, she is glaring at me as if she would cast me into flames."

"Lord Cartwright, too, does not look upon you with favor," Lord Barnett observed. "I fear that your powers are failing, Samantha."

"What?" Samantha gasped.

"Has he once stood up to dance with you?" Lord Barnett demanded. "No, not even once. By all reports, you could not even get him to dance with you tonight at your own ball."

"Oh couldn't I?" Samantha said, her chin coming up. "A hundred pounds says Lord Cartwright dances with me before the night is through."

"Only a hundred? You haven't the courage of your convictions. Make it five hundred."

"Done."

"Done," Lord Barnett said happily, for he had every faith in his champion's dislike of his friend. "But it must be one complete dance. You cannot drag him out onto the dance floor, make your bows, and leave the dance floor and expect payment from me."

"It will be a complete dance, Derek. A waltz, I think. I will accept English bank notes in payment."

Lord Barnett regarded her warily. "What do you know that I don't?"

Samantha's smile was seraphic. "Lord Cartwright's Achilles' heel."

"And that is?"

"His fear of public ridicule."

She bestowed Lord Barnett upon the eager Lady Caroline Evers and then went up to the orchestra which had begun to tune for the first dance. Instructions were given, obedience assured, and then she began to search for Lord Cartwright. She found him in a nest of prominent gentlemen: Charles II, Neptune, Alexander the Great, and Sir Francis Drake by her reckoning. Pausing only for a fortifying breath, she rushed up to her prey.

"I *do* beg your pardon, my lord," she exclaimed. "I was detained by Lord Barnett who was regaling me with the most shocking *on dit* and I quite lost track of the time. Pray say you forgive me and will keep your promise of this first dance. I have been so looking forward to it."

Her expression was one of charming penitence and hope as she met Lord Cartwright's startled gaze without a blink.

"Lucky fellow," said Neptune, "to have the honor of the first dance with so beautiful and delightful a hostess."

"You'll honor me with the next dance, won't you, Lady Samantha?" Sir Francis Drake implored.

"No, no, she has promised the next dance to me, haven't you, Lady Samantha?" said Alexander the Great.

"At this moment, gentlemen," Samantha said, "I can think only of the pleasure of dancing with Lord Cartwright." She smiled expectantly up at her prey.

Being a practical man, he knew a trap when he found himself in one and, privately believing that chivalry was not dead as long as a Cartwright lived, he bowed to his hostess and offered his arm.

"I had begun to fear that you meant to desert me," he murmured.

"Nothing could keep me from our waltz," Samantha gratefully assured him.

Lord Simon Cartwright led Lady Samantha Adamson onto the dance floor and occasioned a great many hushed conversations by so doing.

Lord Wyatt, standing at Lady Cartwright's side, ventured to point out that this was somewhat of an historic occasion.

"Yes, I know," she said with a smile. "I wonder how she did it?"

"But Simon does not dance," Lord Wyatt said.

"Of course he does. Simon dances beautifully. He gets it from my side of the family."

"Why must you toy with me?" Lord Wyatt said with a sigh.

"Because you are such a willing victim, my dear," Lady Cartwright replied with a fond smile.

"Simon has not undertaken a single dance since his father died, as you very well know."

"Indeed. I begin to think we owe a great debt to Lady Samantha."

Lord Wyatt studied the dowager a moment, agreed with the truth of this statement, and then, recollecting the written threat he had received at dinner, cast his eyes about the room for the mistress of his heart. He spied Titania standing bereft of company not ten yards away.

"If you will excuse me, Lady Cartwright," said he, "I have developed a sudden need to partake of the waltz."

The dowager watched in some surprise and then amusement as Lord Wyatt made his way toward her only daughter. Had Samantha a hand in this as well? Meddler seemed a most apt description after all.

"How is it that you are bereft of a partner for the first dance?" Lord Wyatt demanded of Hilary as he reached her side.

"Mr. Dently became suddenly indisposed," Hilary replied, striving mightily not to smile. "I believe the third helping of dates was too much for his . . . constitution."

"Foolish man," Lord Wyatt said with a warm smile as he

took her hand in his, "to deny himself such happiness for the sake of a date. I am far more sensible. Nothing could keep me from your side. Will you honor me with this dance?"

Lord Wyatt's smile, the way he pressed her hand and looked into her eyes, set Hilary's heart to hammering in her breast, her confusion compounded by a new, odd quality to her friend's voice that left her thoroughly nonplussed.

"Oh . . . oh, of course, Aaron," she stammered in reply. "If you would like it. But would you not rather dance with Miss Maxwell?"

"When I may claim instead the delight of my heart? No, no, I wish only to dance with you," Lord Wyatt replied with a look that brought a blush to Hilary's cheeks as he tucked her arm into his and led her onto the floor.

Samantha, meanwhile, was paying the piper.

They had not taken more than two steps in the waltz when Lord Cartwright, his brown eyes lit with amusement, called her to task.

"Come," he said, "tell me why you have so discreetly badgered me into partnering you for this dance. No, no, don't pull that guileless expression on me for it won't fadge. Out with it, Lady Samantha, what are you up to?"

"Why nothing, nothing at all," Samantha breezily assured him. "It is you who have done everything. You've just been so obliging as to win me five hundred pounds."

"What?"

"No, no, don't stop," Samantha said, pushing him back into the waltz. "It must be a complete dance or I don't win."

"You made a wager on me? You gambled that I would dance with you?"

"Such a certainty could hardly be called gambling."

Lord Cartwright's mouth was desperately pinched against a smile. "And what convinced you that you could win such a wager?"

130

"I knew you could not stand idly by while I made a fool of myself before a host of respectable gentlemen."

"Ah. And what drove you to the bet in the first place?"

A sheepish grin tugged at Samantha's mouth. "Lord Barnett said I would lose."

"But of course," Lord Cartwright murmured. "That is your greatest weakness, you know, Lady Samantha."

"What? Derek?"

"No, no. Your inability to walk away from a challenge."

Samantha hung her head. "It is true. I am a trifle stubborn."

"None of this rodomontade if you please, my lady. You revel in pigheadedness and you know it."

Samantha smiled up at him. "Ah sir, you know me too well. The fun will soon leave our acquaintance."

"You undervalue yourself, Lady Samantha," Lord Cartwright gravely replied. "Yours is a bottomless well of tricks to vex and astonish the most determinedly civil gentlemen."

"High praise indeed," Samantha murmured.

"But tell me, in all honesty, Lady Samantha, do you truly enjoy this madcap existence? Do you stuff your days with matchmaking, meddling, and mayhem for your own enjoyment or to fend off loneliness? Does such a life *satisfy* you?"

Samantha's face had gone from white to an infuriated pink.

"And you, sir," she snapped, "do you like sitting in judgment of everyone who comes your way? Do you derive pleasure from eschewing pleasure? Does such a life *satisfy you*?"

Lord Cartwright stared down at her.

"Well," he said, "that certainly put us in our place."

Samantha was startled into a chuckle. "Wretch! You will not even let me argue with you anymore."

The dance ended and they made each other their bows near the doors to the card room.

131

"Simon!"

Both turned to discover a fulminating Lady Jillian Roberts bearing down upon them.

"You were to partner me at whist," that lovely lady declared.

"I *am* sorry, Jillian," Lord Cartwright replied. "I found myself accosted by several loquacious gentlemen and then stumbled into a dance with Lady Samantha. I would be happy to join you in a rubber now."

"That is impossible. The parties are formed, the tables full. I did not know you could be so inconsiderate."

Lord Cartwright again tendered his apologies, Jillian accepted them at last and then declared that she was thirsty. Lord Cartwright instantly went off to procure her a glass of punch.

"You have him well trained, my lady," Samantha commented as she studied the buttons of her left glove. "Have you got him jumping through hoops yet?"

"I will tell you, Lady Samantha," Jillian said in a voice that would have made weaker mortals tremble, "that I strongly resent the indecorous manner in which you treat Lord Cartwright. Your acquaintance is of but short duration, yet you persist in treating him as if he were some adolescent playfellow! Such behavior is extremely objectionable in one of your sex and class and I will not allow it to continue."

"Pray, what have you to say to anything?" Samantha inquired.

"I am Lord Cartwright's affianced wife, or had you forgotten?"

"Oh no. That knowledge is constantly before me like a beacon in the fog."

"I do not understand you, Lady Samantha," Jillian seethed. "Are you *never* serious?"

"No, never. It is too disruptive to the digestion."

"Lady Samantha, I find your conduct reprehensible. I can

no longer tolerate your casual treatment of my fiancé, nor your abuse of his good nature. To converse with Lord Cartwright as you do, to pull him, at whim, from the company of his fiancée and future in-laws, demonstrates a shocking lack of character."

"Lord Cartwright seems a man well able to voice his opinions. I am surprised that you feel compelled to speak for him," Samantha responded calmly.

With an infuriated gasp, Jillian stalked off, Samantha's laughter pursuing her at a discreet distance.

"What are you laughing at with such self-satisfaction? And where is Jillian?" Lord Cartwright demanded as he came up to Samantha, a glass of punch in his hand.

"That is why I am laughing," she retorted.

"At Jillian, or her departure?"

"Both."

"What have you said to her?" Lord Cartwright demanded.

"Everything to infuriate her," Samantha replied happily. "And I am ashamed to say that I enjoyed myself hugely."

"That shows a modicum of right thinking."

"What? Infuriating Lady Jillian?"

"No! Being ashamed for it," Lord Cartwright retorted, struggling to restrain his own smile.

"But I am not so very ashamed, after all," Samantha said, hanging her head.

"That I can well believe. Why do you laugh now?"

"Because I am having a very jolly time tonight."

"At Jillian's expense!"

"But she is so easy to goad. How can I possibly resist?"

"Will power, Lady Samantha. *Will power.* You do not see me goading Jillian, do you?"

"No. Have you wanted to?" Samantha asked with frank curiosity.

"Frequently," Lord Cartwright replied, his brown eyes

twinkling. "Fortunately, *I* have some sense of propriety and decorum."

"Which I lack," Samantha supplied. "But you will notice that I am not the one saddled with a most unfortunate set of in-laws."

Lord Cartwright drew himself to his fullest height. "Madam, you are speaking of the parents of my chosen bride!"

"Have you ever noticed how so many daughters become like their mothers as they advance in age?" Samantha inquired.

Lord Cartwright involuntarily glanced through the door at Lady Winnifred Roberts severely lecturing Lord Horton on his atrocious play.

"Now there's a thought to give a man pause," he murmured.

"But you are made of sterner stuff," Samantha said heartily. "Not even the shrewish prattle of a Lady Winnifred Roberts could turn you from the course of true love."

"No, no, of course not," Lord Cartwright said hastily, and then looked with suspicion down at Samantha as her grin grew. "Wretch!"

"I *am* awful, I own it freely. But you are such a delightful target, how can I resist?"

"You do not seem able to resist very much," Lord Cartwright observed.

"That is very true," Samantha said musingly. "It is undoubtedly a great defect in my character. Have you noticed that the nostrils of both Lady Winnifred and Lady Jillian Roberts squeeze shut when they are particularly incensed?"

Lord Cartwright burst into laughter. "*Odious* woman," he said with an appreciative gaze.

Chapter Twelve

LORD CARTWRIGHT HAD just finished a most delightful gallop through Hyde Park only a week after the Adamson Masquerade Ball, when he was suddenly arrested by the stunning sight of Lady Samantha Adamson riding between Celeste Vandaun and the Marquis of Lockwood. He was not the only one to view this shocking tableau. It seemed that half of the haut ton was present in the park and could do nothing but stare and comment.

It was with relief that his lordship watched Lady Samantha bid adieu to the two lovebirds but the relief was short-lived. She had spied Lord Barnett strolling across the grass arm in arm with a gentleman in a scarlet coat and a good deal of gold braid.

"Brandon?" she gasped. "Brandon, is it really you?" She threw herself off her mare, to the surprise of many around her and, reins clutched in one hand, threw her arms around the scarlet coat. "Good God, you're a colonel!" she cried, hugging him with considerable strength, which he happily returned.

"My dear scapegrace," he said with a fond smile, beaming down at her. He was tall with thick black hair and sparkling gray eyes that surveyed Samantha with the utmost pleasure.

"It has been over a year," said the colonel, "since we last had a lark together and what do I find on my first day back in London, but that you are the talk of the town. And I can see why. We are drawing a crowd."

They were, indeed, the object of speculative survey by a good dozen members of the ton.

"I don't care a jot," Lady Samantha said, dimpling. "It would be far more improper for you to climb onto my horse to hug me than for me to get off my horse to hug you. But what are you doing in town?"

"Now that Nappy is no longer a threat," said the colonel as he studied the lady's mare and found her more than acceptable, "the cavalry has become a bit of a bore. I've decided to abandon scarlet for a frock coat and some other means of amusement."

"I am trying to convince him how well he'd do in Parliament," said Lord Barnett, "but the fellow won't attend me."

"You cannot seriously think, Derek, that I could be happy locked up in a dark room with a hundred other *men*?" said the colonel.

Rolling his beautiful blue eyes heavenward, Lord Barnett gave it up as a bad job.

"For a man with such a fine appreciation of women," said Lady Samantha, "it is odd that you are but a year away from your thirtieth year and still unmarried."

"How can I appreciate the most delightful of the two sexes if I am shackled to a fishwife for the rest of my life?" the colonel countered.

"You and Derek are the greatest thorns in my side," Lady Samantha said with a sigh. "All of my highly developed matchmaking abilities have yet to ensnare either of you into matrimony."

"If you would but accept my suit," said Lord Barnett.

"Give over, Derek," said the colonel with a grin. "You'd harry each other into mutual homicide within a se'ennight of the wedding. As for me, Sam," he said, "you reckon without my mother. A most formidable woman is Lady Dalton. She would put any man off marriage for life!"

"Getting you to the altar, Brandon, is a distinct challenge," said Lady Samantha, "and, as one gentleman recently remarked, I can never ignore a challenge. The gauntlet is thrown. I shall see you wed before the year is out, you mark my words."

"A thousand pounds says you fail," the colonel promptly replied.

"I'll second that," said Lord Barnett.

"Done," said Lady Samantha.

Colonel Brandon Dalton paled. "I fear that smile. That smile had me breaking into a Viennese pastry shop in the dead of night when I was thirteen and she eleven. What do you know, Samantha, that I don't?"

"The perfect wife for you," she replied.

"There isn't such a creature."

"You'll see soon enough," she said. "If I can find the perfect protector for Celeste Vandaun, I can find you a wife."

With a groan, the colonel tossed her back into her saddle, swept her a dashing bow, and returned to his promenade with Lord Barnett, bitterly remarking that once Samantha had a scheme in mind there was no swaying her. He would probably be wed to a freckle-faced harridan before the year was out. Lord Barnett clucked sympathetically.

Lady Samantha, meanwhile, had turned her horse toward the Marble Arch and in this way became aware of the disapproving stares that surrounded her. A flush rose to her cheeks. Her head rose higher and in that moment she saw that Lord Cartwright observed her. The flush darkened, whether from anger or embarrassment he could not tell. With a toss of her head, she wheeled her mare and set her off at a canter.

Forcibly pushing aside the growing unease that plagued

her whenever she returned from a public promenade, Samantha stoically entered her study an hour later to work through the mountain of correspondence that awaited her. Halfway through that day's large post, she came upon a thick letter bearing a crest she knew all too well. She nearly consigned it to her wastebasket, unopened, but decided at last that she could not be so childish. She placed it in one of the cubbyholes of her desk, hoping she would be fortunate enough to forget it was there.

Fortune did not smile upon her that afternoon.

Two hours after hiding it away, Samantha once again held the letter with its grim family crest in her hand. Reginald's existence, she thought, was plague enough. Did he have to compound her misery by forever reminding her of it?

With a heavy sigh, she at last broke the seal and stared with disbelief at a letter, in her brother's inimitable scrawl, numbering ten pages.

"Good God, what have I done now?" Samantha moaned aloud.

Lord Reginald Adamson's letter told her . . . again, and again, and again. He dwelt with particular length on some of the more grievous scrapes of her adventurous girlhood, compared them unflatteringly to her current activities, and then swung into a round denunciation of her guardianship of the Danthorpes. No female of seven-and-twenty, claimed her brother, was a fit guardian for a goldfish, let alone two rambunctious Americans. Disquieting stories had recently reached his ears of Mr. Danthorpe's far from savory frolics. It was said that Peter and his ramshackle friends had pretended to be white slavers and had accosted every respectable woman in sight at Vauxhall!

Samantha, enraged throughout her brother's letter, could not but smile at this. It was rather an inventive lark at that, she thought. Peter may well have been mixed up in it.

She returned to her brother's letter and found a series of

138

dark threats leading up to the ghastly statement: "I have already written to the Tylers to offer my services on their behalf. I mean to take the Danthorpes in hand and remove them from your poisonous influence to the healthful environs of Yorkshire."

Samantha allowed herself to shudder at a threat she knew her brother was fully capable of carrying out. As much as she despised Reginald Adamson, she was well aware that he was a power to be reckoned with in his home county. His contacts were extensive, his influence equally so. Once he got the Danthorpes in hand, it would be hard if not impossible to get them back.

Seriously concerned, Samantha began to pace the room, oblivious to the sunny day outside the floor-to-ceiling windows she walked past, unmindful of the time as the ornate French clock on the mantel struck three.

It finally occurred to her after several minutes of earnest cogitation that she had powerful friends in town. They could advise her on how best to thwart her brother's plans. For some reason, Lord Cartwright's name held prominence in her thoughts, but she ruthlessly dismissed him to the realm of fantasy.

"There must be someone," Samantha muttered as she rubbed her throbbing temples. "Of course! Derek!"

Lord Barnett, though recently returned to his homeland, had already acquired a plethora of powerful friends who saw in him their chance for even greater power through Parliament. Lord Barnett, of all her friends, would know whom to talk to, whom to use, to remove the threat Reggie had concocted. But she would have to act quickly. Reggie would not have issued the threat if he did not mean to take immediate action. Time was paramount.

With a sharp jerk upon the bell rope, Samantha summoned a footman and had her phaeton put to immediately. Not bothering to change her dress, she merely added a driving coat, hat, and gloves and by the time she reached the street her phaeton was ready. Despite the strong wind, the day was mild, the streets dry. She drove her chestnuts at a fast clip to Lord Barnett's town home in Curzon Street. But there she met her first obstacle. Lord Barnett was not at home. When pressed with some asperity to conjure the name of the club or home to which he had gone, the butler at last recalled that Lord Barnett had mentioned something about visiting Mr. Heath, a rising star in Parliament.

But Mr. Heath could not produce Lord Barnett. His lordship had gone off to lunch at Grillon's some two hours before. But he was not at Grillon's. A waiter thought he had heard his lordship mention something about White's and thus, with grim determination, Samantha turned her chestnuts down St. James's Street. Intent only on running her prey to ground, she was unaware of the shocked and titillated stares directed at her by every Bond Street beau lounging in a window or strolling down the street to display the newest heights to which they had wrested their shirt points . . . and their chins.

Those not of the dandy set, but still intent on looking their best, stepped out of Brookes and Boodle's to stare with horror at this *woman* driving unconcernedly down *their* street. Poodle Byng stared, his meticulously coiffured dog barked. Lord Farago's corset threatened to burst.

"I say, Simon," said Lord Horton, jabbing an elbow into his ribs as they exited Brookes, "isn't that Lady Samantha Adamson?"

"Don't be absurd, Cyril, not even *she*—Oh good God!" ejaculated Lord Cartwright as he saw that it was indeed Lady Samantha driving toward them. "She is heedless and headstrong, I know, but I never thought her *mad*!"

"Give her her due, Simon," Lord Horton admonished, "she doesn't seem at all concerned by the stares she's getting."

"She must be used to them after all these years. She knows . . . she must know that no woman of breeding and

140

respectability would dare show her face on St. James's Street. Yet there she drives bold as brass."

"The most amazing thing I've ever seen in m'life," Lord Horton agreed.

She was nearly abreast of them when she suddenly called out: "Derek! *Derek!*"

Lord Barnett, just exiting White's, stared at her, his face pale with shock.

Lord Cartwright could bear it no longer. Outrage, horror, and chivalry all propelled him into the street where he grasped the reins at the chestnuts' heads and pulled them to a stop.

"What do you think you're doing?" Samantha gasped, the color high in her cheeks. "Release my cattle at once!"

"On no account whatsoever," Lord Cartwright replied in a clipped voice as, his hand still around one rein, he stalked back to the phaeton.

"This is the height of enough! How dare you— What do you think you're doing?" Samantha cried as Lord Cartwright leaped into the box and pushed her out of the way.

"Saving whatever tatters remain of your reputation," Lord Cartwright replied, his mouth set in a grim line as he jerked the reins from her hands and, with a vicious crack of the whip, set them trotting hurriedly down the street.

"Stop!" Samantha shouted. "How dare you! Who do you think you are? You can't just manhandle me in this way! I must see Lord Barnett. Stop! Have you run mad?"

"I might ask the same of you, *my lady*," Lord Cartwright retorted as he turned the phaeton onto a less scandalous avenue. "How could even you be so foolish, so consummately idiotic as to drive down St. James's Street in the light of day with all the world to stare and gawk at you? Have you no sense? Have you no consideration for your reputation? By God, madam, if you've no regard for yourself, at least think of your wards! The scandal cannot but affect them."

"I *am* thinking of them!" Samantha yelled. "That is why I went to your precious St. James's Street. I demand that you turn back, Lord Cartwright. I must speak to Lord Barnett at once. The matter is most urgent."

"On no account will I allow you to traverse that street again."

"Who made you God?" Samantha stormed. "You are not my keeper, you are not my conscience, you are not even any relation to me. You've no more right to interfere with what I do or say than has a bootblack!"

"*Someone* has to rescue you from your own folly," Lord Cartwright retorted with some heat. "The horror of it is that you don't even know what you've done. Can you not understand, you pigheaded, sharp-tongued viper that I am trying to help you?"

"I want no help from you!" Samantha cried, the color high in her cheeks. "I want no notice from you! Give me back my phaeton or I shall have you arrested!"

"I should like to see you try," Lord Cartwright said grimly.

"Oh! By all the gods I'll have you thrashed!" Samantha cried.

They continued in high choler all the way back to Berkeley Square, their argument increasing in vitriol with each street they passed until, by the time Lord Cartwright drew to a stop before the Dower House, their voices could be heard up and down the Square.

"Give me my cattle!" Samantha shouted.

"They are confiscated until you return to your senses!" Lord Cartwright retorted. "When there is no more threat of you driving to St. James's Street, then you may have them."

Samantha abandoned her last shreds of restraint and proceeded to curse him in three languages, Arabic particularly suiting her fury as she jumped down from the phaeton, *her* phaeton, and stalked back to her house.

"A pox on you, Simon Cartwright!" she shouted at him.

"You have had your day and I swear by every black fiend in Hades that I shall have mine!" She slammed the front door behind her.

Lord Cartwright uttered a sigh that man, since time immemorial, has uttered whenever arguing with woman. He then drove to the stables behind Cartwright House and informed his stunned head groom that the team and the phaeton were not to be returned to Lady Samantha until the morrow.

He then stalked into his own house, slamming his door with as much fury as Samantha had slammed hers.

The windows rattled.

"I fail to understand," said Lord Barnett an hour later as he paced the length of Samantha's private sitting room, "how a woman of your intelligence, your sagacity, your experience could commit so lunatic an act!"

"I know, I know," Samantha moaned. She was seated at her desk, her throbbing head resting in her hands. "But I told you, Derek, I didn't think of St. James's Street. The waiter said White's. I thought only of White's, not the street where it resides."

"When will you get it through that beautiful thick head of yours that London is not a pleasure ground for you to romp through at your will? You've friends enough to teach you the reefs to avoid, the dangerous fences to hurdle, the bounds of feminine conduct."

"Oh please stop, Derek, I feel bad enough as it is," Samantha pleaded. "I know I've made a hash of things. I've ruined myself and probably Christina and Peter as well. How could I have been so unthinking, so *stupid* . . . ! How can I defend myself after this? Reggie will take them in charge before the month is out and there's nothing I can do!"

Seeing that she really was contrite, Lord Barnett decided to relent.

"There, there," he said, "it is not as black as all that.

Cartwright has put it out that he made you a wager that you would not have the temerity to drive down St. James's Street at the height of the Promenade. He's at Carlton House bemoaning the loss of five thousand pounds even as we speak."

"What?" Samantha's head jerked up and she stared at her friend, her face drained of color. "Lord Cartwright at . . . Carlton House?"

"Prinny's countenance is really the only thing that can restore yours and Cartwright knows it. The wager's a good story, and Prinny took a fancy to you, as who could not? He'll soon set things to rights."

Samantha rose jerkily to her feet. "B-b-but why would Lord Cartwright do such a thing for *me*?"

"Perhaps that Achilles' heel of his?" Lord Barnett hazarded, twirling his quizzing glass. "Or perhaps you were wrong in his weakness. Perhaps Lord Cartwright feels compelled to protect anyone in his ken from the smirks and slights and humiliations he has endured these last few years."

"Has the ton really been so hard on him?" Samantha asked quietly.

"You know what Society is, Samantha. It always likes to see one of its own fall so that it can enjoy a feeding frenzy."

"But 'twas the father's errors, not the son's."

"The father was not around to heckle," said Lord Barnett with a shrug, "the son was."

"Oh, the things I said to him!" Samantha wailed as she buried her face in her hands.

"Knowing you, they were undoubtedly terrible," Lord Barnett said with a smile.

"Oh, Derek, they were awful!" Samantha said, looking up. "The worst I've ever used."

"That is saying a good deal."

"But he was equally rude to me."

"Undoubtedly."

"And he had no right to commandeer my phaeton like that."

"None whatsoever."

"He hasn't even had the decency to return my own team to me!"

"A grievous injury, to be sure."

A smile quivered on Samantha's lips. "You're terrible. I don't know why I like you. I shall have to apologize to the wretched man, I suppose."

"Not every man would be as quick-witted to think of a wager and using Prinny," Lord Barnett conceded.

Samantha hugged herself. "My stomach hurts. I don't want to think about that now. What am I going to do about Reggie, Derek? He will apprise the Tylers and not even *they* can ignore such impropriety. Today has consigned the Danthorpes to Yorkshire, I know it has."

"You were right to seek me out, my Queen of Hearts, though not at White's in St. James's Street. Leave Reginald to me. I promise you continued guardianship of the Danthorpes."

"Are you sure, Derek?"

"How can you doubt me? *Me*, a Barnett of Wortley Hall?"

"You're right, of course, Derek," Samantha said meekly. "I wasn't thinking."

"That trouble seems to have plagued you for the whole of this day, my friend."

"My dear Simon, I just heard!" Lady Jillian Roberts cried as she bustled into the Cartwright yellow drawing room. She was too much an intimate of the family to countenance Clarke announcing her. "Oh, hello, Lady Cartwright."

"How are you, Jillian?" inquired Lady Cartwright as she rose from the sofa with her son.

"Appalled, Lady Cartwright, appalled and horrified,"

Jillian declared, taking her accustomed seat by the fire. "Lady Samantha has finally placed herself beyond the pale. She drove herself down St. James's Street this afternoon!"

"Yes, so Simon mentioned," the dowager placidly replied.

Lord Cartwright, seated beside her once again, said nothing.

"I know you played the gentleman, Simon, and hurried her away as soon as you could—everyone is talking of it!—but not even you could save her from her own stupidity," said Jillian with some satisfaction. "I have just seen Lady Jersey. The Adamson woman will be denied Almack's. The Esterhazys are beside themselves for Lady Samantha had already accepted their invitation to tomorrow night's salon and they dread the reaction of their guests when she is announced. Everyone is talking of her! Well, it is no wonder for who could imagine that *any* woman of breeding would succumb to such mania? Lady Samantha's fall from favor is irrevocable."

"On the contrary, Jillian," Lord Cartwright replied coolly. "Lady Samantha shall be proved beyond reproach. There has been only an unfortunate misunderstanding. Prinny and I were bantering Lady Samantha at the Jerseys' dinner a few nights ago and we jested, all in fun, that not even she would have the temerity to drive her phaeton down St. James's Street at the height of the Promenade. She instantly took up the challenge, in the spirit of the jest we thought, and so we pledged ourselves to an outrageous wager. I believe I promised the sum of five thousand pounds if she completed the drive. Little did we think that she had taken our jest as a serious wager. I only perceived the misunderstanding when I saw her in her phaeton today. She was quite upset when I told her that Prinny and I had not been in earnest. The Prince has promised to smooth everything over so we shall hope that it will all come out right."

Jillian stared at Lord Cartwright with mounting horror.

"Do you ... do *you* actually expect me to believe such a Banbury story?"

"But it is the truth, Jillian," Lord Cartwright said with an easy smile.

Outrage drove Jillian to her feet. She stood in glorious fury looking down at Lord Cartwright.

"You will protect her?" she demanded. "You will shield her from her own impropriety even knowing what she has done? Knowing what she is?"

"And what is she, Jillian?" Lord Cartwright inquired.

The dowager rose quietly and began to make her way from the room.

"Do you not know?" Jillian cried. "Have her beauty and so-called wit blinded you to the horror of her character and the blackness of her soul? She is everything that is loathsome in woman!"

"Loathsome?" gasped Lord Cartwright, rising to his feet. "Lady Samantha? Don't be absurd, Jillian. She is headstrong and often impetuous, but those are errors that will be tempered with age and maturity and association with those who care to teach her how to get on in the world."

"She is anathema to every right-thinking man and woman in the ton!" Jillian countered.

"What's all the to-do?" Matthew demanded as he sauntered into the room.

His mother got a firm grip on his arm, pulled him to her side, and severely shushed him.

"Jillian and Simon are having a row," she whispered as Lord Cartwright informed his fiancée that, for his part, he thought Lady Samantha quite delightful, a breath of fresh air in a staid and stagnant society that had begun, prior to her arrival in town, to bore him to tears.

"But they never row!" Matthew whispered to his mother in astonishment.

"I know," Lady Cartwright said with a smile. "Is it not wonderful?"

They both turned to watch the unexpected drama unfold before them.

"How can you think Lady Samantha delightful," Jillian cried, "when with every day she shows herself to be less and less a lady? Only a fortnight ago you thought her a scandalous harridan!"

"Oh, she is," Lord Cartwright replied easily. "She is also the most entertaining wench I have ever met."

"Simon! How can you speak in such a flippant manner? Such base language is unlike you."

"Actually, it is very like me," Lord Cartwright said thoughtfully. "Lady Samantha has reminded me of it."

"What, will you revert back to the schoolboy under her influence?" Jillian demanded with the suggestion of a sneer.

"A telling blow, that," Matthew murmured.

"No, no, Simon is made of sterner stuff," his mother whispered and indeed she had the right of it for Lord Cartwright replied, after due consideration, that childhood did not seem such a bad place in which to linger. He had always been happy *then* and these last few years of adulthood certainly could not match that claim.

"And I suppose *my* company has only added to such unhappiness?" Jillian said in a scathing voice.

"That is not what I said or meant," Lord Cartwright wearily replied.

"Forgive me. After such unnatural speech I no longer know how to take your comments."

Fifteen minutes later, declaring that this was a stupid argument engaged upon for no good purpose, Jillian departed the Cartwright household with the ominous threat that she would speak with Lord Cartwright when he was more himself.

"Now *that's* something to give a man nightmares," Matthew commented and received a sharp nudge from his mother for his wit.

Scarcely aware of their company, Lord Cartwright, with a barely suppressed oath, stalked from the room.

Chapter Thirteen

"Sam, we can't go to the Esterhazys tonight," Christina cried, wringing her hands. "We mustn't! We don't dare show our faces in town again!"

"I am the one who committed the social solecism, child, not you," Samantha calmly retorted as she stepped into her beige satin gown with the help of her abigail. "Your face will be welcome wherever you go."

"But you don't know what people are saying! You don't know how they stared at me and talked behind their hands when I was coming home from the Hortons' yesterday."

Samantha cringed. She hadn't had the courage to tell Christina of the dozens of notes she had received that day from members of the ton crying off from their rout next week.

"Don't think on the miseries of the past," she advised. "Derek assures me that the Prince will raise us to new heights in the ton and Derek has never been mistaken before."

"Oh, I am so miserable!" Christina cried as she threw herself disconsolately upon Samantha's bed.

"I am truly sorry to put you through all this, Chris," Samantha said, dismissing her abigail. "The last thing I want is to cause you the least difficulty. On my honor, I shall be a model of decorum from now on."

"You haven't got it in you, Sam, and you know it."

"I suppose not," Samantha replied with a rueful smile. "But I do promise to try. Now go and get dressed. You know that there will be at least a dozen of your beaux at the Esterhazys and you don't want to disappoint them, do you?"

"No. No, I suppose not," Christina said, slowly getting off the bed, lost in thought. "Sam, wouldn't it be the most romantic thing if my suitors all defended me in the teeth of even Lady Jersey's disapprobation! It would be like gallant knights battling some fierce dragon to come to my rescue!"

"Depend upon it, they are polishing their armor even as we speak."

"What of Lord Palmerston?" Christina cried, wringing her hands once again. "Do you think . . . *do* you think his feelings will be the same?"

"Of course. He still wants your fortune."

"Samantha, I wish you would not be so prosaic," Christina said petulantly. "Lord Palmerston is the most enthralling man I've ever met."

"Christina, what is so enthralling about an earl in debt up to his ears?" Samantha demanded, hunting through her jewelry box for the pearl necklace she wanted. "An earl, moreover, who has been described on more than one occasion as a rake?"

"Samantha, have you no sensibility at all? *I* shall be his savior! With one stroke I shall rescue him from penury and the evils of the muslin set. He will be my worshipful slave for the rest of our lives."

"I think Mr. Timothy Cartwright more suited to sitting worshipfully at your feet," Samantha said, triumphantly pulling out the pearl necklace.

"He's sweet, of course, but there is nothing in the least romantic about a *farmer*."

Alarm bells went off in Samantha's head. She stared at her ward in growing consternation. "But I thought you were quite besotted with him."

"With Mr. Cartwright? 'Twas just a passing fancy, I assure you. He is not at all the kind of man I could love, let alone marry."

Samantha blinked. "And Michael Palmerston is?"

"But I've told you: he is like a hero in a novel—handsome, world-weary, cynically debased—and I the heroine sent to redeem him!"

Samantha cringed. "You are an intelligent girl, Christina. I only wish you had less sensibility and more *sense*."

Her ward made no reply as she left the room for her head was already busy debating which gown to wear on the night after the St. James's Street debacle. Should she appear retiring and demure? Or assured and vivacious? Which would Lord Palmerston prefer?

Samantha, unhindered by worries over Lord Palmerston's preferences, was suffering a similar quandary. Loathe though she was to admit it, she had been afraid to leave the house today. Until the Prince acted, or failed to act, at the Esterhazys' tonight, she could not be certain of her welcome on any street or in any home in London. She had girded her loins, made up a white flag, and presented herself in Lord Cartwright's study that morning to formally apologize and thank him for all that he had done on her behalf. Aside from taking the flag with a smile and wondering on which wall he should mount it, he had brushed aside all apologies and thanks, assured her the Prince would take care of everything, and had sent her on her way.

Despite such a surprisingly cordial welcome, she had ventured nowhere else. Now she studied herself critically in the mirror. The gown was one of the more decorous confections she had had made since coming to London. For tonight, she would be careful to at least not invite new criticism. Tonight she would remember the rules of the ton, her obligation to Christina and Peter, the threat of Reggie looming on the horizon, and conduct herself in such a way that even Lady Jillian Roberts would approve.

"Well, perhaps I needn't go that far," Samantha muttered. "Then again, perhaps I should."

Peter was to be one of the performers that evening. Fortunately, the Esterhazys had him playing near the end of the evening and, though it was not correct to come in the middle of the salon, Samantha thought that it would be a good deal safer to arrive at the intermission. Hopefully, the Prince would already have made his entrance and begun to weave his tale.

Samantha found it more than a little frightening that her fate rested in another's hands. She had gotten herself into this fix, she would have liked to have gotten herself out. But she was wise enough to see that in this, at least, she needed all the help she could get.

Thus, she and the Danthorpes, after muttering a little prayer on the front walk, entered the Esterhazys' London home a little after ten o'clock that night and were shown into the long drawing room on the first landing of that imposing edifice. It seemed as if everyone in the room turned to them when they entered the doorway. There was a pronounced silence during which Christina wanted to sink into the floor, and Samantha was more than tempted to follow her. Then . . .

"My dear Lady Samantha!" the Prince Regent warbled as he trotted up to them, beaming from ear to ear. "I am so glad you could come tonight," he said, taking her hand as she and the Danthorpes hurriedly made their bows. "I have been wanting to congratulate you on your courage, your daring, nay, your skill! All of London is talking of it! How I wish I had been there to see you driving down St. James's Street! Come, you must tell me all about it. Did Lord Farago really burst his corset strings? Ah, but I was nearly forgetting. First, I must make good on my bet, eh? A debt

152

of honor, after all," he said chuckling. "Here you are, my dear," he said, drawing off a ring from his little finger, "the Emperor's ruby, just as I promised you."

"Oh no, Your Highness, I couldn't!" Samantha cried, aghast as he pressed the ring into her hand.

"But you must," the Prince said simply. "You won the wager."

Samantha collected her wits. "But you were hoaxing me! You hadn't meant it as a real bet. Lord Cartwright has told me all!"

"Tut, tut, my dear," the Prince said, patting her hand. "We may have been bamming you, which was a very ungentlemanly thing to do, you know, but you carried it off superbly. I would be honored if you would accept this small token of my esteem."

Samantha had no choice but to thank her prince and place the ring on her middle finger. It was a loose fit, but she thought it would be safe for the night.

"Come," said the Prince Regent, tucking her arm through his, "let me fetch you a glass of wine and you can tell me all about your little adventure!"

Conversation erupted with as much force as Mount Vesuvius as he led her away. Peter and Christina stared after them dumbfounded before they were rushed en masse by well wishers and sycophants eager to congratulate them. Ellen Sheverton was the first to reach them. She hugged Christina with all the moral support she could summon and stood at her side as the onslaught grew.

Dazed, Christina tried to comprehend that the Prince Regent, the future monarch, had just raised them to the dizzying heights of the upper strata of the Polite World and that they were not merely rescued, they were launched on a monumental tidal wave of success that would make this last month pale by comparison.

She saw with gratitude and relief that Lord Michael Palmerston was one of the first to reach her side. His gaze was as adoring as ever, his smile warm, his attentions devoted. She was unfortunately distracted from so pleasing a conquest by Mr. Timothy Cartwright who had appeared fast on the heels of his rival. More than a little discomposed when her heart lurched at the sweet, amused smile he cast upon her as he took her hand in his and raised it to his lips, Christina was flabbergasted when the tingling in her hand at this contact swept over the whole of her body.

"How courageous you are, Miss Danthorpe, to appear tonight," he murmured, ignoring Lord Palmerston's attempts to reclaim Christina's attention. "But have no fear, the Prince has made everything right. You may move through the ton with impunity."

"His Highness is most kind and gracious," Christina managed and then pointedly turned back to Lord Palmerston. She was not used to being rude or uncivil; it pained her greatly to be so. But she had seen in Mr. Cartwright her nemesis, a formidable obstacle standing between her and all she hoped to make of her future. She thought herself in some danger from Mr. Cartwright, which she could not understand for he was not at all her romantic ideal. Still, the fact remained that his presence had a most pronounced effect upon her ability to breathe and think, that his face plagued her thoughts day and night. Forceful action was required if she was to escape the snare. Thus, she smiled up at Lord Palmerston and allowed him to lead her away, uncomfortably aware that Mr. Cartwright was staring after her, for she could feel the heat of his gaze on her back.

To be so openly snubbed in public was more than any man of honor could tolerate. With a barely suppressed oath, Mr. Cartwright turned on his heel and stalked back to his chair vowing never to think of Miss Danthorpe again, or at least not to think of her with any charity. Never again would the ton see him making a cake of himself by dancing attendance on such a haughty little flirt.

Sadly, for all these fine resolutions, Mr. Cartwright's gaze, quite of its own accord, returned continually to Miss Danthorpe as she moved around the room and seated herself for the second half of that evening's entertainment. To be snubbed was one thing, to be a fool quite another. She was beauty and light and joy, while he was a dull, one-armed farmer. The contrast could not be greater. It had been foolish of him to even dream of winning such a prize. No more would he seek Miss Danthorpe at a party or ball. Never again would he ask to escort her into dinner, or plead the favor of a dance.

For her part, Samantha was playing the role the Prince had chosen for her with all the aplomb at her command as he summoned first the Esterhazys and then the Jerseys into his presence. With the Esterhazys she was contrite; with the Jerseys she was chagrined. They were replaced with the Hortons and then with the Lievens. With the Hortons, Samantha was winningly apologetic, with the Lievens perfectly demure. His Highness was most impressed. Convinced that Lady Samantha had no more to fear from his aristocratic subjects, the Prince then went in search of greater amusement, found it in the plump and pretty Lady Conyngham, and was more than content with his night's work. He discovered that he had quite enjoyed rescuing a fair damsel in distress . . . and bending the ton to his will.

Colonel Dalton drew Samantha away from her new-found supporters to a cozy corner.

"Ah my dear scapegrace," he drawled, "however do you do it?"

"I am almost afraid to ask, but how do I do what, Brandon?" Samantha inquired.

"Get yourself into and out of the most outrageous fixes, of course! To ask your parents why the Emperor of France was so short, while you were standing before the Emperor of France, was bad. The shocking Walter Smedley affair was worse still. But to drive down St. James's Street . . . !"

155

Samantha laughed. "Thank you for placing things in perspective," she said with a fond smile. "I was beginning to actually feel dispirited until you rescued me. How good you are, and what a mean trick I am going to serve you in turn."

"What can you mean?"

"I've found you a wife."

"Impossible!" Colonel Dalton declared.

"What's this? What's this?" Lord Barnett inquired as he drew before them, gazing at the green-tinged colonel with considerable interest. "Are you soliciting Brandon to accompany you on some more of your deviltry, Samantha?"

"No, no, Derek. I would be quite in the way on *this* romp."

"Whatever can you ... Oh dear," said Lord Barnett. "Has the Queen of Hearts struck again? I see by that complacent smile, Samantha, that you have. I fear I shall soon be out a thousand pounds," Lord Barnett said with a sigh. "And after all I've done for you, too, Samantha."

Her heart skittered to a stop. "Reggie?"

"I have spoken to a few friends who are eager to help," Lord Barnett said as he surveyed the room through his quizzing glass. "When I mentioned to Sir Robert Gifford, the King's attorney general, you know, that Lord Adamson would undoubtedly insist on burying Miss Danthorpe in the Yorkshire Dales, insuring that she never set foot in London again, he became quite upset. He voiced his lifelong antipathy to Lord Adamson, his admiration for Miss Danthorpe, and his determination to assist you in any way within his power ... and he is quite powerful. Lord Liverpool was also moved by your plight, and Lady Holland as well. They will write to the Tylers to defend your guardianship. You need no longer fear any action your dear brother may take, Samantha. I have roused the ton to stand against him. He will soon receive a number of letters containing carefully veiled threats. He is stopped before he has begun."

"Oh, Derek!" Samantha cried as she kissed him on both cheeks, "you dear, darling man. I can't thank you enough."

"That is true," said Lord Barnett.

Prince Esterhazy, at the front of the room, requested that everyone return to their seats for the final half of that evening's musical entertainment.

To her surprise, Samantha found that Lady Jillian Roberts, that notable harpist, was to be the first performer. She graciously inclined her head to the applause that greeted her as she climbed onto the low-lying stage that had been erected for that evening, her white silk gown molding itself to her lovely figure as she sat down, pulling the harp to her.

Samantha had never considered the harp a passionate instrument, but it became one in Jillian's hands. Her patrician face was beautiful in its fierce concentration, her hands strong and sensual as they moved over the strings. In this moment Samantha finally saw her as beautiful, passionate, intelligent, and wholly capable of captivating a man, any man. Particularly Lord Simon Cartwright. She saw now that he had not been caught solely by Jillian's strict propriety, but by all the qualities her music revealed. This new understanding served to sink Samantha into something resembling gloom which she could not understand in the least.

Her applause at the conclusion of Jillian's recital was, however, as appreciative as the rest of the audience. She glanced across at Lord Cartwright on the other side of the aisle and saw his smile of pleasure as Jillian made her bow. She hurriedly looked away.

Maria Vincenzo, the opera singer, performed next. She sang a selection from *Cosi fan Tutte* and, as she was in remarkably good voice tonight, the applause at the conclusion of the aria was nearly deafening.

Peter was next. He bowed to the polite applause that sounded tepid in contrast to what Signora Vincenzo had just enjoyed. He sat down at the pianoforte with all of the authority of a man twice his age. With the first notes, as had happened at Cartwright House what seemed a lifetime ago, he held his audience in thrall.

The last stirring notes of the piece drew a thunderous applause from his audience, several giving him a standing ovation, including his sister and guardian. A gasp went through the room as the Prince Regent strode up to the platform to personally shake his hand and compliment him on his performance. Peter's face went from white to red to white again as the applause continued. The Prince beamed at the audience and returned to his chair as Peter, knees a bit unsteady, returned to his own seat at Samantha's side.

"You were wonderful, my dear," she said, squeezing his arm and kissing him on his cheek.

"The Prince, Sam, the Prince!" he managed.

"I know, my love, I know," Samantha said, holding his trembling hand in her own.

The Regent's favorite string quartet concluded the evening's entertainment with Handel. The applause they received at the end, though gratifying, could not compare to what Peter had received and everyone knew it. As the audience rose to slowly make their way to the cold supper the Esterhazys had provided, Peter was surrounded by men and women of every rank who wished to congratulate him, and Samantha, thinking that such universal acclamation was good for any seventeen-year-old's soul, left him to their mercy.

Glancing around the room, she saw that Lord Wyatt and Lord Cartwright were immersed in an animated conversation and felt no hesitancy in joining them.

"My dear Lady Samantha," cried Lord Wyatt, "what a pianist you have in Peter! He'll surpass this fellow Chopin that everyone's talking about, you mark my words."

"Jillian," Lord Cartwright called out to his fiancée who was nearly abreast of them, "come give us the opportunity to congratulate you on your performance. You were magnificent."

"You are overgenerous in your praise, Simon," said Jillian as she joined them.

"Not at all," said Samantha warmly. "I have heard many a harpist in my day, Lady Jillian, and you surpass them all."

"Thank you," Jillian said, barely glancing at her. "As your acquaintance is so notably broad, I must assume that is a great compliment."

"Very great," Samantha replied, having recovered her breath from such a cut.

Lord Cartwright hastily intervened. "I heard Prinny remark that he would attend any musical evening so long as you agreed to perform, Jillian. He was quite enraptured."

"The Prince is very kind," said Jillian.

"And generous," said Lord Wyatt. "Imagine, giving away the Emperor's ruby as if it were so much paste. I've heard it's a marvel, though I've never seen it up close."

"You may gaze to your heart's content, Lord Wyatt," Samantha said as she extended her hand for, though she might hold her tongue, she could not forbear putting Jillian's regal nose out of joint with this princely mark of favor.

"By all the stars and planets, it's as big as an oyster!" said Lord Wyatt, taking her hand and studying the ring. "And you earned every carat, Lady Samantha. To drive down St. James's Street without turning a hair and then have the Prince give his full approbation. What a triumph for you!"

"It felt much more like an acute attack of the ague," Samantha replied. "I owe much to Lord Cartwright and the Prince."

"Lady Samantha is fortunate in her friends," said Jillian with the hint of a sneer. "If you will excuse me, I wish to have a word with Princess Esterhazy."

"She is a wonder," Samantha murmured.

Lord Cartwright found an answering smile on his lips.

"Aaron, my sister is bereft of company. Seize opportunity whilst you may."

"Meddler," said Samantha.

"I leap to obey," Lord Wyatt said as he hurried away.

"They're doing very nicely," Samantha said as she watched her two friends draw together. "If only I could be as certain of Christina and your Timothy. She is being remarkably foolish about her future husband."

"You are determined to have them wed, are you?" Lord Cartwright said.

"But they are perfect for each other!" said Samantha.

"Then why have they avoided each other like the plague tonight?" Lord Cartwright inquired.

"Momentary idiocy. I shall see that it passes."

"You are a formidable woman, Lady Samantha."

"Yes, I know," Samantha said dimpling. "But I am also fortunate in my friends. Instead of exerting yourself in my defense, a man of your correct views should regard me with loathing after yesterday's hobble."

Lord Cartwright considered her a moment. "On the contrary, yesterday you acted impetuously, but without malice, certainly without thinking of the consequences of so rash an act. Tonight, however, you were fully cognizant of the difficult greeting you would receive here, yet you had the courage to not only come, but to make a most impressive entrance. I must admire such an act of courage."

"Oh dear," said Samantha with a comical look, "I very much fear that I shall come to like you after all, Lord Cartwright."

"Now, now, don't think on fantasies. We shall be at loggerheads tomorrow, you mark my words."

"Yes," Samantha said with a smile, "we are both too independent not to butt heads. But for tonight, I am glad to like you."

"And I you," said Lord Cartwright with an answering smile and a bow.

As the Esterhazys once again urged their guests to partake of the cold supper, Samantha abandoned Lord Cartwright and made her way to Ellen Sheverton's side.

"Oh, Lady Samantha. I have been longing to talk to you all evening," said Miss Sheverton. "What an adventure you have had! Lord Farago has spoken of nothing else the whole of this evening."

"Indeed? For a young woman of your lively intelligence, I would have thought a husband capable of more than one topic of conversation to be more appropriate."

"We are not engaged as yet," Miss Sheverton said hastily. "The marriage contract has not been signed."

"Hoping it will be put off, are you?" Samantha said sagely.

Miss Sheverton blushed rosily. "On—on the contrary," she said. "I am very fortunate in my future groom. He is wealthy and kind and he seems fond of me."

"High praise indeed! But you know, I think his primary attribute as a husband is his age."

"It is always best to have a mature husband."

"Very true. But maturity does not always come with age. No, I was thinking that a man of his advanced years cannot expect to live for more than a decade and then you, not yet thirty, will be rich, still in beauty, and free to marry whomsoever you choose."

"Lady Samantha!" ejaculated Miss Sheverton and then cowered behind her fan. "Hush! Someone will hear you. You must not say such things. Indeed you must not!"

"The thought has crossed your mind as well, hm?"

Miss Sheverton peeped up at her, blue eyes dancing with laughter. "Only once or twice . . . a day."

Samantha choked. "Come now, be honest with me, my girl, if you fell in love with a gentleman who, though not able to do your family as much good as Lord Farago, could still ease their financial burden, and love you into the bargain, wouldn't you prefer him?"

"Why tease me with such idle speculation?" Miss Sheverton said, a trifle crossly. "The marriage contract will be signed and Lord Farago and I shall marry by Michaelmas."

"You may well be wed by Michaelmas, but not, I think, to Lord Farago."

Samantha pulled the puzzled Miss Sheverton across the room and stopped before Colonel Brandon Dalton who was about to leave the room in search of a quiet place to enjoy a good glass of port.

"Brandon, stay a moment," Samantha said. "There is someone I want you to meet."

Colonel Dalton turned and stared, not at his friend, but at Miss Sheverton. She, in turn, gripped Samantha's hand with a sudden sharp spasm.

"I believe I mentioned Miss Ellen Sheverton to you earlier this evening," Samantha blithely continued. "Miss Sheverton, I wish to introduce you to one of my oldest friends: Colonel Brandon Dalton. I cannot recommend him enough to you."

Colonel Dalton looked helplessly at Samantha. She smiled at him serenely.

"I really must go and have a word with Lord Wyatt," she said. "I hope you two don't mind if I leave you to your own devices."

She received no reply for neither Colonel Dalton nor Miss Sheverton had heard her. She left them gazing at each other in a rather dazed fashion, fairly certain that she would soon be two thousand pounds the richer.

"Why are you looking so pleased with yourself?" Lord Cartwright demanded as he came upon her once again.

"I've been indulging in matchmaking, meddling, and mayhem."

Lord Cartwright's brown eyes narrowed. "Does the phrase 'out of the frying pan and into the fire' mean nothing to you?"

"Why should I fear the heat when I've a trusty friend ready to rescue me at the least provocation?"

Lord Cartwright returned her smile. "I had best start polishing my armor again. If only I had a white horse."

Chapter Fourteen

THE DAYS IMMEDIATELY preceding and following the Esterhazy music salon saw an ever increasing flurry of social activity in and out of the ton ... which best describes Peter Danthorpe's progress through London town. Matthew Cartwright and his cronies led him on a merry dance from gaming clubs, to the backstage bounty of the ballet, to the forbidden pleasures of cockfights, and thence to the Dionysian delights of several murky taverns.

But all was not rapture, for Peter was constantly plagued by the fear that he would slip up somehow, disgust his new friends with the intellectual breadth of his studies or his many qualms about their more rowdy adventures. Worse, they might discover that at times he longed to remain at his pianoforte rather than journey out with them in search of new fun.

Peter felt himself to be in a fix. Which of the two paths should he choose: his previous monkish existence amongst his books and music with Victor Speer and Madame LeCarron? Or the insane adolescent romps of his cronies? In the end, Peter decided upon the latter. After all, he had spent seventeen years treading the former path, it was time he tried something new, broaden his horizons, as it were.

Samantha had hoped that Peter would return to reason of

his own accord and behave, if not with decorum, at least with sense. She quickly discovered that this was not to be. For two nights in a row, Peter had given vent to huge yawns and had called an early night, climbing up the stairs bleary-eyed as he bade his sister and guardian good night. But when, full of misgivings, Samantha had checked on him later in the evening before retiring to her own bed, she found that not only was he not in bed, he was not in the house. The first night she put it down to youthful adventure. The second night she put it down to deceit.

On the third night, she was grimly lying in wait for him to return from his nocturnal revels when she heard a horrendous crash in the entry hall. Convinced that the house had come under military attack, she ran into the hall only to discover Peter awkwardly trying to reassemble the large Chinese vase that had stood gloriously upon a stand near the stairway and now lay shattered on the floor.

"Good God, what has happened?" Samantha demanded.

"Sorry, Sam," Peter said sheepishly, his face flushed, his black eyes bright. "I . . . uh . . . tripped on the . . . on the stair and fell against the vase and . . . well . . . I'm sure the vase can be mended, Sam. It doesn't look so very badly broken."

"I regret to inform your ladyship," said Garner from the doorway where he still held Peter's torn coat, "that Mr. Danthorpe is drunk."

"I am not drunk," Peter retorted with great dignity.

"Then you have taken to having your clothes laundered in a brewery," Samantha said. "You're reeking, lad!"

"Well, a trifle foxed, perhaps," Peter conceded as his eyes closed and he fell unconscious into Samantha's arms.

"Don't stand there goggling," Samantha hissed at her butler. "Grab his legs!"

Garner hurriedly did so. Together they carried the very young and very drunk Mr. Danthorpe into his bedroom and deposited him unceremoniously upon his bed.

"I wish I were prone to strong hysterics," Samantha said as she surveyed her ward.

Peter began to gently snore against his pillow.

"A pox on all wards, Garner," said Samantha to her impassive butler, "and on all gin hells. You will mention this matter to no one. I want Peter to think that he has passed another night unscathed and undetected."

"Very good, my lady," Garner replied as his brain cogitated on the trap her ladyship undoubtedly meant to lay for Mr. Danthorpe.

And indeed, Samantha was formulating a scheme. She chastised herself as she slowly walked to her own room for not heeding Hilary's warnings about Matthew's friends. She had mismanaged Peter badly and now what was she to do?

She lay in bed thinking the matter over, particularly her own responsibility in her ward's decline into insobriety. She determined that the absence of her personal involvement in his affairs had led directly to Peter's current inebriation. The problem would best be rectified by her active participation in removing him from the dangerous course he had chosen to follow.

Thus, on Thursday night, when Peter again emitted several huge yawns and declared that he was fagged to death, Samantha declared that she, too, was exhausted from the never-ending round of social obligations and that she, too, would call it an early night. She went up the stairs arm and arm with Peter, bade him good night at his door, and then went into her own room.

Rather than changing into her nightgown, however, she changed into a pair of buckskins, shirt, coat, and riding boots, twisting and tucking her golden hair up under a cap. She placed her Harding's pocket pistol in her riding coat and surveyed the effect in her mirror. An impish grin curled across her mouth. She made a very presentable gentleman. Moving stealthily, she went back downstairs and out to the stable where she saddled her dapple gray mare and walked her to the side of the house.

A little more than an hour later she spied Peter climbing out of his bedroom window. With a bit of a stretch he grasped the drain pipe that ran down the wall and slid safely to the ground. He was joined a moment later by Matthew Cartwright who had left his own home by equally secret means.

They hid in the shadows together, talking quietly for a few minutes. Then a chaise-and-four barreled to a stop before them. The driver, with hearty greetings, urged them into the coach, and then, with a neat crack of the whip, they were driving out of Berkeley Square, Samantha carefully following them on her mare.

She had thought that they would go to Covent Garden, an area notorious for cheap liquor and unsavory women, but this was not the case. The chaise-and-four drove at a fast clip south out of town toward Tunbridge Wells. Before it reached that decorous town, however, it turned onto a rutted side road and a mile later pulled to a stop in front of a hulking edifice whose weathered sign proclaimed it to be the Cock's Crow.

The boys leapt from the chaise with glee and thronged toward the front door, a stoical groom keeping watch over the chaise-and-four. With the opening of the tavern's front door came a roar of coarse voices, laughter, shouts, threats, and insults. This was clearly not a place to entrust the safety of a valuable horse. Samantha, therefore, dismounted and led her gray up to the groom.

"Here, you," she said in a rough voice and tossed the startled groom a guinea. "Keep an eye on me horse or I'll have yer guts fer garters."

She thrust the reins into his gnarled hand. "There'll be another guinea fer ye when I come out."

Without looking back, she marched to the front door. It must be confessed, however, that she hesitated before thrusting the door open and entering her first real den of iniquity. She choked on the clouds of cooking and pipe smoke that filled the room, her eyes and throat burning. It took a moment or two to adjust to the dimness of the room and, when she did so, she immediately wished that she hadn't.

She had never been in such a filthy place in her life. The floor was dirt covered with moldy straw, as if the customers were no better than barn animals ... and perhaps they weren't. The floor stank of beer and gin, rancid food, urine, and vomit. The air mixed these odors with the smoke. It was a wonder to Samantha that anyone could live in such stench, but the customers of the Cock's Crow were very much alive. The tavern was packed with nearly two dozen tables, all of them crowded with boisterous men of all ages who were as filthy and as stinking as the floor.

Through the wall of noise composed of tall tales, arguments, and illegal business transactions, Samantha spied the bar and, not wishing to appear conspicuous, shouldered her way toward it. In a gruff voice, she ordered a pint of ale. It was delivered to her in a far from clean glass, but she thought it best not to complain. She tossed a coin to the barkeep and then turned to survey the room and find her ward whose guts she *would* use for garters the minute she got him out of here.

She found him at last in a corner of the room at a large table filled by five other boys, including Matthew. They were all ogling the blowsy barmaid whose large breasts were amply displayed by a dirty white blouse tucked into a brown skirt that stopped well above her rather thick ankles.

Through the din and the murkiness, Samantha saw a thoroughly inebriated patron of the Cock's Crow lurch to his feet and head for the door. She quickly shouldered her way to his abandoned table and claimed a chair before anyone else could act. She now sat two tables away from Peter and could spy without looking suspicious. Wrinkling her nose, she pushed an empty gin glass to the far end of the small table, set her pint of ale down in its place, and leaned back in her chair, prepared for a long siege.

The barmaid had brought a tray of drinks and handed them around to the boys, swatting their hands as they tried to pinch her.

And they were boys. Not one of them, Samantha guessed, had reached their majority, though Peter was clearly the youngest of the six. After a bit of taunting by his fellows, he drained his glass and loudly called for another to the stomping approval of his friends. And for the next half hour that is all they did: drink and insult each other and try to squeeze the barmaid.

Samantha began to think that Peter had embarked on a rather tame adventure when she saw a swarthy, well-dressed man with a knife scar down his face join them to many cheers and offers to buy him a drink. It took but a few minutes for Samantha to ascertain, though she could hear none of their conversation, that this clearly dangerous man held the striplings in thrall. Any adventure that he would throw at them would be the farthest thing from tame.

Before she could become really anxious, however, Samantha was distracted. The front door opened once again and a gentleman whom she instantly recognized stepped in. He scanned the room intently, spied Peter's table, and began to make his way toward it with grim determination. He never reached it, however, for Samantha deliberately stuck her leg out and tripped him.

His natural athleticism kept him from sprawling on the floor, but he did bump into an obese connoisseur of gin at the next table and was forced to make a heartfelt apology before he could turn on Samantha.

"What the devil do you mean—" he began in an angry voice. Then he stopped and stared as he saw the familiar impish grin.

"Lady Samantha!" he gasped.

"Hush!" Samantha said. "Do you want the whole world to know?"

"What in the name of heaven are you doing here?"

"I might ask the same of you, Lord Cartwright. Never did I think to see you descend from your lofty pedestal in pursuit of a glass of gin."

Lord Cartwright blinked and hastily sat down in the chair opposite her.

"Either you have run mad, or I, and I cannot tell which at present," he said. "Lady Samantha, what are you doing here? It is not even a fortnight since the St. James's Street debacle, yet here you sit courting even greater scandal."

"On the contrary, I am trying to avert scandal," Samantha corrected him. "Am I not in disguise? Who in their right mind would recognize me?"

"A telling blow against my sanity. Why are you here, *Mr.* Adamson?"

"I've come to spy on Peter," Samantha said, nodding toward the boys' table. "And you?"

"A similar quest. I had heard Matthew was expected here tonight, and Peter as well, though I hoped that was false. I shall take great delight in wringing my brother's neck."

"How did you hear that Matthew would come tonight?"

"There are reasons women are not admitted to Jackson's Saloon."

"Ah," said Samantha. "I knew I was missing out on a good piece of fun."

"I pray you will miss out on this evening's adventure as well. Return to Berkeley Square, Lady Samantha. I will see that Peter is safely returned to you."

"No, I am his guardian, the onus lies on me."

"Please reconsider. The night could turn dangerous."

"Because of the man with the scar?"

Lord Cartwright gazed at Peter's table, his face darkening as he studied the swarthy man. "So it is he."

"Who?"

"He calls himself Captain Pervis, though if he's ever been in the army I'll make a meal of the swill this place calls food. He's something of a gamester, likes to organize illicit cock fights and dice games. More importantly, it is rumored that he will fence any jewel worth more than a guinea."

"My, my, the people you know, Lord Cartwright."

Lord Cartwright raised a haughty brow. "I don't know him, only of him. I wouldn't be at all surprised if he's trying to rope those boys into stealing from their own homes by making them think they'll be romantic highwaymen without the inconvenience of a horse."

Samantha's eyes narrowed. "We'd better—"

"Pervis!" a giant of a man bellowed from the front door. "You're a dead man!"

He leveled a brace of pistols at Captain Pervis and fired.

The shots were nearly simultaneous, as were the screams and shouts of the other customers as they all dove for the floor. Samantha had just a moment to see Matthew slump in his chair. Captain Pervis, unscathed, jumped up and fired his own gun at his assailant.

In the next moment, the Cock's Crow had become a seething mass of flailing bodies as both Pervis and the giant near the door were rushed. Those not concerned with vengeance were still swept by the violence in the room and began to slash and batter at each other with knives and fists.

"Lady Samantha, get out!" Lord Cartwright shouted. "I'll get Peter and Matthew."

"I'll get Peter, you get Matthew," Samantha retorted, as she jumped to her feet and started toward her ward.

But Lord Cartwright caught her arm and held her still. "Get out while you can! This is no place for a woman."

"Tell that to the barmaid," Samantha retorted just as that capable female broke a bottle of gin over one assailant's head and then decked a scrawny attacker with a rather formidable right hook.

Samantha was jostled by the brawls all around them and thrust into Lord Cartwright's arms.

"You will walk out or I will carry you out," Lord Cartwright threatened, holding her fast.

"In a pig's eye," Samantha stormed, readying her foot for a savage kick at his shin.

She never got the chance. With a far from gentlemanly oath, he jerked her up into his arms and forced his way to the front door, Samantha struggling with all her might. But it did no good. The door was reached and then the blessed clean night air which cleared her head remarkably.

She brought her lips to Lord Cartwright's well-formed ear and screamed with the full power of her not too inconsiderable lungs. With a bellow of pain, Lord Cartwright dropped her in the dirt and clapped his hand to the affronted appendage.

"Very well," Samantha said, rising from her sprawled position on the ground and dusting off her buckskins, "if you will agree not to manhandle me, I will agree not to shriek like a banshee and we can discuss the matter like reasonable adults."

"If I had the time," Lord Cartwright growled, "I would turn you over my knee and give you the spanking you so richly deserve."

"You could try," Samantha retorted. "In the meantime, I believe Matthew to be wounded and certainly Peter is in danger. If we work together, we can get them out quickly before the whole kit and kaboodle are tossed into gaol."

"Very well!" Lord Cartwright seethed. "I haven't the time to argue with you. Are you armed?"

"Always."

"You may guard my back."

"And a very fine back it is, too."

Lord Cartwright evinced no pleasure at the compliment. "You will not move more than an inch away from me while we are inside, is that clear?"

"Oui, mon capitain," Samantha replied, smartly saluting.

Lord Cartwright sighed heavily, grasped her hand in his, and pulled her back into the Cock's Crow, where the brawl had developed nicely. Few of the tables and chairs remained intact. Bodies, breathing but bloodied, littered the odoriferous floor. The customers of that establishment had long ago abandoned fighting a specific enemy. Anyone and everyone was battered at, knifed, and cudgeled.

Possessing far more science than anyone else present, Lord Cartwright began to hammer a path toward his brother and Peter. He was suddenly arrested by a startled "Yip!"

He turned to find Samantha seated on the floor, ruefully rubbing her jaw. A burly, straw-haired fellow stood over her, preparing to do her further harm.

Lord Cartwright caught his arm and spun him around. He then planted him a facer that left the fellow's head ringing. His lordship broke his nose with the next blow, and rendered him unconscious with the third. He then held a hand down to Samantha and quickly helped her to her feet.

"That was masterfully done!" Samantha exclaimed.

"Thank you," said Lord Cartwright. "Shall we proceed?"

They made their way to the corner of the room with only a bit more trouble to find Peter anxiously attending Matthew who was slumped back in his chair and looking very white. Blood seeped from a wound near his temple that Peter dabbed at rather ineffectually with his handkerchief. All their friends had deserted them in the melee.

"Here, let me attend him," Lord Cartwright said.

Peter looked up. "Lord Cartwright! Thank God you're here, sir! Matt's been shot!"

"So I observed," said Lord Cartwright as he inspected the wound. "But not mortally, not even romantically. It's best to get out of here and then staunch the wound. Can you stand, lad?" he asked his brother.

"I-I think so," Matthew said through dry lips.

"Sam!" cried Peter upon piercing his guardian's disguise.

"Hush, brat," she remonstrated.

Lord Cartwright helped Matthew to his feet then put a steadying arm around him. "Put your arm around my neck. That's right. Everyone stay together and we should get out in one piece."

This was a little difficult for there were several in the room who took umbrage at anyone wanting to depart such a wonderful brawl. Peter was knocked to the ground more than once and Samantha was forced to discharge her pocket pistol, the bullet piercing the shoulder of a would-be assailant who finally agreed that she should not be mauled.

Less than five feet from the door with Matthew almost a deadweight in Lord Cartwright's arms, Peter suddenly shouted:

"My lord! Look out!"

Lord Cartwright turned in time to see Samantha swinging a chair down on the bald head of a beefy man who had been coming at him from his blind side.

"He had a knife," she said simply and then pressed forward to open the door for them.

They did not stop their headlong rush until they had reached Lord Cartwright's sporting curricle some fifty yards from the Cock's Crow.

"Are you still with us, Matt?" Lord Cartwright asked as he gently lowered his brother to the ground.

"Barely," Matthew replied. "How did you . . . find me?"

"You are not exactly discreet," Lord Cartwright sardonically replied as he pulled out his handkerchief.

"Here," Samantha said, drawing her own handkerchief from her pocket, "you can use mine as a pad and yours to tie 'round his head."

"You've dealt with bullet wounds before, have you?" Lord Cartwright inquired with a smile. He knelt beside his brother.

"One of the hazards of travel," Samantha replied. "Is it bad?"

"No. The bullet merely creased him, though he's lost a bit of blood. A day in bed and he'll be good as new."

"Thank God," Peter said, shuddering. He then hastily backed away to vomit into the bushes nearby.

Samantha regarded him with little sympathy and then turned back to the brothers. Lord Cartwright finished binding the wound and then stood gazing down at Matthew.

"Well," he said, "you'll live, which is more than you deserve."

A ghost of a smile flitted across Matthew's tightly clamped lips. "I'm going to catch hell the minute I'm better, aren't I?"

"I may surprise you yet," Lord Cartwright said, leaning down and pulling him to his feet. "I'll need your help to get you into the curricle."

With several grunts and gasps, Matthew was installed in the carriage.

"Have you your own means of transportation?" Lord Cartwright asked Samantha.

"I think so," she said, scanning the area for her mare. "I gave a guinea to a groom. . . . He has scarpered, of course, but I think . . . Yes! There she is," Samantha said, striding off. She returned a moment later, her mare, still munching a clump of grass, in tow. "She can carry two."

"But it would be better if she didn't," Lord Cartwright finished for her. "I've room for another foolish stripling, never fear, Lady Samantha. Come, Peter, and support your friend in his hour of need."

"Yes, sir," Peter said looking a bit green in the moonlight. "Of course, sir. I can't tell you how sorry—"

"I'd rather hear it when you're sober," Lord Cartwright interrupted.

Peter blanched and clumsily climbed into the curricle.

"Will you be our outrider, ma'am?" Lord Cartwright inquired with a sardonic lift of one brow.

"It would be an honor, sir," Samantha said with a bow.

175

Before he could offer assistance, she threw herself into the saddle, gathered her reins, and looked down at him. "Well?"

Lord Cartwright laughed. "You're a cool customer, Lady Samantha."

"I told you we'd make a good team. As long as you remember to discuss, not manhandle, we'll get along famously."

"It is a lesson not soon forgot," Lord Cartwright said, rubbing his ear.

"And I shall not soon forget the impressive way you acquitted yourself tonight, my lord. You've a handy pair of fives."

Lord Cartwright began to chuckle. "It seems that since you have come to town I am never out of scrapes and forever rescuing you. I begin not to recognize myself."

"It is your true nature coming to the fore," Samantha assured him.

The next morning, for the first time in her life, Samantha read someone a lecture on responsibility and proper behavior. As Peter was green tinged and bedridden with a monstrous hangover from the previous evening's libations, she felt that her lecture had maximum effect.

Chapter Fifteen

But a week after the Cock's Crow folly, as Samantha termed it, Matthew and Peter had embraced sainthood with all the exuberance of youth, while Christina was swept up into the full Season by the haut ton and only returned to Berkeley Square to sleep, eat breakfast, and embark on another round of social activities with Samantha, more likely than not, unhappily yoked behind her.

She complained to Hilary at least twice a day that, as Hilary was Christina's sponsor, it was not necessary for Samantha to step one foot out of the Dower House. But Hilary was adamant. If Samantha wanted to secure her position, and Christina's, in the ton, then she must be seen in public as often as possible, behaving properly as often as possible.

Samantha thought this a terrible strain.

Had it not been for the many matchmaking opportunities such activity afforded, she might have consigned the Season to perdition without another thought.

The Prince Regent's Spring Ball at Carlton House officially began the social season. Those who were not invited were not worth knowing. Those who were invited congratulated themselves on being as important as they had always considered themselves, and then agonized over sleeves, shoe buckles, hair styles, and gloves.

Samantha, who refused to lower herself to agonizing over anything, and Christina arrived at the ball neither early nor late. Their fame was already such that they no longer had to plot to make an impression on the ton. The ton was fully cognizant of their existence. As was its Prince.

He moved through his guests, speaking for a moment to Lord Barnett, then to Lady Jillian Roberts, chatting briefly with Lady Jersey, and laughing at something murmured by Lord Montclair. His guests argued whether or not the Regent's clothes were à la mode or déclassé, wondered if he looked fatter than last week, and pondered his recent threat to divorce his scandalous wife who was cavorting about Europe, it was said, with an *Italian*.

But every conversation in the room soon took a sudden and universal turn when the Prince led Samantha out for the first dance. Despite his corpulence he made a most graceful bow and Samantha a low curtsy. They swung into the waltz, other couples quickly joining them as the rest of the room buzzed with speculation.

"We seem to be an object of conversation, Your Highness," said Samantha.

"Why else do you think I asked you for this dance?" the Prince retorted with a twinkle. "They are always talking about me anyway, but now they must discuss the excellencies of my taste for selecting so charming and lovely a partner."

"No, no, they will wonder at your noticing such a shocking reprobate as myself," Samantha said with a smile.

"Shocking or otherwise, it is always a pleasure to notice you, Lady Samantha. Ah, if I were but twenty years younger . . ."

"If you were twenty years younger, sir, you would be too young for me!"

The Prince laughed and they continued happily flirting

178

with each other for the rest of the dance. Samantha felt quite safe for she knew His Royal Highness preferred his *chère amies* plump and far older than she.

Lord Cartwright was one of the many to observe this dance, an amused smile teasing his lips. Buckskins one night and an evening gown with a shockingly low neckline the next. It was astonishing, really, that a woman of her imagination had not yet thought to imitate Lady Godiva's antics. A grin replaced the smile. That would be a spectacle he would not soon interrupt.

Several gentlemen who rivaled the Prince, and Lord Cartwright, in their appreciation of feminine beauty took up the next hour of Samantha's time as they each partnered her for dance upon dance until, finally pleading exhaustion, she was able to make good her escape from such flattering attention and devote herself to her real purpose in coming to the ball.

There were matches to be made.

The most imperative was, of course, Christina and Timothy Cartwright. Through deceit, blackmail, and outright trickery, she had contrived to have Timothy present at every dinner and party she had given at the Dower House in the last fortnight . . . to no avail. He would not condescend to speak more than three words to Christina and did his best to keep an entire room of guests between them. Christina, too, had been recalcitrant, refusing to use her considerable skills to lure Mr. Cartwright back into her circle of admirers.

Still, Samantha thought their stony refusal to notice each other was taking its toll. Their gazes continually strayed to each other, each flushed when the other's name was mentioned in their hearing, and both seemed to be suffering from sleepless nights. If she was but persistent, they could not help but post the banns by summer.

Thus, she searched for her ward through the rich gowns and stylish coats of the Prince's guests, spied her at last attended by Lord Palmerston and four other determined gentlemen, and swept up to the group with all the authority of her seven-and-twenty years.

"Gentlemen," she announced, "I have come to steal my ward away from you."

"Do not be so cruel, fair lady!" cried Lord Palmerston in the romantic vein he knew would appeal to Christina. "How can I be happy without the radiant warmth of Miss Danthorpe's sweet smile?"

"Don't take her, Lady Samantha," pleaded Mr. Wilding, a blunt-spoken young man whose black coat had been padded by a master. "She's the only reason I came into this monstrosity of a house."

The others quickly and fruitlessly urged Lady Adamson to abandon her quest.

With murmured apologies and a smile each gentleman believed was given solely to him, Christina took her guardian's hand and walked away.

"Isn't it a bit of a strain being so popular?" Samantha inquired.

Christina laughed. "It gets a bit wearying now and then, but it's rather nice to be so continually admired. When I am gray and wrinkled and fifty no one will be paying me compliments, so I mean to store them up now to warm me in the future."

"How clever of me to have such a wise ward. But let me just give you a hint: if you choose the right husband, you shall have loving compliments the whole of your life, wrinkles or no."

"Lord Palmerston would be such a one."

"Lord Palmerston, if he recollects your name in thirty years, will compliment you only on the size of your fortune, if he has not run through it by that time."

"That is monstrously unfair!" Christina cried. "Why are you so opposed to a gentleman possessed of a noble family,

180

good breeding, and a refinement no other man in this room can match?"

"I think you deserve better," Samantha said simply. "I think you deserve a man who loves you not for your wealth or your beauty or your charming smile, but for your heart and your soul and your mind. Lord Palmerston is all surface. I would wish you a husband with some depth. Ah, Mr. Cartwright, you are just the man I need!" she cried.

Mr. Timothy Cartwright turned from his contemplation of the dance floor, a flush creeping into his cheeks when he saw Christina.

"Samantha," Christina hissed under her breath, but her guardian paid her not the slightest heed.

"You are a man of sound reason and honest opinion, I know," Samantha continued. "Come, Mr. Cartwright, tell me what you think of this so-called ball gown my stubborn ward has insisted on wearing tonight. I think it so much gossamer which leaves nothing to the masculine imagination, but I daresay you will know best."

Christina blushed rosily as Mr. Cartwright obligingly surveyed her from her glossy black curls, to the deep scoop of the white silk bodice that revealed the high creamy curve of her breasts, down the white silk sheath that whispered around her limbs to her white satin shoes peeping out from the gold embroidered hem.

"The gown is . . . delightful," he managed.

"Perhaps," Samantha said doubtfully, "but I still feel it is too suggestive for public display. I will know better when I see how it moves in a dance. Come, Mr. Cartwright, they are playing a waltz. Oblige my curiosity and dance with my ward so that I may judge the full effect of her costume."

"Lady Samantha—!" said Mr. Cartwright, his flush deepening.

She regarded him calmly. "Sir?"

It was an unequal contest. His blue eyes fell first. "If you will oblige me, Miss Danthorpe?" he muttered.

Christina, too, sought to defy Samantha but one look into her steely hazel eyes convinced her of its futility. She placed her hand on Mr. Cartwright's proffered arm and grimly walked out onto the dance floor. As she had done in their first waltz so many weeks ago, she placed both hands around his neck while he stiffly slipped his arm around her waist and they began, like blocks of wood, to revolve around the dance floor.

Samantha watched them with grim satisfaction. Christina's gown was, in point of fact, quite suggestive, which she believed Mr. Cartwright could not have failed to ascertain. Most importantly, however, she had got them into an embrace, however chilly and formal it might be. Physical contact was vital if she was going to make the two erstwhile lovers come to their senses.

When the music ended, however, so did their contact. Mr. Cartwright bowed stiffly, Christina did not even bother to curtsy, and both immediately walked away in opposite directions. But Samantha was content. She had made her point. They would be sensible of it for some time to come.

For entirely different reasons, Lord Michael Palmerston watched their chilly retreats with barely suppressed glee. He was a proud man, a stylish man, a man who enjoyed the many pleasures life had to offer an English nobleman. He understood the intricacies of the oriental and mathematical ties, and the delicacy of conducting a clandestine affair with a married woman. He frequented only the best gaming clubs in London and had been seen to laugh heartily after losing several thousand pounds on a race at Newmarket. He had friends in all quarters of the city, was invited everywhere, knew everyone ... and had a pile of debts that could sink a man of war.

Lord Palmerston was not merely in debt, Lord Palmerston was in serious difficulties. His creditors had turned on him in a most unpleasant manner. Tailors, jewelers, wine merchants, and more were refusing to serve him. Some means must be found of maintaining the style of existence of which he was so very fond.

The answer, of course, was simplicity itself: marry an heiress ... and there was a bumper crop of them this year. A man with his lineage, his features, and his address would have little difficulty in acquiring a suitable wife. In fact, there were three (far from comely) heiresses whom he might have had for a song if he wanted ... but he did not, for Lord Palmerston had seen Christina Danthorpe and, like so many others, had immediately determined that this was the girl for him. Not only was she wealthy, she was a girl a man could not help but want to take to bed ... and Palmerston was fond of the bedroom.

Thus, he had gambled his future on Christina Danthorpe, bending all of his not too inconsiderable energies upon her conquest, and he, with all the conceit that was peculiarly his, thought he had been successful. He had seen some danger in the looks Christina had exchanged with Mr. Cartwright these last weeks, but now, miraculously, the danger seemed to have passed. It was time to think of wedding clothes. With the Danthorpe fortune behind him, the possibilities for extravagance were limitless!

Samantha, meanwhile, wandered the ballroom longing for some real entertainment and spied Lord Barnett lecturing a hapless Member of Parliament on the Corn Law. She swept down upon him, demanded his company on the dance floor, and he very obligingly led her into a cotillion. He was not unaware that the sight of two such Incomparables as he and Samantha dancing together would excite rabid attention and admiration. He was wholly unaware that one of the audience viewed his grace and charm with something approaching ... violence. And Samantha was wholly unaware that the Duke de Peralta and Lady Emma Cartwright were conspiring against her by feeding the flames of this violence.

"They make a handsome couple, don't they?" said Lady

Cartwright, pointing to Lord Barnett and Samantha with her fan.

"Yes," Lord Cartwright snapped.

"Lord Barnett is the most amazing man: intelligent, ambitious, charming, titled, wealthy. He seems wholly formed to attract the devotion of every woman in England."

"A veritable nonesuch," muttered Lord Cartwright.

"Samantha is very fond of him," said the duke. "They've been friends for years, you know."

"He is fortunate in his acquaintance."

"By his own admission, he has even proposed to Samantha on numerous occasions," the duke said.

"Has he, by God!"

Lady Cartwright hid her smile behind her fan. "With such a paragon for a suitor, I would not be at all surprised if Samantha abandons her scruples and marries so worthy a gentleman."

Blissfully unaware of her friends' stratagem, Samantha finally abandoned Lord Barnett to a nest of politicians in one corner of the room and entered upon her second piece of business for the evening. She cajoled the Duke de Peralta and Emma Cartwright into challenging the Shevertons to a game of whist and, once they were safely installed in the card room, commanded Colonel Dalton to lead Ellen Sheverton to the dance floor. He needed little urging. The Colonel and Miss Sheverton floated off as Samantha watched them from the terrace doors.

"What have you been up to now?" demanded an ominous voice.

Samantha turned to find Lord Cartwright staring at her with mock severity.

"Everything you loathe," she replied with a grin.

"I have no doubt. Who is the lovesick gentleman reeling with my sister-in-law?"

"Brandon Dalton of the Derbyshire Daltons. A most respectable family and a most entertaining gentleman. We have known each other for years."

"For someone who has been out of the country for the last fifteen years, you certainly have a broad acquaintance in town."

"Some would even meet your exacting standards."

"Oh, I hope not," Lord Cartwright replied, glancing down at her. "Your acquaintance is the only entertainment I've had all spring. I gather from that smile of supreme satisfaction which I just interrupted that you are meddling in the affairs of my sister-in-law, the *settled* affairs of my sister-in-law," he said severely. "You were not forgetting Lord Farago, were you?"

"Actually I was. Do be an angel and go distract him."

It was a struggle not to smile. "Why should I?"

"Because if you don't, then I shall have to and the man is a dead bore."

The appreciative smile peeped out. "That he is. For that alone I would pity Ellen. I trust Dalton is more interesting?"

"*Vastly* more interesting."

"You speak from experience?"

"Always."

Lord Cartwright chuckled. "Very well, I shall play the knight-errant and rescue you from so abysmal a task. I shall question Lord Farago about his dogs; the man is almost as devoted to the hound as the Duchess of York. It should be enough to divert him for at least the next two hours."

With a bow, he wandered off in pursuit of his boring prey.

In that moment, Samantha conceived a great liking for the proper gentleman. He might be a stickler for decorum, but in every one of her adventures since coming to London he had proved himself a valuable accomplice . . . and handy knight-errant. She thought him much more interesting than Colonel Dalton, and vastly more entertaining than Lord

Barnett. He even rivaled the Duke de Peralta for quantity and quality of charm.

As Lord Cartwright had prophesied, two hours later Lord Farago reclaimed Ellen Sheverton's company and led her into the supper room. Samantha went off to the card room to inform Lady Cartwright and the Duke de Peralta that their services were no longer required. She found, however, that they made up the merriest table at Carlton House and evinced no desire to flee the fate she had chosen for them.

"I'm sorry to interrupt," she said to the chuckling quartet, "but Princess Esterhazy has been asking after you, Phillip, and—"

"She will have to keep asking, Samantha," the duke interrupted. "Emma and I are close to triumph and I'll not let the Shevertons escape so easily."

"Yes, but—"

"You've done your duty, dear," said Lady Cartwright, "now go away."

Samantha bowed very low and was just rising when Lord Wyatt, Hilary in tow, burst into the room and dashed up to inform her, in a far from coherent manner, that Hilary had been so good as to accept his hand in marriage.

"It's amazing, incredible, glorious, unbelievable!" Lord Wyatt cried. "I can't . . . I don't know how to tell you how happy I am."

"You are making an excellent job of it, I assure you," Samantha said with a grin.

"This is all well and good," said Lady Cartwright dampingly, "but there was a time when a gentleman asked the *parent* of his paramour for the young lady's hand in marriage. The only question I recall answering tonight had to do with the stakes at this table."

Pandemonium ensued as Lord Wyatt fell to his knees before his future mother-in-law to plead his cause while Hilary, laughing until the tears streamed down her cheeks, tried vainly to pull her ardent lover back onto his feet and to

186

stop making such a cake of himself. Two dozen players of cards watched the scene with the greatest delight.

So public an announcement could not fail to spread through Carlton House like wildfire for, though Hilary was a relative nonentity in the haut ton's firmament, Lord Wyatt was the second son of the Duke of Hensley and thus a more than suitable topic for gossip.

"Your first great success," Lord Cartwright murmured to Samantha as they, and a dozen other friends of the newly betrothed couple surrounded Hilary and Lord Wyatt, champagne glasses dutifully in hand.

"No, no," Samantha said with a smile, "they contrived the whole by themselves. I only provided an occasional nudge. That is the genius of my work."

Lord Cartwright choked on his wine. "I have never met a woman who combined modesty and arrogance into such a devilish whole. Is it nature or contrived for your own amusement?"

"Oh nature, certainly, sir. No woman of breeding would admit to contriving her arrogance."

"The very devil," Lord Cartwright said, smiling down at her. "And what, as a woman of breeding, do you think of the greatest palace in London?"

"I like it," Samantha promptly replied. "I know it is not fashionable to do so, but when have I ever heeded fashion?" She glanced around the packed ballroom. "Some may sneer at its opulence, at the traceried ceiling of the Conservatory encrusted with gold ornamentation, the ostrich plumes in the Throne Room, the velvet carpets in the Crimson Drawing Room, the forest of ionic columns in the Circular Dining Room, but they're all short of a sheet. Carlton House, of any palace I've ever been in, is dedicated to the goddess of us all: Beauty. Yes, there is extravagance here, but it bespeaks merely a childlike pleasure in beauty and opulence that any mortal must embrace."

"But this is dreadful, Lady Samantha!" exclaimed Lord

Cartwright. "I find myself more and more in agreement with you with each passing day!"

"Speaking from vast experience, I should warn you, my lord, that there are dangerous shoals ahead if you pursue such a course."

"I think," Lord Cartwright murmured as he gazed down at Samantha, "that I will enjoy every rock and storm."

Chapter Sixteen

On the succeeding afternoon, Samantha and the Danthorpes returned to the Dower House after a brisk, though decorous, canter through Hyde Park and were just turning to the stairs when Garner arrested his mistress with the ominous words:

"May I speak with you, my lady?"

Fearing murder or at least mayhem to be the tidings he undoubtedly bore, Samantha ordered the Danthorpes upstairs to change their clothes, and turned with trepidation to her butler.

"Tell me the worst," she said. "Has Monsieur Girard quit again?"

"Thankfully not. However, your brother, Lord Adamson, is in the front drawing room, my lady. He has insisted on waiting for you there this last hour."

Even Samantha could not help but pale at such a declaration. " 'Tis a blow, Garner. A palpable blow."

"Yes, my lady. I have, of course, offered his lordship every hospitality of the house, but he will neither eat nor drink. He will barely speak save to criticize the furnishings of the drawing room and demand of me every five minutes why you have not yet returned."

"You have had a trying hour, Garner. Would you care to lie down?"

A momentary smile flitted across the reserved butler's mouth. "Thank you, no, my lady. I live but to serve you."

Samantha returned the smile. "Oh, but this is dreadful, Garner! Could you not say that I've left the country indefinitely?"

"I was tempted to do so, my lady, but Lord Adamson forestalled me by claiming that he knew you were in town and refused to leave the premises until he had spoken to you."

"Bellowed at me, more like," Samantha murmured. "Well, delay him a bit longer, Garner, while I change."

Garner gravely bowed and returned to the drawing room to announce to his lordship that he expected her ladyship shortly. Lord Adamson harrumphed, muttered something about featherbrained gadding about town, and continued to pace the thick Chinese carpet with a violence that made Garner fear for the carpet's survival.

Fifteen minutes later, dressed in a blue satin scalloped gown trimmed in silver ribbon, Samantha entered the drawing room if not with trepidation, at least with considerable caution. She had not seen her brother in six years, though they had exchanged letters on a regular basis during that time. She had but a moment to observe that Lord Adamson, lacking both height and beauty, had grown decidedly stout in the last several years. His face was florid, his pale brown hair noticeably thin at the top of his head, his brown eyes rheumy as he whirled around at her entrance and glared at her.

"So, you deign to come back to your own house, do you?" he snapped as he advanced upon her.

"How good of you to pay me a call, Reggie," Samantha said imperturbably. "You're looking very well. Have you been in town long? Would you like some tea? My chef is known for the delicacy of his pastries."

190

"Oh, you're cool as a cucumber, aren't you?" Lord Adamson sneered. "Quite the lady of the manor. Well, I know better, miss, and so does the whole of London and a good part of the country!"

"I have advised you time and again, Reggie, not to listen to gossip. It makes you bilious. Would you care to sit down?"

"Look at you!" Lord Adamson said in disgust. "Tricked out in the first stare of fashion, I've no doubt. Leading a gay life of dissipation from one end of town to the other for the last four months when you haven't even had the decency to visit your own family! Your own flesh and blood! I might have known *you* would be so unfeeling, so uncivil, nay, so *cruel* as to disappoint the only relations you have in the world by selfishly pursuing your hedonistic revels!"

"Hedonistic?" Samantha said, arching one brow. "Why Reggie, you've been reading Mr. Johnson's famous *Dictionary* again."

For one terrible moment it seemed as if Lord Adamson's round head would explode.

"By *God* I'll take a horsewhip to you one of these days, Samantha, see if I don't!"

"But what a scandal you would cause if you did, my dear brother."

"Scandal?" Lord Adamson snorted. "A lot you care about that! Moving into a house that no woman of principle would inhabit, driving about town without a chaperone, galloping in Hyde Park, flirting with every gazetted fortune hunter in London, giving some swarthy Spaniard the run of your house, letting a slip of a girl parade herself in front of every able-bodied man in the ton, driving yourself down St. James's Street—oh yes, I heard about that! The whole county heard about that!—and parading yourself on the Prince Regent's arm as if you were no better than a *courtesan*. Oh no, Samantha, I don't think you care anything about *scandal*!"

"You dare to impugn the honor of the Prince Regent?" Samantha coolly inquired. "Careful, Reggie, lest you speak treason. The Prince is a trifle sensitive about what people say of him."

"I wish to God you had a particle of that sensitivity!" Lord Adamson declared feelingly. "Then perhaps you would be more circumspect in what you do and say in public. Parading yourself in front of every dandy and rake on St. James's Street. I still can't believe it. You've no sense, Samantha, and you never had. Any fool without a smattering of education would know that a bubbleheaded female of seven-and-twenty is not merely unsuitable but *unfit* to be guardian to a pair of youngsters like the Danthorpes. But not you. *You* keep them dangling after you like a pair of adoring puppies, ruining any chance they might have of presenting a decent character in the ton. And *then* you have the effrontery, the damned *gall*, to have Sir Robert Gifford and Lord Liverpool threaten—yes threaten!—me should I try to do the only right thing and rescue those unhappy children from your shameful abuse. No, don't try to pull an outraged face on me. I know what I know."

"On my honor, Reggie, I have never spoken to Sir Robert or Lord Liverpool in my life."

"Honor? What honor?" scoffed Lord Adamson. "You don't even know what the word means. But I do, by God. I'll not let the Danthorpes stay another day under this roof, Lord Liverpool's protection or no. I have written to the Tylers to implore their immediate return to England that they may rescue the Danthorpes from your ruinous mismanagement. I have assured them that I shall keep the Danthorpes safe until their return!"

"Why, how presumptuous of you, Reggie. What would the Tylers think of you removing from town two of the Prince Regent's particular favorites? They must wonder why you would not consider the friendship of our Regent sufficient protection to shield the Danthorpes from any harm."

"*Prinny's* protection? Bah! As soon have a fox watch the henyard. Did you know that the members of White's are actually betting on whom Miss Danthorpe will marry?"

"I believe the gentlemen of the ton are sporting enthusiasts."

Lord Adamson smacked his hand upon his knee. "I might have known you would not take your responsibilities to the Danthorpes in a serious light! Samantha, you cannot continue to let the Danthorpes be the center of gossip! It's bad enough you hire a French—*French*—piano instructor for Peter and let him run tame at Jackson's, a den of iniquity if ever there was one! You've actually hired some foreign tutor for him when he should be at school getting caned at least twice a day. How could you, even you, allow a boy of seventeen to put himself forward at music recitals when he hasn't even left the schoolroom?"

"Peter has the talent to begin to make a name for himself now which cannot but benefit his future career. Did not today's admirals and generals join the military when they were not yet out of short pants?"

"That's neither here nor there," Lord Adamson said, waving away such a retort. "You've done even worse by Miss Danthorpe! You're spoiling her, Samantha. Yes, and worse! You're ruining her with an expensive, not to say shocking, wardrobe that's the talk of the town, letting her ride a high-spirited bonesetter in any weather, letting her flirt with every man who's willing—and I've heard they're all willing! But the worst of it all, Samantha, is that you've had a complete stranger sponsor her debut when Lydia or my wife should have done so!"

"I had no idea Lady Adamson was eager to abandon her children to launch Christina into Society," said Samantha with commendable surprise.

Lord Adamson flushed and blustered a bit. "Yes, well, be that as it may, *Lydia* would have been perfectly suitable—"

"But, Reggie, you know how Lydia detests London. The frolics of the ton are anathema to her—she frequently says so."

"She needn't put herself out. Lord Bathgate has indicated to me his perfect willingness to take the Danthorpes in hand if you'd let him."

"What a charming debut for Christina: a sojourn amongst the Bathgate sheep."

"They could come with me!" Lord Adamson declared. "I've written you time and again that I'm willing to take them. I'm *wanting* to take them. I'll do a much better job of keeping those two out of mischief than a rattlepated female like you ever could!"

"We must leave that to the realm of conjecture and fantasy for you can't have them."

"Why you—you damned hussy!" sputtered Lord Adamson. "Never have I encountered such willfulness! Such stubbornness! Have you no thought to the Danthorpes? Have you no concern for *their* well-being?"

"But their well-being is uppermost in my thoughts every moment of the day," Samantha assured her brother. "That is why I'd rather feed them to the crocodiles of the Nile than hand them over to you."

This was, of course, too much for Lord Adamson and he spent the next twenty minutes striding up and down the drawing room ranting at his youngest sister with all of the heat and eloquence which his fiery temper and limited intellectual resources gave him. Samantha's morals, character, and lack of obedience to the head of the family— Lord Reginald—were severely remarked upon. In fact, every aspect of her life was brutally condemned.

She listened to it all without a word until, when her brother finally stood before her panting for breath, she informed him that, as she had no intention of surrendering the

194

Danthorpes to him and as he had threatened to stay until she did hand them over to him, she recommended he send for his wife and family to take up lodging in the Adamson town house in Grosvenor Square for he was going to be staying in London for some time to come.

"Aye, I'll be staying," Lord Adamson said murderously. "You'll soon tire of playing Prince's favorite and children's guardian and sail off to some new adventure in some heathen land. And when you do, I'll be here to see that the Danthorpes receive the care they need and deserve!"

He stalked from the room and thence from the house. His sister, when she heard the front door slam, hurled two vases and a porcelain statuette against the nearest wall with such violence that they shattered into powder.

A lifetime's experience of her brother's rages had taught Samantha the futility of raging at him in kind and so she had learned to hold her tongue before him, whatever the provocation. Once free of his company, however, her own rage could boil over as it did now with a violence that threatened the safety of every furnishing in the room.

Ten minutes of cursing her brother to every torture and misery devised in millennia of human history had done little to soothe her wrath when Garner, with understandable trepidation, ventured into the drawing room.

"What do you want?" Samantha demanded as she spun around on him with a fury that made the butler take three steps back to the doorway.

"Your pardon, my lady," he said soothingly, "but Lord Cartwright has called and wishes to speak with you. Shall I tell him you are not at home?"

"Tell him to go to the devil!"

"Very good, my lady," said Garner, beginning to close the door.

"No! Wait!" Samantha said hurriedly. It had occurred to her that even the scullery maid could not but be aware she was in the house after this tantrum. Simply because her

195

brother had enraged her was no reason she should insult her neighbor. If she could feign calm in Reginald Adamson's presence, she could certainly do the same in Lord Cartwright's presence. "You may show him in, Garner," she said.

"Here?" inquired the butler with some alarm.

Samantha glanced around the room. It looked as if it had been sacked by Attila and his untidy Huns.

"Your point is well taken, Garner," she said. "Where have you installed his lordship?"

"In the downstairs front parlor, my lady."

"I shall attend him there. You offered the usual tea tray?"

"Yes, my lady. He refused."

"Why do none of my gentlemen callers want to partake of the bounty of my kitchen?"

"Perhaps they are fasting, my lady."

Samantha was startled into a chuckle. "You are a priceless asset to my household, Garner. Remind me to give you a raise."

She went downstairs and, drawing a calming breath, entered the front parlor to find Lord Cartwright studying a painting of plump, naked female bathers by Fragonard which she had recently acquired.

"I am sorry to keep you waiting, Lord Cartwright," she said.

"Not at all. I have been here for just a minute . . . admiring the view." Lord Cartwright's bland expression became one of concern as he turned to her. "I beg your pardon, Lady Samantha, but you appear flushed. Are you ill? Should you be up?"

"I am not at all ill, Lord Cartwright. Thank you for your concern. If I am flushed, it is but the residue from a recent tête-à-tête with my brother."

"Your brother?"

"The plague of Yorkshire! The dullest, severest, most

pompous, self-righteous, self-centered, asinine *boor* ever to slander humanity by his very existence!"

Lord Cartwright could not but smile at this description. "He is recently arrived in town?"

"The travel dust was still upon his clothes. He could not wait to visit me after six years' separation to charge me with every unnatural crime a woman could commit."

Lord Cartwright's brown eyes widened at this. "What could you say to provoke such an attack?"

"I?" cried Samantha. "I said nothing! I was an exemplar of good manners. I turned aside every insult with a mildness that would have done a saint credit!"

"I did not mean to cast any aspersion—"

"Didn't you?" Samantha said bitterly. "Every time we meet you cannot wait to criticize some new act or conversation of mine. Your opinion of me is almost as harsh as that of my brother!"

"Lady Samantha, we have had our differences in the past, I know. But often I was as much to blame as you. And now that I know—"

"Blame?" seethed Samantha. "Who are you to blame me? By what right do you condemn any act or word I speak? Of all the sanctimonious, self-righteous—"

"Lady Adamson," Lord Cartwright broke in firmly, "if you will but let me complete a sentence you will hear me agree with everything you say. I've no right to blame or condemn or criticize. It is the height of effrontery to act otherwise."

"Fine words," Samantha stormed, "when only last night you called me an arrogant devil!"

"You have taken my words wholly out of context!" Lord Cartwright declared, his own temper beginning to govern him. "I meant no slur as you well knew last night! If I had wished to criticize, I would have mentioned the shameless way you flirted with Lord Barnett for half the night!"

"Why you—you swine! You take a single dance with

197

Derek Barnett and blow it into an open affair in the middle of the Prince's ballroom!"

"I never accused you of having an affair."

"You said my conduct was shameless. What other meaning am I to impute?"

His lordship knew a strong desire to shake his hostess. "Lady Samantha, if you will but govern your own prejudices and hear what I am saying—"

"I hear you perfectly well and these ham-handed pronouncements of yours will shortly get you thrown out of my house if you do not try some other means of communication!"

Goaded beyond what any mortal man could tolerate, Lord Cartwright thereupon grasped Samantha with barely suppressed violence.

For one wild, heart-shuddering moment she thought he meant to kiss her. And she wanted him to!

In the next moment he had thrust her away from him.

"I will call on you again when we are both calmer!" he said in a strangled voice before striding from the room.

She stared after him, heart pounding, breath coming in gasps, face flooded with heat as the full knowledge of her traitorous yearning struck home.

As for Lord Cartwright, it required several hours of walking London's crowded and far from clean streets before he could bring himself to any semblance of calm. He returned home disheveled and in a foment of thought. Eschewing all company, he locked himself in his study, removed his coat and neckcloth, and sat behind his desk staring up at the excellent Jacobean woodwork of his ceiling. After considering the matter in all its aspects, he wrote to Lord Derek Barnett seeking an interview that evening. A reply in the affirmative returned with the footman and Lord Cartwright presented himself in Curzon Street at seven o'clock that night.

An hour after Lord Cartwright had left him, Lord Barnett

discovered that Jillian Roberts was to attend Lady Jersey's card party and, by bringing his considerable resources into play, was able to obtain an invitation for that night and succeeded in being placed at Jillian's card table.

Chapter Seventeen

A WEEK HAD passed since Lord Cartwright and Samantha's quarrel. She had successfully contrived to avoid him for the whole of that week, but her thoughts could not be so well schooled. *Had* Lord Cartwright meant to kiss her? No! It was impossible! But the way he had looked at her . . . Samantha's heart lurched. No man had ever gazed at her with such barely suppressed fire. Endlessly she went back and forth: had he meant to kiss her? No, of course not! And yet . . .

The trouble was, she always bumped up against the shocking knowledge that *she* had wanted to kiss *him*. She could not imagine what had caused such a quirk. Other men had indicated that they wished to kiss her, some had even done so. She had felt nothing—not excitement or fear or distaste.

Certainly not this hurricane of emotion that continued to batter her a week after nothing had happened. What was wrong with her? She did not love Lord Cartwright. *That* was impossible. She had too much strength of will to fall in love with any man.

But why did she fear meeting him again?

"It is only because I acted badly and am ashamed for it," she muttered as she dragged a brush through her hair late one night. "I shall have to apologize to him *again* and I dread it. That is all."

Relieved at so rational a solution to so nagging a worry, she went to bed and proceeded to toss and turn the whole of that night.

Her next meeting with Lord Cartwright came much sooner than Samantha wished under auspices she could not avoid. The Cartwrights gave Hilary and Lord Wyatt a betrothal ball and, as best friend and matchmaker, she was compelled to attend. Lord Wyatt and all five Cartwrights stood at the entrance to the Cartwright ballroom already half-filled with guests when Samantha and the Danthorpes slowly approached them. Lord Cartwright's height and breadth of chest and shoulders would have made him stand out in any crowd. Samantha could not seem to pull her gaze from him. She managed to murmur a hello and congratulations to Hilary and Lord Wyatt, but then Lord Cartwright laughed at something Colonel Dalton said as he passed through the line and her gaze was once again painfully fixed upon Lord Cartwright's strong, handsome face.

This comingling of temptation, fear, and curiosity was something she had never experienced before. It left her feeling off balance and unsure of herself. Lord Cartwright, who had been as sensible of her approach as she, was struggling under equally strong emotions. Thus, they murmured their "good evenings" to each other with equal wariness and consciousness before Samantha and the Danthorpes escaped into the ballroom.

Samantha abandoned Christina to her suitors and Peter to his friends and admirers. She glanced back at Lord Cartwright who was still receiving guests. Heat surged into her face and she quickly walked to the opposite end of the room to collect herself.

She acceded to any gentleman who asked to dance with her, refused wine, drank champagne punch, conversed with the utmost civility, and noticed none of it. She was unaware that Colonel Dalton and Miss Sheverton had already danced twice together. She did not see the Duke de Peralta expertly flirting with a variety of wealthy women in the ballroom. She did not care that Christina and Timothy Cartwright assiduously avoided each other for the whole of the evening. She was distracted and distracted to such an extent that she did not even know Lord Cartwright had come to her side until he spoke.

"It is a pleasure to see such happiness, isn't it?" he said.

She jumped, held a gasp firmly between her teeth, and looked rather blindly to the dance floor where she dimly perceived Hilary and Lord Wyatt dancing together.

"A great pleasure," she managed.

"Hilary has already received letters from the Duke and Duchess of Hensley couched in the greatest terms of affection. It is agreed that she and Aaron are to spend the summer at Danville, the Hensleys' main country seat. A date in September has finally been established for the wedding, I believe."

Samantha, grateful to his lordship for undertaking so innocuous a conversation with her, replied: "So Hilary informs me, though the question of whether it is to be a town or a country wedding has yet to be decided."

"They are both perfectly malleable on the subject," Lord Cartwright continued imperturbably. "The wedding is the thing, location is of little consequence to either of them. The Hensleys, however, have very firm opinions on the subject which has put my mother's back up and so the battle is fairly joined."

"I would think anyone, even the Duke and Duchess of Hensley, to be unequal to any battle Lady Cartwright cares to wage."

Lord Cartwright's smile was genuine. "We Cartwrights can be formidable when we put our minds to it."

Samantha was able to laugh. "Sir, you underestimate the matter, I do assure you!"

"Well, if anyone is a judge of formidableness, it would be you, Lady Samantha."

She took a fortifying breath. "That brings me to an overdue apology. I behaved very badly toward you the last time we met and I am sorry for it."

"Are you?" said Lord Cartwright with an odd look in his brown eyes. "I've come to relish our contretemps. They always show me new horizons to explore."

Samantha gazed at him quizzically, but received only a bland smile in return before his lordship bid her adieu and strolled off to attend to the rest of his guests.

On the next evening was fixed an excursion to the Vauxhall Gardens. As both Christina and Samantha had no desire to be confined in a box with the elder male Cartwrights—for reasons they had no wish to publish to the world—Samantha fobbed off Lady Cartwright's suggestion that she and the Danthorpes join the Cartwright box by claiming a prior promise to make one of Lord Barnett's party. That the gentleman had no knowledge that he was going to Vauxhall that evening troubled her not at all. She was, it must be confessed, somewhat taken aback by his ready acceptance of the scheme, but then she was still ignorant of his interest in Lady Jillian Roberts, who he knew would make one of the Cartwright party.

Thus the Berkeley Square residents ventured forth to the Vauxhall Gardens on a delightfully mild night, the stars thick above them, the promise of good food, fun, and fireworks bidding them on. Not wishing to spoil the evening's entertainment, Lord Cartwright forbore picking a quarrel with Jillian, as had recently become his habit, and instead devoted himself to recounting to Lord Wyatt, in Hilary's hearing, the various adventures he had led his sister into in their youth. Hilary was kept in a continual blush that amused her brother and charmed her fiancé no end.

For her part, Samantha quickly tired of the crush of applicants to Christina's heart. Fortunately, the orchestra began to play and her ward was quickly promised to every dance. She strolled off on the arms of Lord Palmerston and Mr. Wilding, the rest of her admirers trailing behind her in a grumbling pack. Lord Barnett, spying Jillian walking on the arm of her sister, suddenly announced that he saw an old friend that he must just have a word with, and he hastily decamped.

"Well, Peter," Samantha said with some amusement to the only other occupant of their supper box, "do you think, if I let you off your leash, that you can contrive to stay out of any serious mischief? You note that I will allow you minor mischief. But no playing at being a white slaver, if you please."

Peter flushed at this reminder of his disreputable past, assured his guardian that he would be the soul of decorum, and ran off to join Matthew on the Dark Walk.

Samantha knew a momentary discomfort at finding herself alone in her box which she quickly dispelled by making her own exit and looking out for her own fun amongst the Chinese lanterns, fountains, and cascades. She found it soon enough in the idiocies of her own class. She was just passing one of the lesser supper boxes near the Orchestra Pavillion when she was arrested suddenly by the promise of great mirth.

"Pink? Are you sure, Archie?" she overheard a man cry.

"I assure you, Bartley, that pink will make me the most influential arbiter of male fashion since Beau Brummell," Archie replied.

Samantha backed inconspicuously closer to this couple to more easily overhear what was being said.

"But I look quite bilious in pink, Archie," the poor Bartley protested. "Could you not settle on some other shade? Yellow, perhaps, or green? I look quite smashing in green."

"No, no, the gypsy was emphatic. She said that pink would be my hallmark. I tell you, Bartley, pink will grant me the success I have so long deserved. Think of it! I shall be the envy of Braxton, Drake, Byron!"

"Byron's in disgrace, Archie," Bartley pointed out.

"You are not taking my point," Archie said testily. "At the end of one month, any man who values his position in the ton will be wearing pink pantaloons, pink waistcoats, pink morning coats, pink cravats!"

"Not . . . cravats!" Bartley said faintly.

"*Pink* cravats," Archie sternly reaffirmed. "At the end of four short weeks *I* shall be the most sought-after man in London."

Samantha could bear no more and scurried away to hide herself behind a shrub. She was convulsed with laughter for the next several minutes.

"Are you enjoying yourself?" Lord Cartwright gravely inquired, his brown eyes twinkling merrily as he came upon her.

"Pink!" she gasped.

"I beg your pardon?"

"No, no, it is I who beg *your* pardon," Samantha replied with an enforced sobriety. "Being from a barbarous clime, I had not known the importance of that color nor the intensity with which men of discerning dispositions discuss its many merits."

"*You* have been talking to Archie Baldwin," Lord Cartwright declared, instantly enlightened.

"Oh no," Samantha said meekly, her golden head bowed. "I could never find the courage to enter so awesome a presence. I eavesdropped. Shamelessly."

Lord Cartwright began to chuckle.

"It is not a laughing matter, sir," Samantha reproached him. "Do you not realize that we have in our midst a man whose awesome intellect has illumined the key to power and success in our time? Archie Baldwin could be our next Napoleon! Cannot you see him on his gallant steed, crossing the Alps à la Bonaparte, resplendent in pink Hessians, pink breeches, pink coat, and pink epaulets?"

Lord Cartwright roared with laughter, for he *could* imagine such a scene.

"You are the most absurd woman," he declared, still chuckling.

"Why thank you."

"No, no, thank *you*. London was not half so amusing before you swooped down upon us, like a chicken hawk spying a fat hen."

"That was meant as a compliment?"

Lord Cartwright smiled inscrutably. "I confess to being somewhat disappointed at not finding you in a fix from which you need to be rescued."

"Oh come now," Samantha said, her lips quirking, "I have not gotten into a scrape all week."

"Have no fear, Lady Samantha, something may yet occur, in fact, something already has, in a minor sort of way. You will probably not care to hear that no lady makes a promenade of the Vauxhall Gardens by herself. To do so leaves her prey to the inebriated—and they are always inebriated—male revellers of every class."

"What," Samantha said, peering up at him, "are you foxed?"

"No, you odious woman. I am simply trying to instruct you in the inherent dangers of English pleasure gardens."

Samantha sighed with great weariness. "You are, as usual, being presumptuous, my lord. I cut my wisdom teeth long ago. I do not carry this very handsome walking stick as a mere affectation."

Lord Cartwright considered the tall, gleaming mahogany stick. "No?"

"No. It can be, and has been, put to a variety of painful uses. I am too much a woman of the world, my lord, not to know how to defend myself."

"One would hope such skill lies within such a determined scapegrace," Lord Cartwright agreed.

Samantha sighed once more. "And the man calls *me* odious. Come," she said, slipping her arm through his with apparent calm, "lead me to your box so that I may pay my respects to your mother and I will amuse you by ridiculing myself with a tale from my misspent youth. It has to do with a gentleman by the name of Walter Smedley."

Alas, Lord Cartwright was not destined to hear the diverting tale for, as they approached the Cartwright box, they found it a scene of riotous upheaval.

"What's the to-do?" he murmured.

"Miss Sheverton appears to be at the heart of it," Samantha replied, peering closely into the crowd.

She had the right of it. No sooner had they come within hailing distance than Miss Sheverton, her heart-shaped face aglow, called to them in a voice that could be heard across half of Vauxhall.

"Simon! Lady Samantha! I am betrothed to Colonel Dalton! Lord Farago is in such a fury and I don't care. I am so happy!"

Lord Cartwright stopped dead and looked down at Samantha. "Not another one," he said with a sigh.

Samantha looked demure and tugged him toward the box. "You will soon come to regard Brandon as another brother, I am sure of it. He comes from a perfectly respectable family, although he cannot claim a perfectly respectable past. He has, however, a number of sterling qualities that will endear him to you. He is faithful in all his friendships—and he will be faithful to Miss Sheverton. He is loyal even at the risk of his own life. He is intelligent, well educated, well traveled, and adept at talking himself out of any difficult situation that comes his way. I speak from experience. He has recently left the military and now, with a sufficient income, finds himself at loose ends. He loves to travel, as does Miss Sheverton, I believe, and speaks several languages fluently. I thought he might make you an excellent man to manage your Continental business interests."

Lord Cartwright once again stopped and stared down at Samantha. "Did you indeed?" he inquired.

Samantha smiled sunnily up at him. "After all, not even you can be in ten places at once and at the pace you are advancing your financial enterprises, you will soon have to be. Brandon might be useful in relieving you of some of that burden."

"My nerves are but a shadow of their former selves since meeting you. Very well, Lady Samantha, meddler extraordinaire, I shall interview the gentleman."

"You're a gent, guvnor."

Lord Cartwright laughed. "Your servant, madam," he said, raising Samantha's hand to his lips.

The touch was almost a kiss of air. Fire curled up from Samantha's fingers and spread through her with a rush.

"My lord," she managed before Lord Cartwright pulled them into the midst of their ecstatic friends and family.

Chapter Eighteen

FEELING SOMEWHAT MORE at ease with Lord Cartwright, Samantha felt the breadth of her vision widen once more and what she saw was most distressing. Christina and Timothy Cartwright were being difficult. Their continued estrangement demanded that she exercise every matchmaking skill at her command. Alas, she was too late. On the day after Miss Sheverton's announcement at Vauxhall, Mr. Cartwright refused all future social engagements which might bring him into further contact with Christina. He found it too painful watching her flirt with her myriad of more worthy suitors. To hear her speak was torture. To hear her laugh mangled his heart. Being a practical gentleman, he chose not to inflict such misery upon himself when he could avoid it.

It took Christina nearly a se'ennight to realize that Mr. Cartwright meant never to see her again. At first she felt relief that she would no longer spend an evening in a ballroom surreptitiously watching Mr. Cartwright's every move and longing to be with him rather than the more suitable Lord Palmerston or Mr. Wilding. But the pain she felt at the next ball she attended when Mr. Cartwright was not there and would not come no matter how long she waited soon dashed any feelings of relief. Anger succeeded pain. How dare Mr. Cartwright make her long for his company and deliberately withhold it from her? Sadness soon rose to dominance. She had made her choice and must abide by it, no matter the cost.

Fear quickly supplanted every other emotion for it came to Christina late one night as she lay sleepless in her bed that perhaps she had made the wrong choice after all. It was inconceivable to her that Mr. Cartwright could so easily supplant the romantically dissipated Lord Palmerston in her affections. Yet he seemed to have done so with very little effort. She began to wonder if she had perhaps chosen the wrong romantic ideal.

This thought was so unnerving that Christina was once again relieved that Mr. Cartwright was not close at hand to incite such wayward thoughts. She decided her best defense would be to plunge into company with Lord Palmerston whenever she was tempted to dwell upon the absent Mr. Cartwright. As her thoughts were frequently tempted in that direction, she spent more and more time in Lord Palmerston's company . . . to the disgust of her guardian.

Samantha had a shrewd understanding of Christina's dilemma and, while disparaging her ward's slavish devotion to novelistic love, was glad to see Christina brought to such a desperate stand. Now all she had to do was bring Mr. Cartwright up to snuff. Working from the simple premise that, if Mr. Cartwright could be brought into company with Christina and Lord Palmerston, he would be made jealous and, if jealous, he would act, Samantha blithely assured him that, while she would join the Cartwrights (and Lord Wyatt, of course) at the Hortons' anniversary ball, Christina was pledged to a small dinner party at the Esterhazys. This was, of course, a blatant falsehood, as Mr. Cartwright quickly discovered.

Entering the crush of the Hortons' ballroom with his mother on his arm, Mr. Cartwright knew a sudden fury when he saw Christina dancing a reel with Lord Palmerston. His fury increased as he observed the radiant look she cast upon her partner, and the frequency with which Lord Palmerston kissed her hand whenever they came together . . . an act which was not a part of the accepted dance steps!

"Where is Lady Samantha?" Mr. Cartwright demanded of his mother in grim tones.

"I think I see her talking with Lord Barnett," Lady Cartwright replied. "Do you see the Duke de Peralta anywhere?"

"If you'll excuse me, Mama," said Mr. Cartwright, "I must have a word with our neighbor."

He stalked toward Samantha, who was teasing Lord Barnett about his recent preoccupation. She was entirely sensible of Mr. Cartwright's approach and turned just as he opened his mouth to accost her.

"Ah, there you are, Mr. Cartwright!" she said gaily. "I have been looking for you this half hour. If you'll excuse us, Derek, I must discuss a private matter with Mr. Cartwright."

Lord Barnett bowed and Samantha, ignoring the fulminating glare of Mr. Cartwright, took his arm in hers and led him away.

"If you were a man," said Mr. Cartwright, "I would call you out for what you have done!"

"But what have I done?" Samantha inquired innocently.

"You have lied to me! You have practiced deliberate deceit!"

"Lied?"

"Miss Danthorpe is here tonight!"

"Well, yes, of course she is . . . Oh, you mean . . . Yes, I thought she was going to be at the Esterhazys' tonight, but she is actually invited for tomorrow night. It seems I got the dates muddled up. With the plethora of invitations that deluge our house night and day, I am amazed I remember as much as I do of our engagements."

Mr. Cartwright believed not a tittle of this, but he was

too well bred to tell her so. Thus, he stood glowering at Samantha, trying to think of something cutting to say.

"They make a handsome couple, don't they?" Samantha said, indicating Christina and Lord Palmerston on the dance floor.

"Indeed," Timothy said grimly.

"I wonder if I might ask your advice on a matter of some import. Lord Palmerston has asked for a private interview with me tomorrow morning—"

"He *what*?!"

"—and I cannot but suspect his purpose. His attentions to Christina have been too pronounced to be misconstrued. His family and presentation are all that I could ask," Samantha blithely continued, "but there is a hint of . . . wildness in his character that worries me. What sort of husband do you think he would make?"

"Husband? He is not fit to be Miss Danthorpe's boot-black!" Timothy stormed.

"Certainly he is in some financial difficulty as I understand it, but—"

Timothy clutched her arm. "Good God, Lady Samantha, he is leading her out onto the balcony! *Do* something!"

"Goodness, whatever for? Christina is well able to take care of herself."

With an oath, Timothy stormed off.

Samantha watched him go, a seraphic smile on her full lips.

Having danced a reel with vigor, Lord Palmerston declared that his partner appeared flushed and overheated and suggested the cool night air on the balcony as a restorative. Well aware that Mr. Cartwright was now present in the ballroom—her heart had experienced a painful spasm at his entrance—Christina was eager for distraction. She accepted Lord Palmerston's offer, took his arm, and allowed him to lead her out onto the balcony.

There he guided her to a darkened corner, somewhat removed from the other couples seeking fresh air.

"Are you feeling better, Miss Danthorpe?" he asked.

"Yes, thank you," Christina replied.

"The moonlight casts you in its spell," Lord Palmerston said in a reverent voice. "How lovely you look tonight, Miss Danthorpe."

"Thank you."

"I remember the first moment I saw you. You were a vision, an angel in white. I thought my heart had ceased to function, so stunned was I by your beauty."

Normally, Christina was willing to listen to any inventive flattery, but unease oppressed her tonight. "Please, my lord. I wish you would not."

"But I must and shall speak all that swells my heart!" Lord Palmerston declared as he grasped Christina's hand and passionately began to kiss it.

"L-L-Lord Palmerston!" Christina gasped, jerking her hand free before she knew what she was about.

"From that first moment I adored you," Lord Palmerston feverishly vowed, undeterred by such a response. "I have loved you every minute since that night. Loved you and wanted you. I am not a man governed by society's rules. I care not that the world will think me imprudent for this night's work. I can no longer remain silent. I love you, Christina. Love you, adore you, worship you. Say that you will marry me!"

"M-m-marry you?"

Lord Palmerston held out his arms as if courting a quiver of Cupid's arrows. "I offer you my heart, my soul, my very life, and all the protection of an ancient and noble name and estate."

Christina knew that she should be in ecstasies, or at least very happy at achieving the culmination of all her dreams. She felt, instead, a little depressed and more than a little frightened.

213

"I-I-I don't know what to say."

"Say that you love me! Say that you will marry me as soon as we may secure a license."

"Oh," said Christina, forcefully pulling herself together. "Oh, of course I love you. I must love you. Yes, I'm sure that I love you."

"My darling!" cried Lord Palmerston. He pulled Christina to him and forced his mouth down upon hers.

As she neither fainted nor felt any passionate response to this embrace, Christina began to wonder if the novels she had read had somehow gotten such declarations of love all wrong, or if she was perhaps not feeling very well tonight.

Samantha considered her ward—standing pale and silent before her, hand clasped tightly by Lord Palmerston—with the greatest consternation. That Lord Palmerston meant to offer for her ward this morning, she had known. That he would try to cut the ground out from under her by proposing to Christina first, and winning her acceptance, she had not expected. She stood on the edge of a precipice that could easily cast her out from Christina's regard forever.

"I have listened very carefully to your declarations of undying love for my ward, Lord Palmerston. I would now like to hear what you have to say, Christina."

"S-s-say?" Christina replied, blushing furiously.

"Yes," Samantha said, sitting back in her chair. "Is your devotion to Lord Palmerston as deep and abiding as he claims his is for you?"

"Oh. Oh, yes, of course."

"He is the companion you wish at your side for the rest of your days?"

"Yes."

"No other man could ever please you as much as Lord Palmerston?"

"No. Certainly not, Sam."

"You would withstand any privation to marry him?"

214

"Oh yes!" Christina replied with the first spark of animation she had displayed during this interview.

Samantha was again silent for a moment. "I will speak to you both with the honesty which your mutual declarations require. I cannot approve of this marriage."

"But Samantha—!" cried Christina.

Samantha held up her hand. "No. Hear me out, Chris. You have known Lord Palmerston only four months. You have conceived a violent affection for him. I must ask myself: can such an affection last? Four months are not sufficient to provide an answer. In this same period of time, I have been informed by people of the highest repute that Lord Palmerston is so severely in dun territory that he is threatened with gaol if he does not repay his creditors and quickly."

"I have made a full confession of my difficulties to Christina," Lord Palmerston declared.

"Yes, of course you have, as any gentleman would," Samantha calmly broke in. "You have also, I am sure, informed her of your excesses amongst the muslin set, your seduction of a number of willing wives throughout the ton, and the sad saga of your last mistress, an opera dancer, I believe, whose eye you blacked during one of your frequent rows."

"Samantha, how could you?" Christina hotly demanded. "How could you throw up Michael's past like this?"

"I merely wanted to point out that such a past would be of concern to any guardian solicitous of a ward's well-being."

"No one regrets more than I the errors of my youth—" Lord Palmerston began.

"We'll take it as read, my lord," Samantha broke in, determined to thwart any more of his melodramatic monologues. She had heard enough of them this morning to last her a lifetime. "I freely grant you all heroic reformations and good intentions. The fact remains, however, that on

215

the surface you are very far from being a desirable husband for my ward."

"*Samantha,*" said Christina.

"I said on the surface," Samantha continued imperturbably. "I am quite willing to believe that beneath this reprehensible facade of which Lord Palmerston has freely admitted, lies a character of the greatest worth and a heart that cleaves solely unto you, Christina. Fortunately, you need not be guided by my concern. Exert a little patience, and on your twenty-first birthday you will be entirely free to marry Lord Palmerston."

"But that is two years away!" wailed Christina.

"Lord Cartwright and Lady Jillian Roberts have been engaged for longer than that period," Samantha retorted. "I do not deny you full access to Lord Palmerston in the ensuing two years. You may see him every day if you like and dance with him every night. The two years will serve to reassure your aunt and uncle and myself that Lord Palmerston fully deserves you as his wife, and they will serve to solidify your affection for each other through a steadfast commitment witnessed by the whole of the ton."

"But two years is such a very long time," Christina complained. "Ye gods, Sam, it is four-and-twenty *months*!"

Samantha played her trump card. "I thought you said that you would be willing to undergo any privation to marry Lord Palmerston."

"Yes, but—"

"I fully see that two years of waiting to marry the man you love is a very great privation. I cannot, however, in all good conscience, ask you to do anything less. Do not the heroines of your beloved novels suffer before they are united to the men they love?"

Christina was stymied for she knew that any heroine worth her salt would leap gladly at such an opportunity to prove the steadfastness of her love, even though it meant

216

waiting a lifetime. And Samantha, after all, had only asked for two years.

For her part, during the whole of this dialogue Samantha had been surreptitiously studying Lord Palmerston. She had watched him change in hue from purple, to green, to white. The fury and the terror swelling his breast were revealed in his dark eyes. They both knew that he could not wait two weeks, let alone two years, to announce his forthcoming marriage to an heiress. His need for funds was desperate and immediate.

"I see through you clearly enough, Lady Samantha," he said bitterly. "You have no faith in my love for Christina nor in her love for me. You believe that we will tire of each other before a year has passed. Nay, 'tis worse than that. You are already planning the ways you can detach Christina from my regard. You are already plotting against a pure and hallowed love!"

Both Samantha and Christina were impressed by this little speech: Samantha for its calculated artfulness, Christina for its romantic glow.

"No matter what you say or do, Samantha," she cried, bright color staining her cheeks as she clasped Lord Palmerston's hand fervently to her breast, "you cannot keep me from Michael's side. I will marry him! I will!"

"Yes, of course you will," Samantha said soothingly. "And so far from keeping you from Lord Palmerston, I give him free access to my house as long as you dwell here. He can squire you every minute of the day if you like."

Christina's heroism was severely dampened. With Samantha for her guardian, Juliet would have been an old lady of sixteen when she wed Romeo and probably a grandmother at thirty-five. Where was the drama in that?

"Oh," she said. "Well, that is something, of course."

"Christina!" cried Lord Palmerston, his hands gripping her shoulders as he stared beseechingly down into her eyes.

"How can I live two days, let alone two years, without you as my wife, as my best self, my heart, my soul?"

"But if we are with each other every day—" Christina began.

Barely able to choke back a laugh, Samantha rose from her chair.

"I'll leave you two to discuss the matter in private," she said.

She trusted Lord Palmerston's desperation would soon drive Christina out of her nonsensical rose-colored cloud. She ought to let him get on with it. She walked sedately from the parlor and went to inspect the morning post.

It was the only glaring error she had ever made in her hitherto illustrious matchmaking career. Lord Palmerston's desperation made him far more clever than she had anticipated.

For the next hour, alternately clasping Christina to his bosom or kissing her, he wept, he pleaded, he recited all the horrors that delay in their marriage would bring. He carefully turned all that Samantha had said on its head and painted it in the light of tyrannical demagoguery designed to destroy all of Christina's hopes and dreams.

"Her heart is cold and barren," Lord Palmerston declared, his hands cupping Christina's face. "How can she know what we feel, what we suffer, when she has never been woman enough to love! Oh, my darling, I long for us to become one heart, one soul. I cannot wait two years to marry you. I cannot wait two months. I must have you as my very own now and forever. You trust in my love, don't you?"

"Yes, of course, Michael," Christina murmured into his shoulder.

"Then prove your love for me. Let us elope."

"Elope?" Christina squeaked, staring up at him, aghast.

"Now! This very night! We shall drive a thundering team

of horses to Gretna Green and be wed before the week is out!"

"B-b-but . . . but *elope*?!"

Lord Palmerston covered her face with kisses, talking quickly all the while. "Once we are married and your guardian and the Tylers see how happy we are, how devoted we are, they will not turn against us. They will see how wrong they were to prohibit a union both as necessary as it is inevitable. We were meant to be man and wife, Christina. No mere convention should keep us from doing what God intends."

With several more like arguments, each couched in the most romantic and exciting terms, Christina was slowly brought to agree that eloping was the only option before them. Lord Palmerston was casting her in the role Samantha had sought to deny her. She would be a heroine, daring the scorn of the world to wed the man she loved.

Chapter Nineteen

THAT CHRISTINA HAD no wish to attend the Duke of Wellington's dinner party at Apsley House that evening surprised Samantha not at all. She understood that the interview with Lord Palmerston could not have been easy for her and that she had a great deal to think over. It was a pity Samantha did not comprehend the full scope of her ward's thoughts.

She sailed off to Apsley House with Peter in tow and did not return until after two o'clock in the morning. Guardian and ward mounted the stairs, arms about each other's waist as they discussed the Great Man and his Great Guests. While suspecting no calamity, Samantha nonetheless felt an urge to check on Christina before retiring to her own bed and therefore just opened Christina's door a crack and peeped inside.

The peep was not satisfactory. She opened the door wider and discerned that Christina was not in bed, that she had not even been in bed. Striding quickly into the room, she spied a letter addressed to her lying on the mantel. She quickly took it down. The letter was long, it covered both sides of the page, and it was difficult to read for Samantha's hands were shaking so badly after the first sentence that she could not hold the paper steady. At its loving but resolute conclusion she emitted a far from ladylike bellow of rage that brought Peter running in stocking feet and shirtsleeves into his sister's room.

"Ye gods, Sam, what a noise!" he said. "What's happened? Where's Chris?"

"Your sister," Samantha shouted as she turned upon her ward in towering outrage, "your bubbleheaded, nonsensical, melodramatic ninnyhammer of a sister has eloped with Lord Palmerston!"

"She *what*?" Peter demanded, unsure of whether to laugh or curse.

"I will kill her," Samantha stated grimly. "I will strangle the wretch with my bare hands, and then I will lynch Palmerston, and then I will keel-haul your sister!"

"Sam, not even you can kill someone twice."

"Oh! When I get my hands on her! And on him!" Samantha growled as she stalked from the bedroom and into her own room, yelling for her abigail in a decidedly dangerous tone of voice.

"What are you going to do?" Peter demanded as he followed her.

"Go after them, of course!" Samantha said, beginning to pull off her jewelry. "They cannot have been gone above five hours. I will hopefully come up with them by morning and, when I do, they will both rue the day they were ever born!"

"But you can't go after them alone!" Peter remonstrated, his adolescent sensibility severely shocked by such a scheme. "I'll come with you. It will only take me a minute to change."

"You will do no such thing!" Samantha thundered. "Have you forgotten that Reggie is in town? You must stay behind to spread some believable tale excusing Christina's and my absence from London. Not even a hint of this affair must reach my sainted brother's ears for if it does, you will

221

find yourself packed off to the black depths of Yorkshire with no hope of reprieve!"

"But—"

"*No!* I shall send a quick note to Victor Speer. He shall come and act your chaperone while I am gone."

As Samantha's abigail scurried into the room just then and was as quickly sent to fetch traveling garb from the wardrobe, Peter could only mutter a grudging acquiescence and leave the room. Standing on the landing, however, his admirable mind considered the difficult situation his sister had put them in, his guardian's volatile temper when thus aroused, and the horrors of Reggie and Yorkshire.

This last decided him. Stopping only long enough to put on shoes, he ran from the house, across the Square, and pounded on the Cartwrights' front door. Clarke, with severe disapproval stamped upon his face, opened the door and, when forced to confess that Lord Cartwright had not yet retired for the night, grudgingly granted him entrance into the house.

The family party was reduced for Hilary, Lord Wyatt, and Matthew were still frivoling at the Esterhazys' rout. Lord Cartwright, however, his mother, Timothy, and the Duke de Peralta, were all found in the front drawing room and evinced varying degrees of surprise when they saw Peter, disheveled and half-dressed, enter at such an hour. His dramatic announcement of his sister's stupidity and Lord Palmerston's perfidy created all the sensation his adolescent heart could desire. The sensation doubled when he announced that Samantha meant to pursue and recover Christina by herself.

"She would," Lord Cartwright said with disgust as he started from the room. The others quickly followed him.

The five trooped across Berkeley Square and into the Dower House. Garner, made busy by his mistress's infuriated orders for her team to be put to and a food hamper prepared for her journey, greeted this party with admirable calm. He did not even protest when, having informed Lord Cartwright that her ladyship was in the library, the Cartwrights, the Duke de Peralta, and Peter trooped off to the library without waiting for Garner to announce them.

They found Samantha, reoutfitted in a burgundy traveling dress, sturdy boots, driving gloves, and hat, bent over a map laid across her desk.

"Not even you could be such a thimble-cap as to drive alone at night through England," Lord Cartwright stated without preamble as he advanced into the room.

Samantha came erect. "How did you—" She spied Peter. The color rose in her face. "I'll have you flogged, brat!"

"You'll do no such thing," said Lady Cartwright as she put a protective arm around the nervous youth. "Peter was perfectly correct in coming to us. Samantha, you cannot honestly mean to attempt such a rescue by yourself!"

"I am fully capable—" Samantha began.

"You are more than capable," Lord Cartwright ruthlessly interrupted, "and, I had hoped, wiser. No unmarried young woman, whatever her station, can expect to travel the length of the country and go unnoticed and unscathed. Once noticed," he pressed on over Samantha's burgeoning retort, "you would be ruined and not even the Prince could help you then!"

"Christina is my responsibility and I will fetch her," Samantha stated flatly.

"Very well," said Lord Cartwright. "But you will not go alone. I shall act as your escort."

"I don't *need* an escort!"

"God give me strength," Lord Cartwright implored. He strode up to Samantha, placed both hands on her shoulders, and shook her. "*Remember St. James's Street!* Lord Farago bursting his corset strings, Poodle Byng gaping at you, his dog yapping, Lord Barnett white with horror."

Samantha stared mutinously up at him. He glared back.

Her gaze dropped to the top button of his yellow waist-coat. "Oh very well," she muttered.

"I knew you would act sensibly," said the dowager, giving Peter a reassuring squeeze. "And never fear, my dear, I, too, shall protect your reputation. I shall come along as your chaperone, or at least your duenna."

"Oh come now, Lady Cartwright—" Samantha began.

"My mother is right," Lord Cartwright interrupted. "For an unmarried man and an unmarried woman to travel alone together would be ruinous."

Samantha sighed heavily. "Oh honestly. Very well, I shall have a duenna."

"Excellent," said Lady Cartwright, beaming.

"In that case, I, too, shall partake of the adventure," pronounced the Duke de Peralta. "Lady Cartwright will need a protector on such a dangerous journey. There are highwaymen and footpads on every inch of English roads. Anyone knows it. I shall be her chevalier."

"Now, Phillip, that is quite unnecessary," said Lady Cartwright, placing a hand on his arm.

"My dear, I insist," said the duke.

"What none of you are remembering," said Mr. Cartwright for the first time since his earlier horrified ejaculation at Peter's announcement of the elopement, "is that Christina is not alone. Lord Palmerston is with her and I doubt if he will surrender her quietly. As Simon means to protect Lady Samantha and the duke means to protect Mama, *I* shall deal with Palmerston personally."

"This is not a bloody parade!" Samantha shouted.

"Of course not," Lord Cartwright said soothingly. "We'll all fit nicely into the Cartwright coach. There will even be room for Miss Danthorpe when she has been recovered. One carriage does not a parade make, Lady Samantha."

"I don't know why I ever thought I liked you," she muttered, rolling up the map.

"Give us ten minutes to order our carriage and change

into suitable attire and we'll be off," Lord Cartwright said with a suspicion of a smile.

"You would not, perhaps, like to call out the Bow Street Runners as well?" Samantha sweetly inquired.

"I don't think that will be necessary," Lord Cartwright replied as he ushered his family and the Duke de Peralta out of the library.

Peter was left to withstand the withering glare of his guardian.

"I assure you, Sam," he said hastily, "I was only thinking of your welfare . . . and Yorkshire."

This stopped Samantha. "Yorkshire," she muttered. "Listen carefully, Peter. In ten minutes we've got to concoct a plot to pull the wool over the eyes of my sainted brother and *you're* going to have to be the one to pull it off."

Peter was all eagerness to obey.

Ten minutes later he waved good-bye to the Cartwright coach as it barreled out of Berkeley Square. He then ran back into the Dower House silently blessing his sister for throwing such adventure his way.

Samantha, however, was still mentally cursing Christina for her folly and, when she glanced at Mr. Timothy Cartwright, who sat opposite her in the forward seat with Lord Cartwright and the Duke de Peralta, her spleen rose up and would not be quashed.

"I blame you, Mr. Cartwright, for this whole miserable expedition," she said bitterly.

"Me?" gasped Timothy.

"Yes, you! If you had not been so missish about courting Christina and teaching her her own heart, she would never have succumbed to Palmerston's blandishments and run off like this."

"I have acted with the greatest propriety and have kept Miss Danthorpe's best interests at the forefront of my every thought," Mr. Cartwright retorted.

"Balderdash," said Samantha. "You have acted the coward from first to last. Bonaparte didn't turn a hair on your head, but a pretty girl with a large fortune sent you running off with your tail between your legs!"

Timothy flushed. "You are insulting, my lady!"

"And you have driven me to it!" cried Samantha. "Of all the mutton-headed love-besotted dolts I have had on my hands, you take the prize, Mr. Cartwright. Any fool can see that you're madly in love with Christina and that she is head over heels in love with you, and rather than doing everything in your power to secure your happiness and hers, you have chased her off into the arms of a coldhearted fortune hunter!"

"You are too severe, Lady Samantha," Lord Cartwright remonstrated over his tongue-tied sibling's angry gurgles. "My brother may have been foolish in discounting his own many admirable qualities, but Miss Danthorpe is an intelligent young woman wholly capable of pursuing any man she chose. It is her folly, not my brother's, that has led her to choose Lord Palmerston."

"Had Mr. Cartwright fixed his interest with her this would never have happened!" said Samantha.

"Had Miss Danthorpe more sense than sensibility this would never have happened!" Lord Cartwright retorted.

"Oh yes," Samantha said scathingly, "I know full well that sense is your god, but for lesser mortals, Lord Cartwright, it runs a poor second to the dictates of the human heart!"

"Miss Danthorpe does not act from love," Lord Cartwright stated. "She acts from the feverish imaginings acquired from a lot of silly novels. She has not consulted her heart one jot; it is all melodrama."

"What do you know of the feminine heart, you great lump of ice?" Samantha cried. "Christina's actions are perfectly understandable. She is running from something she wants but fears and the fear is ruling her."

"What has fear to do with love?" demanded Lord Cartwright.

"How can you have advanced to the age of two-and-thirty so disgustingly uneducated?" Samantha said. "To love is to be vulnerable and to be vulnerable engenders fear. In Christina's case it is very much worse, for she has believed in a romantic ideal for so long that to find it shattered with one glance from your brother's blue eyes has quite overset her reason. It is a frightening thing, my lord, to find you want something other than what you have pronounced to yourself and the world."

This was not an argument that Lord Cartwright could hear with any calm and the battle was fiercely joined. His mother and the Duke de Peralta watched on in silent glee, for an argument on such a subject could not but further their own schemes. Mr. Timothy Cartwright was also silent for, though Samantha's accusations had been made in the heat of the moment, he perceived that there was some justice in taking some of the blame for Christina's elopement onto himself. He had much to think over.

Chapter Twenty

THE RESCUE PARTY drove through the night without respite, stopping only to change their horses and inquire at every tollgate for news of Lord Palmerston's coach. They very soon ascertained that their unanimous belief that his lordship would take the fastest and most direct route to Gretna Green was fact. Time was of the essence for Palmerston. He had not only to elude his creditors, but anyone Samantha might send after him for he could not suppose that she would tamely allow him to carry off her ward without making some push for her recovery.

Fortunately, as Samantha informed her companions some time after she and Lord Cartwright had argued themselves into silence, Lord Palmerston was saddled with Christina and she could not but help them in their endeavor. Christina, while appreciating the need for urgency, was still not a great traveler. She would insist on stopping at varying points along the road north to rest and refresh herself with hot food and clean clothes. The rescue party, on the other hand, eschewed such niceties and had every hope of catching the elopers by noon the next day.

As it happened, they came upon their quarry very much sooner than that, and it was entirely Miss Danthorpe's doing. With each change of horses, she had gotten out of

Palmerston's chaise to walk, to eat, and once even to change her traveling dress, her erstwhile bridegroom gnashing his teeth and pulling his hair at these delays. Finally, body aching from the furious pace Lord Palmerston's chaise had set, heart sore from her decision to flee Samantha (and Mr. Cartwright), head throbbing with self-recriminations and self-doubts, she had insisted on stopping just before dawn at the posting inn where they were to change their team. Lord Palmerston argued all the dangers in vain. Christina would not continue another inch until she had been revived by a few hours sleep in an adequately comfortable bed.

Fearing discovery above all else, Lord Palmerston had thereupon determined to drink Christina under the table and compromise her in such a fashion that even Lady Samantha would agree that a marriage must be accomplished forthwith. Unbeknownst to his lordship, however, Christina had a very strong head for her age and sex and she was not at all as incapacitated as he had hoped when he began to make love to her.

She cried out at such familiarities and darted away from his arms. Lord Palmerston, believing the wine and his own noted successes in previous seductions were superior to any argument for modesty or decency that Christina might make, pursued her around the private parlor, caught her once again in his arms, and tried to swamp her maidenly fears with sensuality.

Christina had admitted to herself earlier that evening that she was extraordinarily foolish on a number of subjects, but there was a strong bar of American practicality that supported her character.

She savagely kicked Lord Palmerston in the shin and escaped his clutches.

Lord Palmerston roared with pain and fury at such treatment and lunged for her once again. But Christina was agile and easily eluded his grasp. Grabbing the fireplace poker, she raised it over her head.

"Take one more step toward me, Palmerston, and I shall brain you!" she cried.

Lord Palmerston was no man's fool. He stood quite still. The threat had cleared the fog of rage from his head and he realized he had made a capital error. It was time to regroup.

"Christina, I cannot apologize enough for my abominable behavior," he said humbly. "The wine and my long-standing desire for you must have overwhelmed my reason. I beg your forgiveness. Put down the poker. I'll do you no harm."

"I do not forgive you and I'll not put down the poker!" Christina said heatedly. "Nothing can atone for your conduct, Lord Palmerston. I find I don't want to marry you after all. I shall hire a carriage and return to London alone."

In vain did Lord Palmerston argue, plead, weep, and prostrate himself before Christina. She would not be moved.

Grimly he picked himself up from his knees. Inexorably he advanced upon Christina.

"You will marry me," he said. "My safety, my future, my *creditors* demand it! Even if I have to ravish you on the floor of this filthy posting house, you *will* marry me, Christina!"

He suddenly reached out and caught her wrist in one hand. His other hand forcibly held back the arm that sought to brain him with the poker.

"Oh! You monster!" Christina cried as she struggled in his grasp. "You mercenary, unprincipled monster. Unhand me!"

"Not until you are bound to me by ties that cannot be broken!"

"*Help!*" Christina screamed with all the force of her not too inconsiderable lungs. "Innkeeper! Help! Oh, help!"

The innkeeper and his eighteen-year-old son had heard

the growing commotion from within the parlor with more and more unease. At this summons, therefore, they prepared to burst into the parlor. They were forestalled, however, as two women and three men, clearly members of the Quality, ran in through the front door.

"Where is she?" demanded the ravishing blonde.

"Through that door, miss," stammered the innkeeper, pointing to his only private parlor.

Samantha leading the charge, the rescue party burst into the parlor just as Palmerston wrestled the poker from Christina's hand. He received yet another kick in the shins for his pains and thus, doubled over as he was, could not in any way anticipate the blow Mr. Timothy Cartwright leveled at his square chin. Timothy might have only one arm, but it was strong.

Palmerston toppled to the floor.

"Timothy!" shrieked Christina.

He paid her not the slightest heed.

"If you please, Simon," he said.

"With pleasure, brother," Lord Cartwright replied. He pulled Palmerston back to his feet and Mr. Cartwright once again knocked him down with the greatest relish.

Samantha, meanwhile, was returning the poker to the fireplace. "A good choice for a weapon. How very silly of you, Christina, to let Palmerston take it away from you." She stalked up to her ward, grasped her by the shoulders, shook her hard, and then hugged her fast. "Oh Chris, are you all right?"

Christina began to laugh and cry at once from the tumult of her emotions.

"Oh yes, Sam," she gasped. "I can't tell you—"

Indeed, she could not, for Mr. Cartwright, seeing Lord Palmerston had no desire for a fight (he was, in fact, unconscious), had followed fast on Samantha's heels. Without a thought to propriety, kindness, or the titillated gaze of the innkeeper, his son, and two curious chambermaids, he tore

Christina from her guardian's grasp and spun her around to face him.

"Timothy!" she cried. "I mean, Mr. Cartwright, whatever do you mean—"

Again she was unable to complete her sentence for Mr. Cartwright, deeming words inadequate to the occasion, pulled her to him and kissed her with an insensibility which, nerves already dazed, she readily returned, experiencing none of that reluctance she had felt in Lord Palmerston's arms.

"She's doing that very well," Samantha remarked to the Duke de Peralta. "I wonder who she's been practicing on?"

Mr. Cartwright pushed the stunned Christina far enough away to glare down into her stunned black eyes.

"You will stop acting like a nonsensical, overly romantic, caper-witted schoolgirl and marry me by June!" he stated.

"Yes, Timothy," said Christina with admirable meekness.

Mr. Cartwright blinked at this sensible reply and then roughly pulled her back into an embrace of even greater duration.

It was some time before calm, let alone decorum, could be restored to the room. Timothy and Christina, resting safely against Mr. Cartwright, his arm around her, his lips at her ear as he whispered all the love that was in his heart, were preoccupied. Lord Palmerston was still unconscious. Samantha, Lord Cartwright, Lady Cartwright, and the Duke de Peralta, therefore, were left to attend to the practicalities of the situation.

"Very well," said Samantha, "Christina is far safer than we had dared to hope. But how are we to keep her safe?"

"The ton will not have failed to notice that she and Palmerston disappeared from London at the same time," Lady Cartwright agreed.

"As they are betrothed, could not Miss Danthorpe and

Mr. Cartwright continue on to Gretna Green?" the duke inquired. "April is as good a month to marry as June."

"I suspect Christina has been put off elopements for life," Samantha said wryly.

"Besides," said the dowager, "these border marriages are not at all the thing, you know."

"Quite," said Lord Cartwright firmly. "I propose another solution to these self-inflicted difficulties which even Lady Samantha must approve."

"You hold us in thrall," Samantha informed him. "We hang on your lips. Pray continue."

Lord Cartwright cast her an amused glance and continued. "Palmerston's departure from London is easily explained away. Losing all hope of attaching Christina, pursued by a host of determined creditors, he has fled abroad. As for the timing of his departure, it was brought about by Christina informing him that she had just accepted my brother's proposal and meant to wed him soon."

"Admirable," Samantha agreed. "But what of Christina's absence?"

"Why, she is with us, of course," said Lord Cartwright.

"And why have we been absent?" asked his mother.

"Miss Danthorpe, being notably romantic, conceived a great desire to view her future home. My brother, wholly besotted, at once agreed to the scheme. Finding no fault with their plan, we all agreed to make up a formal party and journey to Grenwick together. It is but thirty miles away. We should be there this afternoon."

Samantha stared up at Lord Cartwright. "That, sir, is brilliant. Even I could not have conceived so satisfying a story. It answers every difficulty. I congratulate you."

"I am overwhelmed by your approbation," Lord Cartwright murmured.

Palmerston groaned and regained consciousness.

"There are, however, a few loose ends," Lord Cartwright said, walking over to the groggy eloper. "Your carriage is hereby confiscated," he stated. "You are ruined, Palmerston. A man with no money, no friends, and no principles must walk through life. In your case, perhaps you had better run. I understand your creditors will not hesitate in extracting their pound of flesh. I strongly recommend a trip abroad. Tomorrow would not be too soon."

"Innkeeper," Lord Cartwright said to their anxious host, as the duke and Timothy released Lord Palmerston, "you would do us all a great favor if you would lock this miscreant in your cellar until tomorrow morning. He will cause you little trouble. I see no need to feed him. You may release him on the morrow and think no more of the matter. Here is a little something for your trouble," he said, handing him several guineas.

"I'll have him locked up right and proper, me lord," said the innkeeper. "Here, you Johnny," he called to his stalwart son. "Help me get this bloke downstairs."

Palmerston protested all the way out of the parlor, but to no avail. He was not Johnny's equal in strength.

Samantha, asking for a stay of but ten minutes, procured paper and pen and wrote a hasty letter to Peter giving him the particulars of his sister's rescue and ordering him to solicit Lord Bartlett's and Colonel Dalton's aid in putting abroad the story Lord Cartwright had so brilliantly fabricated. Pressing the sealed letter and several additional guineas into the innkeeper's hand, she asked that the letter be sent express, thanked him for his many kindnesses on her ward's behalf, and then returned to the Cartwright coach. In but another minute the party set off for Grenwick.

It lacked but twenty minutes to midnight. Though not chilled, Samantha pulled her shawl closer around her as she strolled Grenwick's formal gardens. It was a pretty place, testament both to Mr. Cartwright's taste and hard work. Christina would be happy here. A smile touched Samantha's lips. So much adventure to achieve so rational an end! But the happiness that Mr. Cartwright and her ward radiated more than made up for the frustration she had endured while furthering their match. She heartily wished them joy and felt confident that they would fulfill her wishes.

The lovers and the rescuers had spent the day exploring Grenwick's grounds and making wedding plans. Christina had finally retired to her hastily arranged bedchamber an hour earlier. Lady Cartwright and then the Duke de Peralta had soon followed her excellent example. Mr. Cartwright and his brother were talking together in the lower drawing room whose French doors led out to this garden. Samantha smiled as she saw the two brothers together. So much sincere affection and goodwill in one family. She could never have suspected such a phenomenon from her own familial experiences.

How much the Cartwrights had taught her in only four months! She was the better and the wiser for having known them. She had found her first true female friend in Hilary, a whimsical scapegrace of a brother in Matthew, a devoted slave in Timothy (she chuckled at this), a loving guide in Lady Cartwright, and in Lord Cartwright . . . ?

Lord Cartwright had helped her move from the shadow of responsibility to its reality. She had undertaken the guardianship of Christina and Peter more as a lark than anything else. She had meant for them to amuse her as so much of the world did not. But Lord Cartwright, alternately shocked and outraged, amused and despairing, had slowly guided—yes, guided—her toward becoming responsible not merely for the Danthorpes, but for herself as well. Never again, would she be able to act on the wildest impulse, ignore the boundaries of social decorum, or denigrate herself by her own actions in whatever city she inhabited.

She had learnt self-governorship, never having known that she needed the lesson. She knew it now. Her face flamed with heat when she recalled the many instances when she had heaped abuse on Lord Cartwright's handsome

235

head, when she had added to his misery rather than lightened it, when she had scorned the very things his character and honor most valued.

What an odious thimble-cap she had been! How could even she have been so foolish as to not value the friendship of so worthy a gentleman? He had of his own accord assisted her out of every scrape she had fallen into or created through her own folly. Christina owed the salvation of her reputation to his lordship's particular genius. Why he had, almost from the start of their acquaintance, insisted on acting the knight-errant to Samantha's talent for trouble she could not guess. But she was sincerely grateful that, however much she had provoked him, he had stood fast as her friend.

Seeing but not hearing his laughter at something Timothy had said, Samantha thought Lord Cartwright quite the most charming man she had ever met, despite his occasional lapses into chilly reserve. How fortunate to have gained his friendship. How reasonable that she should love him.

Love him?

Clutching her shawl, Samantha stood staring into the drawing room in something akin to shock. All this time she had thought she merely admired Lord Cartwright's many worthy qualities when in fact she, who had prided herself on never being susceptible to masculine charms, was in love! Not merely in love, no, that was too pale a description for the depth of her feelings. Simon Cartwright was the perfect friend, lover, and companion to her days. He was everything she had lacked in her life and yearned for.

He glanced toward her through the open doors and smiled.

Her heart turned over.

Oh, she loved this man. Loved him! There was glory in that. But with this admission of love rose the specter of Lady Jillian Roberts. Oh, monstrous to be in love and not enjoy its fruits! Lord Cartwright was betrothed to another woman and as a man of honor, even should he return Samantha's regard, which she could not think possible, he would not bring scandal to an already injured family by retracting such an engagement. The golden light that had filled Samantha's heart was quickly snuffed out.

She loved in vain. What god had she offended to bring so much misery into her life?

Bidding his brother good night, Lord Cartwright stepped out into the garden and approached her with a light step generated by the pleasures of his brother's conversation and a beautiful spring night.

"I never thought I could utter such a statement," he said as he drew before her with a smile, "but my stolid brother is quite giddy with happiness. You have done your work well."

"I?" Samantha said as she struggled to bring her pounding heart and blushes to order. "Mr. Cartwright managed Christina very well on his own, I thought."

"Oh yes. But only after you had brought him to fever pitch by your insidious manipulations these last few months."

Samantha dropped a small curtsy. "A matchmaker is always happy to accept credit where credit is due."

"And what of a friend?" Lord Cartwright said quietly. "Will she, too, accept credit where credit is due?"

"I-I don't understand you."

Lord Cartwright took her hand in both of his, his brown eyes holding her gaze in thrall. "For some time, now, I have wanted to thank you on my own behalf. Since you moved into the Dower House, I have found myself not merely remembering, but partaking of the pleasures of life: its laughter and friendships, absurdities and joy. Your impulsiveness and warmth have taught me to remember that the world is not so important that it cannot be laughed at. I find I have shrugged off Hamlet's dark mantle for the more indecorous costume of Puck!"

Samantha could not but laugh. "You must not lay such a change at my door, sir. Not even I could be so improper as to clothe you in forest leaves."

"On the contrary," Lord Cartwright said with a gentle smile, "through your often infuriating challenges to my claims of superiority, your pointed discourses on the truths of life, and the warm generosity of your heart, I have learnt who and what I am. I am very grateful."

Samantha was grateful to the night which hid her blushes as his lordship continued to hold her hand and made no sign that he intended to let it go.

"You must not paint me in a more flattering light than I deserve," she said, a trifle breathlessly. "I have treated you abominably on many occasions. You must own it."

"Oh I do. But it was no less than I deserved. Any woman of independence would be affronted by such a great block of ice as I was before you came to town."

"N-n-no man of your character could ever be compared to ice, Lord Cartwright. To a volcano, perhaps, but not ice."

"Precisely," Lord Cartwright said with a smile. "If you have abused me, I have returned the honor more than once. 'Twas an odd way to make a friend. And we are friends, are we not?"

Samantha trembled at the warmth in his voice, the intensity of his gaze. "Oh yes," she said, "though it cannot but outrage your fiancée's finer feelings. Lady Jillian Roberts thinks me a reprobate."

Lord Cartwright studied her a moment and finally released her hand. "Ah yes, Jillian," he murmured. "I was forgetting. Will her disapproval keep you from my friendship, Lady Samantha?"

Samantha breathed a silent sigh of relief at this release. "You know me well enough by now, my lord, to think that disapproval ever stops me from doing anything I like. And I confess to liking your friendship. It has certainly stood me in good stead these last few months, for all I kicked and complained at the lessons you sought to impart. Your steadiness and honor have taught me that I, too, possess such qualities and ought to make use of them. I, also, have reason to be grateful for a friendship . . . your friendship."

"Then we are well matched," said Lord Cartwright, smiling down at her in the moonlight.

Samantha could not regard him with composure. She looked away and pretended to study the fountain gently splashing to her left.

"It is late, Lord Cartwright, and I find after the excitement of these last two days that I am a little fatigued. I think I shall retire. Good night."

"Good night," said Lord Cartwright, raising her hand to his lips, "my lady."

Samantha briefly closed her eyes against the heat coursing through her veins and then, with a half-choked adieu, hurriedly made her escape.

She achieved none of the sleep she had espoused.

The following morning, she had intended to be the last one down to breakfast but found that the Duke de Peralta and Lady Cartwright had thwarted her. They had not yet appeared. Christina and Mr. Cartwright, who only had eyes and conversation for each other, could offer her little protection from Lord Cartwright's company and she found her heart and nerves required all the protection they could get.

She busied herself unnecessarily at the side table procuring tea and toast for her breakfast and then sat where she must sit: between Christina and Lord Cartwright at the foot of the table.

"It is a beautiful morning," said he to Samantha. "We should have an easy journey back to London."

"I surprise myself by saying that I will be glad to get back, but I will," Samantha replied. "I dislike leaving the maintenance of an important pack of lies to anyone but myself. Peter, Hilary, Derek, and Brandon are doing their best, I'm sure. But I won't feel really secure until I have seen the announcement of Christina's engagement in the *Gazette* and told everyone who will hear me of the pleasure trip we have just taken to Grenwick."

Lord Cartwright's reply was forestalled by the entrance of his mother and the Duke de Peralta who came, not from the stairs, but from the direction of the front drive. They were already in traveling attire.

"Buenos días!" said the Duke de Peralta jovially, which was surprising for the duke was not known for his fondness of early morning hours.

"We cannot stay," said Lady Cartwright as she went around the table kissing her sons, Christina, and even Samantha. "But I did want just a chance to say good-bye."

"Good-bye, Mama?" said Mr. Cartwright. "You are leaving for London before us?"

"No, my boy," the duke said, "we are leaving for Gretna."

"Gretna?" cried the four people at the table.

"Phillip suggested, and I thoroughly agreed, that someone really ought to finish Christina's adventure for her," said Lady Cartwright calmly. "Besides, I've never eloped before and I've always secretly wanted to."

"Eloped?" said Lord Cartwright faintly.

"Phillip and I are going to marry."

"What?" ejaculated Samantha.

"I cannot thank you enough, Samantha," said the duke as he raised her hand to his lips, "for introducing me to Emma. I love her more than I can say and she is so kind as to return my regard."

"B-b-but Phillip," said Samantha, "she is not rich!"

"Not in money, perhaps, but her heart . . . Ah, Samantha, for Emma's heart I shall learn to economize!"

"Good God," said Samantha, "you *are* in love."

"Isn't it wonderful?" Lady Cartwright said, dimpling. "And at our age, too. Well, good-bye, my children. I shall return to you an impoverished duchess in about a week."

"Muy amada mia," said the Duke de Peralta as he offered his arm to his bride and led her from the room.

The Cartwright brothers, Christina, and Samantha dazedly followed them out to the front drive where Palmerston's chaise and coachman were waiting, the duke's and dowager's valises already secured behind.

"Dispenseme usted. You do not mind my commandeering the chaise you commandeered from Palmerston, do you?" the duke inquired of Lord Cartwright as he helped his bride into the carriage. "I thought it should be put to some good use, and the coachman needed employment."

Lord Cartwright laughed and heartily shook his future stepfather's hand. "I make you a wedding present of it, sir, and gladly."

"We shall deal well together, I think," the duke said, twinkling down at him as he mounted the carriage step. "After all, we both have excellent taste in wives."

He directed a speaking glance at his future stepson, who calmly returned it, and then closed the door.

The word was given to the coachman and the Duke de Peralta's chaise set off for Scotland.

"My word," Christina said as they watched it disappear around a curve in the drive.

"My mother is eloping with an impoverished Spanish duke two years her junior," said Mr. Cartwright in a strange voice.

"I wonder what story I can fabricate for this turn of events?" Lord Cartwright said.

Samantha collapsed on the front steps and buried her head in her arms.

"Lady Samantha," Lord Cartwright said with mock severity as he sat down beside her, "I would have appreciated just a hint of your plans for my mother."

Samantha raised her head, tears of laughter streaming down her face. "On my honor, sir, I had no hand in *this* match. But by God I wish I had!"

Lord Cartwright joined her laughter to such an extent that they had to lean against each other for support, Christina and Mr. Cartwright looking on with some surprise.

Chapter Twenty-one

THE DUKE AND Duchess de Peralta returned to London eight days later. The duke removed himself from the Clarenden and into Cartwright House where all continued in harmony for the duke thought only of his wife and had no wish to interfere in the workings of the household. The de Peraltas learned that, according to the story put abroad by Samantha and the Cartwrights, they had been married in the rectory attending Grenwick and had been spending the last week in romantic solitude, enjoying the pleasures of spring and their recent marriage. They accepted the story with equanimity.

The ton was, of course, titillated by so precipitate a marriage coming so fast on the heels of the engagements of a Cartwright son and daughter. Society was, therefore, disposed to welcome the duke and duchess everywhere so that the union could be marveled at openly and the couple thoroughly questioned on every aspect of their courtship and marriage. Close association with Samantha had taught the duke and duchess the fine art of dissembling and they carried off their newfound popularity with consummate skill.

The ton found that it was swimming in scandal-broth. First there was the startling escape of Lord Palmerston from London and his pressing financial responsibilities; then the

243

marriage of the Duke de Peralta to Emma Cartwright; and then the engagement of the greatest heiress Society had harbored in a century to a one-armed second son of a debauched baron. Never had the occasions for gossip been so great.

A marriage requires a celebratory ball and, as Samantha was his closest friend, she assured the Duke de Peralta that it was both a pleasure and an honor to organize a ball on his behalf. As for Christina, a betrothal requires a betrothal ball and Samantha leapt into this breach as well with a determination none could check. Her reasons were entirely selfish: she wished to be distracted from painful thoughts and feelings. And she wished to grasp any and all excuses to avoid Lord Cartwright's company. Thus was she busy from dawn until dusk for the fortnight after Christina's failed elopement.

On the night of her ward's betrothal ball, Samantha surveyed her ballroom. It was glittering, it was hot, it was packed with every possible variety of guest. Christina and Timothy were beaming at each other nonstop. In short, she had created another success. If only Lord Cartwright had not extracted the promise of two dances from her, she might have been content.

But each time he took her in his arms and swept her out onto the dance floor, Samantha shivered as the most delicious heat poured over her skin and every coherent thought left her brain save one: she loved this challenging, witty, honorable, generous man more with each passing hour. No amount of hiding away could change that. She would have to run away, if only to preserve what peace of mind she had left. Impossible to be near Lord Cartwright and not eventually reveal the true state of her heart and mind. Impossible to court such disaster. Once the Tylers or Oxford claimed Peter in the fall, she would flee England, purchase passage on a suitable ship and sail ... it mattered not where.

It was with a feeling of relief that she curtsied to Lord Cartwright at the end of their second dance and, claiming the duties of a hostess, escaped the pleasure and pain of his company. But her eyes continually strayed toward him, her heart knew only misery whenever she saw him with Lady Jillian Roberts. Her thoughts were in the greatest tumult when she saw them argue, as they always did when they came together.

As her gaze and thoughts were directed solely toward Lord Cartwright, Samantha quite missed that Lord Barnett was dancing attendance on Jillian with a determination that brought a continual blush to that young woman's ivory cheeks. She did not see Lord Barnett lead Jillian into a dance, despite her lavender gloves. And Samantha missed entirely the odd spectacle of Lord Barnett then pulling the stunned Jillian out onto the terrace.

Lord Cartwright, however, had seen it all. With an amused smile, he went to partner Christina, who was glowing, in a cotillion.

The day following the Danthorpe–Cartwright betrothal ball was cold and damp and Samantha was feeling aggrieved. It was just such a day as this that reminded her why she had avoided returning to England for so many years. If she had simply held to that determination and taken Christina and Peter to any other country to await the Tylers, she might even now have been enjoying sunshine, gaiety, and would never have met Lord Simon Cartwright who insisted upon growing more handsome, more charming, and more interesting to her every waking thought with each new day.

Garner entered her sitting room just then and gravely announced that Lord Adamson had come to call.

"Oh no," Samantha said with a groan.

"Quite, my lady. Shall I say that you are ill and unable to receive visitors?"

245

"You would not be telling a very great falsehood. But, no, I shall not play the coward with him. Show him up! No! I won't have him pollute my only sanctuary. I shall come down."

With noticeable reluctance, Samantha went downstairs and into the front parlor where her brother stood staring with undisguised horror at Fragonard's bathers.

"There you are," intoned Lord Adamson at her entrance. "I wonder you have the temerity to see me! Are you not ashamed of what you have done?"

"You know me too well, Reggie, to believe that I am ashamed of anything that I do," Samantha coolly replied. "What is my newest crime?"

"How can you stand there and play the innocent," demanded Lord Adamson, "when you know full well that you have betrothed Miss Danthorpe without first seeking my permission."

"*Your* permission?!" gasped Samantha. "You are under the mistaken impression, Reggie, that you have any power over me or the Danthorpes. Let me disabuse such a rattle-pated notion this instant! I owe you no obedience. You have no rights over me and no power. It is time you realized that."

Lord Adamson exploded at this and proceeded to rake Samantha over the coals with all the fervor his limited imagination could sustain. Her character, morals, breeding, presentation, conversation, actions, friendships, and disregard for every social convention were severely disparaged.

During the course of this diatribe, Lord Cartwright gained entrance to the house and Garner, while believing Samantha fully capable of dealing with her disagreeable brother, thought it kindest to provide her with some sort of rescue, if only to protect the parlor's furnishings. He, therefore, ushered his lordship down the hall to the front parlor, both overhearing a good deal of Lord Adamson's discourse.

"You've no family feeling!" Lord Adamson stormed.

"No regard for what *I* endure daily on your account! *You* do not care that I am laughed at for *your* excesses, ridiculed for your indecorous behavior, cut by every leader of society because of your mismanagement of the Danthorpes, let alone your own affairs. Marrying off the Dowager Cartwright to a Spanish pauper! Detaching Miss Sheverton from the husband of her parents' choosing and uniting her instead with one of your dissolute friends! Betrothing your ward to a nobody!"

"You must be more circumspect when discussing my brother," said Lord Cartwright, entering at this point, "for I might feel compelled to plant you a facer." He smiled at Samantha's startled look and continued. "As for Society cutting you dead, Lord Adamson, I'm afraid you've only yourself to blame. Samantha Adamson, though a sad scapegrace, is so well regarded by the haut ton that your insistence on disparaging her in every conversation you undertake cannot but disgust your listeners."

"How dare you, sir?" sputtered Lord Adamson.

"I am renowned throughout the ton for my honesty and chivalry. It is time for you to bid adieu to your sister. I wish to engage her in a private tête-à-tête."

"How dare you?" Lord Adamson blustered. "How dare you even try to hint me from my own sister's house?"

"My, he is thickheaded, isn't he?" said Lord Cartwright to Samantha and won a warm smile in return. He turned upon Lord Adamson and began to remove his coat.

"My lord," said Samantha, "there is really no need. I am fully capable—"

"I know," said Lord Cartwright, "but I'm having such fun. As hints make no impression, Lord Adamson, I shall have to apply brute force," he said, laying his coat over a chair.

"You—you wouldn't dare," said Lord Adamson, lifting his double chin.

"Wouldn't I?"

"You have no right."

"I have every right!" thundered Lord Cartwright in so loud a voice that Lord Adamson staggered back and Samantha stared at him in astonishment. "I value what is good and beautiful and honest in this world as you do not and cannot. You are so blinded by your implacable hatred of one so superior to you in character, talents, and feeling that you make yourself ridiculous before the whole of the ton as you do here today. You disgust me. Leave this house and do not dare to disparage your sister in company or to her face again!"

"I am your superior in age and station and—" began Lord Adamson.

"You insult me, sir," Lord Cartwright scathingly retorted. "You are not even superior to the lice infesting your thinning hair."

Lord Adamson turned purple with rage. "Had I less regard for my position, I would call you out!"

"You don't honestly think you could best me, do you?" Lord Cartwright said coldly. He opened the parlor door and bowed to the glowering Lord Adamson. "Good day, sir."

Lord Adamson departed with rancor.

Lord Cartwright leaned against the closed door. "I trust, sweet Samantha, that I have said nothing that you would not have said?"

"You were rather magnificent," Samantha said in little more than a whisper.

"Thank you."

"Do you not get tired of always rescuing me?"

"No, my love, I rather enjoy it. I shall be happy to enter into the lists whenever your odious brother comes to town."

Samantha uttered a small, shaky laugh. "Y-y-you must be drunk, disguised, bosky. No sober man would willingly walk into the Adamson battlefield."

"Ah," said Lord Cartwright, walking up to her, "but any sober man would move heaven and earth *and* decorum to claim such a prize. Let me be your knight-errant from now on, Samantha. I have routed the dragon harrying your castle and by right you are mine. My heart and soul have ever been and will always be yours."

"Do not," whispered Samantha and, had she seen the expression on her own face, she would not have been surprised when Lord Cartwright suddenly pulled her into his arms. He kissed her with a passion and a need that left her insensibly returning the embrace. "This is madness," she murmured as Lord Cartwright pressed kisses to her brow, her temple, her jaw.

"Madness not to," said he with a groan as his lips captured hers again.

In the next moment, Peter burst into the room and stopped dead upon finding his guardian clasped in his patron's arms.

"Good God, Sam, what are you doing?" he exclaimed.

Samantha was overcome by a fit of giggles as Lord Cartwright calmly ordered his protegé out of the room to think upon the social requirements of knocking on every closed door one encounters. Peter hurriedly backed from the parlor, closing the door behind him.

"Another lesson most kindly imparted," Samantha murmured, her eyes twinkling mischievously.

"The boy still has too many rough edges to suit me," said Lord Cartwright. "Where were we?"

"Doing our best to forget the world. Simon, this *is* madness," Samantha said, pulling free. "I'll not bring dishonor to you."

"Dishonor?" demanded Lord Cartwright, staring at her.

"You are engaged to Jillian Roberts and that must take precedence over whatever we feel for each other."

"I think not," Lord Cartwright retorted.

"Simon, I will not harm a woman who has done me no harm."

"Samantha, I honor your scruples. That is why I have taken matters into my own hands."

Samantha stared at him. "What have you done?" she said faintly.

"I have become the King of Hearts."

"W-w-what?"

"I," pronounced Lord Cartwright, "have become a matchmaker."

"But . . . but men don't *do* that!"

"I have," Lord Cartwright said happily. "I inquired of Lord Barnett if he would be so good as to woo Jillian and he confessed himself most willing and has been so successful in his endeavors that they are to be married. Jillian informed me of it not ten minutes ago. Have you ever considered honeymooning in China?"

Samantha tried to take it in but her heart was beating with so much violence and there was such a roaring in her ears that she had some difficulty in doing so. "You are . . . free?"

"On the contrary, I am a prisoner of love, my love for you."

Samantha could not but laugh. "You are the most absurd man and I think . . . yes, I think that I am the happiest woman on earth."

"Come, give me your love in return."

Lord Cartwright held out his arms to her and Samantha, who was both mortal and sensible, flew to him. All coherent conversation ceased for some time.

By the time sanity was restored to the room, Samantha was lying happily in Lord Cartwright's arms on a green satin chaise, his fingers gently sifting through her soft hair.

"*Very* satisfying," she murmured as her fingers tenderly caressed his cheek.

"Isn't it?" Lord Cartwright replied with a smile, and a kiss. "I find that I am the happiest man on earth. There now remains the matter of apprising the ton of this most happy exchange of partners and I have come to the conclusion that the most expeditious and proper means is for Jillian and I to send a notice to the papers announcing the mutual dissolution of our engagement."

"Yes but, Simon, do but think of Jillian and your own family. Will not such an announcement create a scandal?"

"Not at all," Lord Cartwright calmly replied. "It is already widely acknowledged that Jillian and I are not suited, nor has Lord Barnett's pursuit of her gone unnoticed. Jillian and I have each proved ourselves honorable people, beyond reproach, in fact, for the steadfastness of our commitment to each other in the most difficult of times. And I have been so very successful at being unreasonable with Jillian when in company that no one could blame her for not wishing to marry me."

"How clever we all are," Samantha murmured, kissing him once again. "One match dissolved, two others made, and no scandal arising from any of it. Although there is one point that still has me uneasy. When do you plan to pay me your addresses?"

"Samantha, what are you talking of?" demanded Lord Cartwright in some surprise. "Have we not settled it between us that we are the happiest people on earth?"

"Indeed, we have," said Samantha, "but our happiness has *not* been formalized. You have kissed me with a freedom that inspires some hope of your intentions, but a woman in my position cannot be too careful. Jillian now has Derek, but I am bereft of a husband and I have taken a fancy, of late, to acquiring one. You have not yet asked me to marry you and I am not such a madcap that I would ask *you*."

"Rescuing you from St. James's Street and the Cock's Crow *and* your brother was just the same as paying you my addresses."

"Nonsense! I once rescued Walter Smedley from a pack of irate Turks and, by your logic, we should now be married with six bald babies hanging on my skirts. But you will notice my gown is free from any and all encumbrances."

"Who," said Lord Cartwright, his lips trembling, "was Walter Smedley?"

"Did I never tell you of him? He was someone I met when my family was visiting the Turkish court. He wanted to interest the Sultan in some Arabian horses and the Sultan took the offer in quite the wrong way."

"We shall discuss your scandalous past later," Lord Cartwright intoned, "and, depending upon that discussion, I will then formally make an offer for your hand."

"What," said Samantha, folding her arms across her chest, "and deprive our marriage of any future conversation? No, sir, you will propose to me now or not at all!"

Lord Cartwright, with a sigh uttered since time immemorial by man forced to concede to woman's whim, went down on his knee before her just as Christina hurried into the room.

"Samantha, I *must* borrow—Good God, Lord Cartwright, what *are* you doing?"

Lord Cartwright's shoulders shook as Samantha sternly instructed Christina on the propriety of knocking on any and all closed doors she encountered. Christina hurriedly backed out of the room, closing the door after her. She then ran across the Square to inform the Cartwrights that Samantha and Lord Cartwright had finally come to their senses.

"Where were we?" Samantha asked Lord Cartwright, but he was too overcome with laughter to begin his addresses. "Oh honestly," she said. She dropped to her knees on the floor and kissed him. This effectively stopped his laughter and led to the happy denouement both had thought impossible but a few months before.